PB— AXH—278

MY LADY
Pocahontas

MY LADY Pocahontas

a novel by
Kathleen V. Kudlinski

MARSHALL CAVENDISH

ACKNOWLEDGMENTS

For generously sharing your knowledge and enthusiasm, many thanks are
due to the staff and interpretive guides at Jamestown Rediscovery, the
National Park Service personnel at Colonial National Historical Park, the
helpful representatives of various native tribes, the interpreters at history
museums, and the reference librarians at too many facilities to mention.

Text copyright © 2006 by Kathleen V. Kudlinski • All rights reserved. No part of this book may
be reproduced or transmitted in any form or by any means, electronic or mechanical, including pho-
tocopying, recording, or by any information storage and retrieval system, without permission in
writing from the publisher. • Marshall Cavendish Corporation • 99 White Plains Road,
Tarrytown, NY 10591 • www.marshallcavendish.us • Library of Congress Cataloging-in-
Publication Data • Kudlinski, Kathleen V. • My Lady Pocahontas / by Kathleen V. Kudlinski. •
p. cm. • Summary: Nuttagwon, daughter of a minor Pamunkey chief, is still a girl when
Pocahontas's vision of peace between their people and the newly arrived English colonists bonds the
two in a lifelong friendship as they work together to make the vision a reality. • ISBN-13: 978-0-
7614-5293-5 • ISBN-10: 0-7614-5293-1 • 1. Pocahontas, d. 1617—Juvenile fiction. 2.
Jamestown (Va.)—History—Juvenile fiction. 3. Virginia—History—Colonial period, ca. 1600-
1775—Juvenile fiction. [1. Pocahontas, d. 1617—Fiction. 2. Pamunkey Indians—Fiction. 3.
Indians of North America—Virginia—Fiction. 4. Jamestown (Va.)—History—Fiction. 5.
Virginia—History—Colonial   period,   ca.   1600-1775—Fiction.]   I.   Title.
PZ7.K9486My 2006 • [Fic]—dc22 • 2005051325 • The text of this book is set in Adobe
Garamond • Book design by Sonia Chaghatzbanian • Printed in The United States of America •
First Marshall Cavendish hardcover edition • 10 9 8 7 6 5 4 3 2

mc Marshall Cavendish

*To my best friend and fellow traveler
through book after book, Hank Kudlinski*

contents

MY LADY
Pocahontas

PART I

FRIENDS

WEROWOCOMOCO

1607

1
SPIES

NUTTAGWON'S HAND FROZE ON THE HEAD OF THE FAT LITTLE puppy squirming in her lap. She looked up at a short, slender girl sneaking through the reeds to the river's edge to stand behind her. The girl's eyes held mischief and her cheeks were dimpled, but her tattoos made Nuttagwon's mind race. *Pamunkey.* She read the tribal pattern. *The vision people. Beaver Clan, like me.* But this girl had the mark of the Powhatan himself. She wore a white feather in her hair, the sign that she had already been given a vision!

"Are . . . " Nuttagwon paused, trying to calm herself and the dog, "are you Pocahontas?" Even in her far Appamattuck village up in the hills, she had heard stories of the Supreme Chief's daughter.

Instead of answering her, the other girl grinned and said, "You are Nuttagwon, come to beg for food from my father. And yes, for now, I am known as Pocahontas."

How did Pocahontas know so much about her? Nuttagwon wondered. *And what did she mean by* "For now"? Nuttagwon glanced around. The riverbank was empty except for the two girls and the puppy. Behind them, in the distance, Pamunkey women worked in the sunshine in front of the longhouses, chatting and laughing. They looked well fed even after the winter. So did their children, playing nearby.

"The white men have landed downstream." Pocahontas looked out over the reeds at the river flowing toward the Chessiopiac Bay. "We can't simply stay here playing with a puppy. Not when we could be spying on them."

"You would go to the strangers?" Nuttagwon asked. She'd heard enough to know Pocahontas loved risks, but this was as foolish as stepping into fire. "What if they capture you?"

"I will not go alone." Pocahontas offered Nuttagwon a canoe paddle. "There are things we must learn, and soon."

"We?" Nuttagwon thought fast. *We?*

"It is something I must do, and you with me."

Nuttagwon's stomach tightened. Whenever a Pamunkey spoke that way, it had something to do with their vision. There would be no talking Pocahontas out of going. *Not that I would dare try,* Nuttagwon thought. Visions were sacred and very private, and Nuttagwon wished with all her heart that she could have one. Then she could be a help to her Appamattuck tribe, and not just another mouth to feed.

"Pocahontas." Nuttagwon took a deep breath. Every nerve in her body said, *run.* Even her mother had warned her of the wild Pocahontas. "The men will return from hunting soon. Take a tall man with you instead of me. He could watch for danger."

"I can hide in a tuft of reeds," Pocahontas said. "No man can. You are even shorter than I am and skinny as a mink.

You will fit in beside me where no man could find cover. This very night, I will report to my father the numbers and strength of the strangers. I might even learn a few words of their language."

Nuttagwon felt like a rock as the stream of Pocahontas's words poured over her. She clung to one word. "Hide?" she asked. "We would just hide?" Trade and warfare were the work of men. But a girl could spy. *And*, Nuttagwon thought, *if that girl kept Supreme Chief Powhatan's daughter safe, he might be kind to her village.* She pictured many baskets of corn arriving in time to save her sick relatives. She took the paddle.

The puppy bounced and scampered around their feet as the two girls made their way to the canoes. Pocahontas chattered as they walked. "For now, spying is all we will do. We will see how these people decorate their hair and how they tattoo their faces!" She tripped over the dog, but still she didn't stop talking. "They might have dogs, too! Strange hunting dogs—and maybe fuzzy puppies. You'd like to see them, wouldn't you?"

"How do you know that?" Nuttagwon asked. "I've only been here a few days."

Pocahontas laughed. "Werowocomoco is not like your little village in the hills. Here, if you listen and watch, there are no secrets. And if there *are* secrets, someone is sure to tell them." Pocahontas pointed to a two-man canoe pulled up into the reeds, and Nuttagwon set her paddle inside. "Besides," the stream of words flowed on, "you have already made friends with every dog in the town and not one of the other girls."

That's not true, Nuttagwon wanted to say, as she helped Pocahontas drag the canoe across the mud into the water. She looked up. The sky was clear and the water smooth. That could change in a moment at the harsh God Okeus's will. "Wait," Nuttagwon said. "I have tobacco." She reached into a pouch strung around her neck and pulled out a pinch of the holy herb. Begging Okeus to withhold storm and wind until they returned, Nuttagwon sprinkled the tobacco on the water. "There," she said, and the knot in her stomach relaxed.

"You sit in the front," Pocahontas directed. "I'll steer." She hissed to quiet the puppy's mournful whimpers as the dog stood in the mud at the river's edge. "Hurry, now," she commanded Nuttagwon.

"Go find your mother, little one." Nuttagwon patted the dog good-bye and climbed over a basket toward the bow of the dugout. She glanced at the bold pattern woven into the basket, then looked inside. Her mouth watered. There were four corn cakes and a dry gourd full of strawberries ready for a mid-day meal. How had Pocahontas known she would agree to come along? What else could this vision-seer predict?

Pocahontas steered the canoe along the riverbank. Nuttagwon kept silent as they ducked under tree branches and pushed aside the soft new cattail leaves that whipped their naked arms. "We are as clever as my father's best scouts," Pocahontas whispered.

Nuttagwon shivered in the warm sunshine. It was wrong to go in secret. They hadn't asked permission to take the canoe. She'd left chores undone. Her parents had no idea

4

where she was. With each paddle stroke, Nuttagwon thought of more reasons why she should feel shame. Instead excitement bubbled up inside her.

Even the water spirits were different here. At home, brooks babbled over stones, sparkling and chuckling downhill. Like the wind, the waters talked to anyone who would listen. Here, wide, muddy rivers wandered silently across the land, plodding toward the ocean. Twice a day they seemed to rise up and change their minds, heading back inland and mixing with the salty water.

Around a bend, the canoe swerved as Pocahontas backpaddled. A forest of bare sticks poked up from the water on the far side of the river. Pamunkey men stood thigh deep with harpoons poised by the narrow end of the fish trap. Other Pamunkeys swept fish nets through the water. Like Nuttagwon, they were under the rule of the great Powhatan. The Supreme Chief commanded tribute from many different tribes. From her Appamattuck village in the mountains all the way to the sea, and from the Chessiopiac tribe in the south almost to the Patowomekes in the north. Thirty different tribes. A hundred and thirty towns all together.

Pocahontas eased the canoe along, and both girls bent low. The men were focused on the shadows underwater, watching for fish. If they glanced up, perhaps they might mistake the canoe for a log floating in the rushes. *More likely*, Nuttagwon thought, *they would see that it was a stolen canoe.* She did not want to imagine what might happen if she and Pocahontas were caught sneaking downriver now.

Nuttagwon made no sound as they slid along with the

current. The wind cooled the front clean-shaved half of her head. Her braid fluttered against her back like a freshly caught fish. She breathed in short gasps as Pocahontas steered them toward the far bank.

As the canoe began drifting downstream, Nuttagwon turned around, and Pocahontas threw a strawberry at her. Nuttagwon caught it and scowled.

"Eat it." Pocahontas laughed. "I knew you wouldn't let it fall into the water! And you'll want a corn cake, too. Eat your fill." Nuttagwon gobbled down the entire cake and a handful of berries as well. When she finished eating, she brushed the crumbs off her chest, licking her fingers to savor the last of the toasted corn flavor.

"Maybe we should go home now," Nuttagwon said, looking at the sun.

"It is only mid-day. The strangers are just up around the bend."

Nuttagwon pressed her hand to her belly to still the fluttering there. Were these strange men the ones from under the world? The ones who would bring destruction to their way of life? Not everyone believed the tales, but Nuttagwon always listened to them. If the prophecies were true, now she would be part of the story!

When tall naked spires appeared over the treetops, her breath stopped. Cords the thickness of a man's arm stretched between the posts. Others hung, tied like giant spiderwebs. Pendants fluttered from the tops of the posts, colored blood red and berry blue. One man climbed up the webbing; another stood on a platform near the top.

From the rear of the dugout, Pocahontas back-paddled, then steered the boat into a little creek shaded by tall ferns. Pocahontas climbed out and waded ashore. Taking a deep breath, Nuttagwon joined her in the undergrowth.

Suddenly, a strange barking noise pierced the forest. Nuttagwon thought it might be a fox. She listened closely. The bark was too loud for a red fox, too deep for a grey. It was neither the bay of a proper hunting dog nor the guttural howl of a wolf. What was this animal?

A man's voice rang out sharply. "Kwy-it!" The animal whimpered and was still.

Nuttagwon mouthed the strange command the unseen man had yelled. "*Kwy-it?*"

The two girls made a wide circle downwind of the animal and the man who controlled its voice. They belly-crawled up a rise and lay down in the ferns at the top to look at the boats in the river below. Nuttagwon's eyes ached as she tried to take in all the strangeness.

"Wonderful!" Pocahontas whispered.

The floating watercraft were three times the length of the longest war canoes. They were many times wider and higher, and there were three of them. Great tall poles grew from the middle of each boat and climbed upward into the sky. Vast pale sheets looped along crosspieces. Were they leather or woven grass mats? Nuttagwon could not tell, but she memorized the huge red-cross pattern decorating them.

Just as a smaller boat began moving away from the shore toward the mother craft, a growl sounded right behind Nuttagwon. She froze. Very slowly, Nuttagwon turned and stared up into the black eyes of a dog. His head was as big as a bear's, and he had teeth to match. His ears drooped down instead of pointing up, and his shaggy hair curled softly. This was like no dog Nuttagwon had ever seen, but he *was* just a dog. A nervous one and still young, perhaps.

Nuttagwon gauged his mood. His tail quivered and his mouth hung open as if he were smiling. He wasn't squinting, either, and his lips were soft around his mouth. This dog did not mean to attack—yet.

Nuttagwon eased herself up onto an elbow and extended her hand toward the dog. He growled and stepped forward. The growl deepened, and he flashed his teeth at Nuttagwon and pulled his ears back so they lay against his head. His teeth flashed. She willed herself not to flinch and scolded "Kwy-it" with all the fury of the man's voice.

The dog wilted. His tail and ears flopped down and his lips slid back down over his teeth. Nuttagwon cooed. The dog rumbled uneasily, but when Nuttagwon snarled "Kwy-it" again, the dog gently sniffed her knuckles. Nuttagwon heard Pocahontas slowly release her breath.

Nuttagwon let the dog get his measure of her scent. When his tail began wagging, she rubbed a fluffy ear. He sat, then lay down beside her, rolling over and spreading his legs to the sky. Nuttagwon scratched the dog's tenth rib. Soon he was wiggling helplessly in pleasure.

"Heer-boi!" A nearby man barked another strange command. Nuttagwon froze, but the dog leaped to his feet. "Heer-boi," the man called again and the dog was off, one of his great paws scraping Nuttagwon's leg as he passed. She listened to him crashing downhill and splashing through some water.

"Heer-boi," Pocahontas said beside her, very quietly.

"Kwy-it!" Nuttagwon answered, and the girls grinned at each other.

When the woods were quiet, they eased down the rise toward the sound of voices. Moving from tree to bush to reedy tussock, they finally got a good view of the boats and the landing.

"Look at the strangers!" Pocahontas whispered. Nuttagwon was already staring. The men had not shaved either side of their heads. Most were dark-haired, but a few had pale locks. One of the short ones who was strutting about and shouting even had hair as yellow as corn pollen. From his eyes down, his face, like all the others', was shaggy, leaving no space for paint or tattoos. A few smooth-faced boys looked normal, but the rest seemed more like animals.

When Nuttagwon forced herself to look below their furry chins, all she could see were clothes. These people wore clothing all over their bodies! Some of it was shiny, like copper metal, but white. Their chests were hidden behind the metal, and a jointed metal apron covered their legs. A few even had hats of this strange white stuff, sparkling like river ice in the sunshine.

Beneath the metal, they wore a fabric more finely woven than sweet-grass cloth. It was so thin that they needed many layers to stay warm, even on a fine spring afternoon. The only skin that showed was on their hands. Hairy hands.

What would it feel like to be buried alive in clothing,

Nuttagwon wondered. Then she wiggled, glad to feel the soft fern fronds tickling her naked back. She pressed herself into the cool, damp earth, sighing and letting the earth's spirit fill her with strength.

Pocahontas put a hand on Nuttagwon's arm. "Be still," she whispered, soft as a rustle in the grass. Her head was cocked and her eyes were closed. Nuttagwon listened to the gibberish rising on the wind and could make no sense of it. Instead she tried to memorize the patterns woven and stitched into the stranger's clothing and painted on the sides of their boats.

Another enormous dog galloped across the beach below them. This one was nut brown with great white spots and strange floppy ears. As he ran, his ears flew up and down. Nuttagwon had to smile. The strange barking sound of his breed floated up to the girls. "*Tie-nee!*" a boy yelled, and the huge dog lunged upward to knock him over. Dog and boy rolled over and over, wrestling and laughing. The strangers' dogs acted like overgrown puppies! So did the boys.

"*Tie-nee.*" Pocahontas repeated the word softly, "*Tie-nee.*" Nuttagwon liked the sound of the new word. Although she did not say it aloud, she stored it in her mind.

"We must go," Nuttagwon finally said, looking at the sun. Pocahontas nodded, and they backed out of their hiding place and snuck down to the canoe. The tide had turned, so the current helped sweep them homeward.

With every stroke Pocahontas practiced out loud the words she'd heard, while Nuttagwon paddled silently and looked at the scratches that the big black dog, Here-boi, had left on her thigh. The marks were bloodless but white against the brown of her leg. They made her smile. *The first contact I made with these strangers was with a dog,* she told herself. *I have learned strange words and spoken them, too.* She wondered what her friends would say, or her mother.

"Do they have women?" Nuttagwon spoke aloud. "Or mothers?"

"All beings have mothers," Pocahontas said.

"Do you think their mothers have hairy faces?" Nuttagwon wondered. The idea made her giggle and Pocahontas chuckled, too. "Can you imagine wearing clothes all over your body?" Nuttagwon asked.

Pocahontas spread her arms wide to show her nakedness. A thin string tied about her waist held a soft pad of moss between her legs. Otherwise, she wore only tattoos. "This is how I would rather live," she said. "Even after I become a woman, I will leave off my apron when I can."

Nuttagwon went back to paddling. "A good greasing gets me through until the snow falls in the hill country. Then I have leathers, of course."

"I have feather cloaks and beaded leggings for ceremonies," said Pocahontas.

"The only leather I saw was on the men's feet," Nuttagwon commented, "and nothing was fringed, beaded, worked with porcupine quills, or worn fur-side out."

"Except their faces!" Pocahontas answered, and the girls started giggling again.

"What would Okeus say if he saw their hairstyles?"

Nuttagwon asked. At the mention of the strict god, they stopped laughing.

"Perhaps Okeus did not come to tell the men to shave the right half of their heads?"

"But Pocahontas, what if he did, and the strangers are disobeying Okeus?" The thought silenced both girls. They paddled quietly, the current sweeping them toward home where they knew what to expect. Sunset was coming and soon everyone would gather at the water's edge to give thanks to Ahone, the maker of stars and moon.

Smells of home floated on the breeze—cook fires and succotash stew, sweet grass, tobacco, and venison. Nuttagwon sat up taller, straining to see Werowocomoco, so much grander than her own village. First, she saw wisps of smoke spiraling up over the treetops. Then she saw the canoes in the shallows left by returning fishermen. And on the bank, she saw the Supreme Chief Powhatan. He was waiting for them, his face frozen in anger.

2
WELCOME

May 1607

NUTTAGWON HELD HER BREATH AS THE BOW OF THE CANOE glided right up to the Supreme Chief's feet. She glanced at the fury in the Powhatan's eyes before looking away.

"You can make no excuse for this, daughter. You risked your life and the lives of others." Nuttagwon prayed to sink through the bottom of the dugout and into the cool mud beneath the water. There would be no food for her village now, she was sure. Their starvation would be her fault and she deserved whatever punishment the Powhatan meted out.

"Dear Father." Nuttagwon jumped at Pocahontas's sudden joyful voice from the back of the canoe. "Their leader is called *Kaptinzmit*," Pocahontas gushed. "He walks as you do, seeming to own the very air around him." Pocahontas's words came as fast as the river, but they were cunning. "No one would dare to challenge you, Father," Pocahontas went on, "but there are, among the strangers, men who would challenge this Kaptinzmit."

How does she know all this? Nuttagwon wondered. She turned in surprise to look at her new friend.

"Why are you startled? Were you not watching by my side?" Pocahontas chided. "Do you not remember the sandy-haired stranger stamping about, making noise with his moccasins?"

Nuttagwon felt foolish. She *had* seen—but she had not understood.

"Father," Pocahontas went on, "I will be more valuable than we dreamed. When a boy wandered through the crowd, Kaptinzmit rested his hand on the youth's head. Others only cuffed him aside. This leader enjoys children." Pocahontas raised her arms. "I can be a child." Nuttagwon blinked at the change in her new friend's voice. It was thinner and higher and more nasal. If she had not been looking, Nuttagwon would have thought a little girl spoke. A white-feathered little girl.

The fury in the Supreme Chief's face gave way to affection. "Daughter," he said, "anyone who mistakes you for a mere child is a fool."

"She *is* a child, and you seem to forget this, my Chief."

They all turned to see a young man silently paddle another dugout alongside the girls. A long, shiny lock of hair dangled from the side of his head that most men shaved clean, and a turtle-shell rattle lay across his knees. *A priest*, Nuttagwon thought. *And handsome.*

"That's Uttamatomakkin," Pocahontas whispered to Nuttagwon. "He tries to keep order in all of Werowocomoco."

"Pocahontas is only one woman-child among many," Uttamatomakkin repeated to the High Chief, "and reckless."

"Do not underestimate this girl," Powhatan said softly. "I

have many daughters, but this one has a mind unlike any other. Visions come to this little one, even without fasting. And she has the honey tongue of a diplomat." He looked fondly at Pocahontas, then turned to Uttamatomakkin. "We will need to use the talents of all in the fight ahead, Tomakin."

"The fight?" Nuttagwon pressed her fingers to her lips to silence herself, but it was too late. They were all looking at her.

"You are . . . ?" The Powhatan waited.

"This is Nuttagwon," Pocahontas volunteered. "My new friend came from a far and hungry Appamattuck village to plead for help from your highness."

"Nuttagwon," she went on, "this is my father, Wahunsenacah, Supreme Chief of the Powhatan Confederacy."

"She is more of a friend than Pocahontas deserves," Tomakin said. "I watched one of the stranger's dogs start to attack these girls where they hid." Cold water seemed to wash over Nuttagwon as she listened. This Tomakin had seen them? He had followed them?

"But for little Nuttagwon," the priest went on, "your daughter might have been killed or worse—revealed and captured. Your high-spirited Pocahontas chooses her guardians well."

Nuttagwon stared at the paddle in her hands. A hot rush of blood reddened her face as she struggled with what to say.

Pocahontas seemed to know. "Tomakin," she said, "will you make a ceremony tonight to adopt Nuttagwon and her gifts into our family?"

Nuttagwon stiffened. She already *had* a family. She pictured her mother, gaunt and loving, and her father, always tired now. How could she consent to leave them? How dare Pocahontas ask this? Anger flooded her mind. *Be calm*, she told herself, willing the spirit of still water to enter her veins. Instead waves crashed.

"I can't," she began, but the Powhatan, Wahunsenacah, interrupted.

"This seems a good plan, Daughter," he said. "These Appamattucks, I do remember them arriving. Her mother's sister is Totopotomoi, the Weroansqua in charge of a large town." Nuttagwon felt Pocahontas staring at her as the Powhatan went on. "Her father is only a lesser Weroance of a tiny village. We will send her parents off after the dawn's prayers with ten bushels of corn and seed to plant." Nuttagwon gasped. That was more than her father had hoped for! "And," the Supreme Chief said, "we can spare three men, their wives, and their children to work their fields through harvest."

"Oh," Nuttagwon paused to calm herself. "I cannot ask this."

"After harvest, I will expect your people to return a full tribute as well as my tribesmen, if they choose to return," Wahunsenacah said. "Your village, from what I have heard, is beautiful."

"Thank you," Nuttagwon answered, feeling trapped. She pictured three new longhouses built in her little village. There would be new children laughing and strong new backs for the fields. That would mean more hunters, too. Her mouth watered, imagining the feasts.

But she swallowed hard. If the Supreme Chief had his way, she would not be there to share in the bounty. Her cousins would feast. Their weak little babies would grow healthy. Her mother would be soft again, and her father strong, but she would not see it. "Might I go home now? I would come back to Werowocomoco after the harvest, too," she tried to bargain, but the Powhatan interrupted.

"The next time you spy, Daughter, I will send a party of guards along—and this little Nuttagwon as well."

"They do need minders," Tomakin said. "Though the strangers neither heard nor saw them, the girls left the shapes of their bodies crushed into the ferns. A blind man could follow their careless tracks."

"Enough, Uttamatomakkin. These girls have brought me useful news," the Powhatan said. "And Pocahontas has much more to share. I will see you all at the meal tonight. Anath."

"Anath." Nuttagwon mumbled a good-bye.

"*Fayre thiwell*," Pocahontas said.

"*Fayre* . . . ?" the Supreme Chief repeated.

"That is the stranger's way of saying anath," Pocahontas explained. "Try it again. *Fayre thiwell.*" Nuttagwon could not believe what she was hearing. Her new friend was correcting the Supreme Chief of the entire Powhatan Confederacy. She was not even in line to inherit the throne, but nothing she did seemed to irritate her father. He repeated the foreign words over and over until Pocahontas agreed that he had gotten the sounds right.

"*Fayre thiwell*, girls," the Chief finally said, then looked at Nuttagwon. "My wives will welcome you into the royal longhouse this evening." He turned and strode toward town.

Uttamatomakkin back-paddled his canoe furiously and headed upstream without another word, a white feather dangling from the knotted hair on his right side, and his priestly lock fluttering from his left.

Pocahontas tugged at Nuttagwon's braid. "We will have all of our adventures together now!"

Nuttagwon refused to turn around. "We need to beach the canoe," she said dully, "and then I must find my mother."

The path winding beside the tobacco fields looked different as Nuttagwon hurried past. *This will be my home*, she lectured herself. *My new home.* She blinked back tears as she tried to decide how to present her sudden new life to her mother. Knee-high bean sprouts filled the cornfield. Nuttagwon waved to the girl standing watch on the platform by the field and swung past the refuse heap at the edge of town. She held her breath against the sharp smell of so many people's garbage. *My people's now.* The small house she and her mother had erected together lay just beyond the next field. Nuttagwon paused, still as ice, closing her eyes and pressing her feet into Mother Earth. "Blessed Ahone, help me now," she prayed.

A late snow goose flew overhead, its wing beats strong against the wind. *Hurry*, Nuttagwon thought as it rushed north to join its tribe. *The others have left, but you will be fine.* Nuttagwon's heartbeat matched the sure strokes of the white wings rowing through the sky. Energy flooded her body. She knew this wasn't a true vision—there was no fasting, no chanting, and no herbs—but she had felt the strength of the goose's spirit. For now, it was all she needed.

As Nuttagwon walked into the clearing, her mother looked up from the cook fire and brushed the bangs from her eyes. "Wingam!" she cried out joyfully. Nuttagwon jumped at the sound of her secret name.

"Mother." Her own voice sounded old, Nuttagwon realized. She felt old. Nuttagwon pulled the image of the snow goose into her mind. "I have wonderful news," she said.

"What happened, Wingam? Are you not well?"

"I am in good health." Nuttagwon spoke quickly. She tried to make her voice sound happy. "Our village is saved! The Great Powhatan told me that he will send many bushels of corn home at the next dawn."

"The Supreme Chief spoke to you?" Her mother rose to her feet and wiped her hands on her short leather apron.

"Yes, Mother." Nuttagwon plunged on. "And he will send a handful of hunters, their wives and children, to help as well. They will carry the bounty to our home, and then they will stay on for the harvest season. Our fields will be worked and our forests hunted with new energy."

"The Supreme Chief spoke to my daughter?" Nuttagwon's mother repeated.

"Our bellies will be full," Nuttagwon said.

"Then why is there no joy in your voice?"

Nuttagwon made herself stand tall. "I am lucky." She used Pocahontas's term. "I will stay on at Werowocomoco and live in the royal longhouse within the royal stockade. The Powhatan instructed me to move in there tonight."

Nuttagwon's mother put both hands to her mouth. "You

are too young, daughter. The Chief is an old man. Surely he can find wives of his own without reaching for children!"

Nuttagwon took a deep breath. "I am to be a guardian of Pocahontas, not wife to her father."

"You? A guardian?" Nuttagwon's mother put her hands on her daughter's shoulders. "This is madness, little one. You're not big enough to be anyone's guardian. Besides, I do not want you spending time with that Pocahontas. She is trouble. All the townswomen agree."

Nuttagwon held herself still, though she ached to melt into her mother's arms. This was worse than the pain of hunger, harsher than having to beg, crueler than the loss of friends to the sickness that swept the village. Nuttagwon took a shuddering breath. "I will miss you," she said firmly.

"This has truly happened, then?" Nuttagwon's mother backed away. "We gain the food we need, but we lose you? This seems a harsh bargain."

"I will come to the village when I have fulfilled the vision."

"A daughter of mine has been given a vision? Wingam, you have not begun your moon-times yet, nor have you fasted." There was wonder in the woman's voice. "There have been a few white feathers in our clan, but . . ." she stopped. "This is that Pocahontas again, is it not? What foolishness has the Powhatan's favorite filled you with? *Visions?* Ha!"

"I need to get my things, Mother," Nuttagwon said. She hurried into the hut. The fire was low, so Nuttagwon piled on extra fuel. It would be a bad omen to have it die when things already seemed so dreadful.

Her mother's voice bored through the grass-mat walls straight into her heart. "That girl wants to leave all tradition behind. She will ruin your life with her wanton ways." When the hearth flames began flickering, Nuttagwon rolled up her sleeping mats. She wiped her eyes as she looked about at the worn traveling baskets that they had brought from their home in the hills. Her head filled with echoes. In her mind, she could hear her aunts and uncles talking, and the crying sounds of her village.

These memories mingled with the laughter and warm voices of the Beaver Clan women of Werowocomoco. Her clanswomen had helped tie the saplings into place and unfurl the wall mats to build the hut. They had shared fire and food. She clung to their strength. The clan would support her if she needed it in the future.

Nuttagwon stepped out of the hut and gasped. Her mother had already smeared her face with the black ashes of mourning. "I wove those mats for you with my own hands," she said.

Nuttagwon hugged the smooth old mats to her chest. "They will give me strength. Mother, the Powhatan will need my talents in the fight ahead. He said so himself. You cannot doubt his vision."

In response, her mother lifted off her own necklace. A perfect shell bead of deepest purple dangled from the end of its thin leather thong. Nuttagwon held her breath as her mother settled the wampum bead around her daughter's neck.

"Thank you," Nuttagwon whispered.

Her mother pushed her toward the path that led to the town center.

A tall unfamiliar girl stepped out from behind a long-house beside the path. She wore Pamunkey markings and carried a tightly woven basket of corn flour. "Are you going home to your little backwoods village now?"

"No." Nuttagwon wondered who this ill-mannered girl was. "I am moving into the royal stockade for a time."

"Oh-ho!" the tall one crowed. "I suppose you think you are better than us? That will last only as long as you keep Pocahontas's attention."

A girl with many tattoos scurried to join them. "One moon," she said, "and you'll be back grinding corn with us—or grubbing in the gardens."

"Two days, I give her." A third girl limped up. "Is this the one?"

Nuttagwon stared at the three Pamunkeys. None of them wore the apron of a woman, yet, though all looked to be near their moon-time, and they all seemed to be friends. "Am I *what* one?" she demanded.

"The one with the secret."

"What secret?" How could they know of the spy mission so quickly?

"Then there *is* a secret," the tall one said triumphantly. The three girls linked little fingers with each other. "You can tell us."

Nuttagwon remained silent. The tall girl's face hardened. "You cannot keep a secret from all our eyes and all our ears," she said. "We know Pocahontas took you out on the river. We know that gorgeous Tomakin left soon after. And neither of your canoes returned for most of the day." The other girls were nodding. "Matachanna is hoping to marry him.

Wouldn't she be thrilled to know that you were off seeing her sweetheart?" They all made clicking noises with their tongues. "And you not a woman yet." The tattooed girl stared at Nuttagwon's flat chest.

Nuttagwon pulled the sleeping mats up to hide her nipples. The woven grasses felt warm and soft, smoothed by many seasons' use. "Who is Matachanna?" she demanded. "And who are *you*? Why didn't you greet me before?"

"Oh-ho. Our little troublemaker wants our names before she spills her secrets," the tall one said.

"Stop it, Ofanneis," the tattooed girl said. "This is enough." She turned to Nuttagwon. "Pay us no mind. We are old friends, skilled at mischief. I am Cheawanta, of the Otter Clan, out of the Rabbit Clan."

"Thank you," Nuttagwon said. She gave her name and her clan relations and waited until Cheawanta explained that Matachanna was Pocahontas's older sister.

Then Nuttagwon turned quickly. "I am expected at the Supreme Chief's longhouse, but I will be back to exchange proper greetings. That is a courtesy that everyone, even in my 'little backwoods village,' knows to do." The other girls hissed.

Nuttagwon's back burned with the heat of their glares as she hurried on. She felt as lonely as the single white goose she'd seen earlier, winging its way through the wide spring-blue sky.

3
GIFTS

"Come." Pocahontas beckoned Nuttagwon. She
pulled aside the deer-hide flap at the royal longhouse door.
Nuttagwon ducked and entered, then stood blinking at the
haze in the smoky interior. There would be no mosquitoes in
here. Pocahontas gestured toward a shadowy corner and said,
"The light sticks."

Nuttagwon laid her sleeping mats on a bench, then
grabbed a pine stick and lit its knotty end in the low fire on
the floor. A light flared up, gleaming against the glossy fur of
pouches hanging from the ceiling—beaver, otter, wildcat,
and skunk. Furry deerskins and bear pelts lay thick on low
sleeping platforms around the edge of the room. Fancy dancing rattles and feather cloaks hung from the rafters with
other finery.

Pocahontas laughed aloud, then explained, "Thank you.
Through your eyes I see all this anew. I thrill to anything
new." She paused. "You will find my jewelry in that wildcat
pouch."

"Your own pouch is not in one of the back rooms?" Nuttagwon pointed toward the door at the rear of the entry room, wondering how many bedrooms this huge longhouse held, lined up one behind the other.

"Let the older women sleep in the back rooms with their children. I choose to sleep by the door to see everyone who comes in and out," Pocahontas said. "Sometimes I even sneak out at night wrapped in black furs."

Nuttagwon stared at a corn-husk doll that leaned against a perfect wolf pelt the color of a midnight sky. "I'll need the paint pot from that basket over there, Nuttagwon," Pocahontas prompted. "We must be ready for the feast, even before evening prayers."

Evening prayers. The thought jarred Nuttagwon into action. She would see her mother at prayers and her father, too. Nuttagwon reached up to unhook the jewelry bag. She nearly dropped it, it was so heavy.

"The front of my head is as prickly as a porcupine." Pocahontas rubbed her scalp. "I wish I had thought to shave it smooth today. I have plenty of sharpened shells to use, but . . ."

Nuttagwon was running her hands through the long, soft fur of the wolf skin on Pocahontas's sleeping platform. "I have always slept on a reed mat," she said slowly, "with another thrown over me for warmth, in a house made of woven mats." She stared up at the thick bark walls of the longhouse and the smoke hole at the top.

Pocahontas took the white feather from her long black braid. "Nuttagwon, this was all a surprise to me, too, when

I first came here. I said farewell to my mother and her village as a very little girl. Like you, I once lived in a reed hut with the forest sounds to sing me to sleep at night."

"I did not know that."

"I am just the daughter of one of my father's many wives. They come here from the countryside and only enjoy this luxury until they conceive a child by Wahunsenacah. Then they are sent home to their villages until the babies are born. My father overlooks the very smallest villages, like yours, as he searches for wives." Pocahontas held a feather comb out to Nuttagwon and turned her back. Nuttagwon took the comb and began to work through the long black locks. "When they are a few years old," Pocahontas went on, "the Powhatan's children are sent back here to Werowocomoco, alone."

"You never saw your mother again?" It was hard for Nuttagwon to say the words.

"I hardly missed her," Pocahontas said firmly. She tied a leather apron around her waist and went on. "Here I had more than a dozen new mothers—the Powhatan's new wives. His family is friendly. You will see. Hand me the paint pot and tell me about yourself."

Nuttagwon gasped. Pocahontas, still a girl and not even in line to be a Weroansqua, was going to paint herself? And *red*?

"Do you sing?" Pocahontas prompted.

"Of course," Nuttagwon answered, looking away from the paint. "I can play the flute, too, but music is not the talent Ahone gave me."

Pocahontas dipped her fingers into the oily red paint and

poked at Nuttagwon with dripping fingertips. "So what is your gift?" Nuttagwon laughed and jumped aside. "Ah, you dance? Or win at foot races?" Pocahontas smeared the thick color over her face and shoulders. "You create new stews from old game?" Still, Nuttagwon did not answer. "You can retell the old stories word for word?"

"I am an Appamattuck, a member of the Powhatan Confederacy," Nuttagwon answered. "I can do what must be done. I had just begun training as a healing woman before I left home. I never have seen a vision, as you have, but I do see patterns."

"Do not be so sure you want a vision." With one finger, Pocahontas ran a line of red down the front of her body from her chin to her waist. "You see patterns?" she prompted.

"Like the one on your apron."

Pocahontas looked down. "But it is blank," she said.

"Sometimes I can see a pattern that will fit," Nuttagwon said, "and sew it in beads. Patterns to edge a pot. To embroider a moccasin. To cut a tattoo. I just," she paused, "see them."

Pocahontas leaned forward so Nuttagwon could lift strings of beads over her head. "I need more necklaces," she demanded. "I must look important tonight." Then she asked, "Nuttagwon, do you always work from the old patterns?"

"They are always the best."

Pocahontas slid the precious white feather back into her hair. "Could you make *new* patterns for me?"

Nuttagwon stood silent, struggling to imagine breaking the old patterns. It had taken days for her to copy the cookpot design and weeks to learn the ancient moccasin pattern. The elders had been amazed at how quickly she picked up and remembered designs. It would be years before she would have them mastered, of course. *Change them?* She closed her eyes and pictured the classic designs woven into her mother's headband.

That pattern could be worked upside down, she thought. She visualized it huge, then very tiny. Nuttagwon saw the sharp angles woven into curving waves instead, and the dots enlarged into flying birds. Her mind rebelled against the changes, but the old patterns kept dancing behind the lids of her eyes. They shifted color and fled tradition—yet they were still beautiful! Nuttagwon opened her eyes and reached out to steady herself.

"I could make decorations for you that no one has ever seen before." Nuttagwon's words tumbled out. "Those baskets could have new colors." She looked around at the treasures of the longhouse. "I can already see new beading for your earrings and a new star shape on your paint pot."

"This comb?" Pocahontas asked. Nuttagwon nodded. "That ladle and cup?" Nuttagwon nodded again. "My cloak? The canoe?" Pocahontas was grinning. Nuttagwon was, too. "You could ornament everything to look new, couldn't you?"

Nuttagwon's mind swam with the strange patterns and colors that the hairy people on the beach used. She pictured the intricate design on the bow of their boat. Nuttagwon imagined copying it onto a canoe here at Werowocomoco—perhaps even onto the Supreme Chief's canoe! She caught her breath. That canoe, like the other belongings she'd thought to alter, were all Powhatan's bounty, tribute brought to him from all over his Confederacy. Nuttagwon hung her head. How had she dared tell Pocahontas that these treasures could be improved?

Pocahontas put her hand on Nuttagwon's shoulder. "You are a wonder! A maiden who can bead my skirts, grease my hair, and join in my adventures, too! I cannot wait to see the changes you will bring to my life."

"Your life?" Nuttagwon echoed weakly. "Cheawanta said this would last only a few days. . . ."

"Cheawanta?" Pocahontas asked. "She is the kindest in the pack, but she plays no part in our future."

Nuttagwon felt the tension leave her shoulders. *Our* future? "I will decorate you so beautifully that men will flock to you," she said. "We will make sure you marry well."

Pocahontas was suddenly silent.

"Isn't that what you want?"

"I never want to leave Werowocomoco, Nuttagwon. My father is here. Fifteen thousand members of Powhatan's Confederacy send corn and tobacco, skins and shell beads to him in tribute. I would not want to go to an ordinary village and be wife to a lesser man. I must be in the center of all that is new and exciting and powerful."

"But unless your mother is a Weroansqua, your future is as an ordinary woman," Nuttagwon said gently.

"Both Father—and my vision—say otherwise."

"Your vision showed that *you* will become a Weroansqua?" Nuttagwon took a step backward. "*And* a blessed woman, too, with visions of the future?" She put her fingers to her lips to stop the rude questions spilling out.

Pocahontas shook her head. "No," she murmured, "I will be none of those." A look of sorrow suddenly made her face look old. As the firelight flickered, she extended a finger toward Nuttagwon. "I will need a true friend, for strength—and for life."

Nuttagwon stared at the outstretched finger.

"Please," Pocahontas begged. Her voice was suddenly high and small. She sounded very young—and scared.

Nuttagwon linked fingers with her. "The name beneath my name," Pocahontas whispered, "is Matoaka." Nuttagwon felt chill bumps rise along her arms. *Matoaka?* The name itself meant "white feather." Pocahontas had been marked as a visionary while still a baby?

When she could breathe, Nuttagwon whispered back, "My first-given name is Wingam." The thought of saying her true name outside of her family, beyond her clan and far from her village, made Nuttagwon gasp with fear.

"I will be a sister to you, Wingam," Pocahontas promised.

A scratching sounded at the door. "Pocahontas," a woman called quietly.

"Matachanna!" Pocahontas answered, then explained, "My older sister, Nuttagwon—one of dozens—but powerful. She may marry Uttamatomakkin."

Matachanna entered. "Father asks if you have lost your way. I wonder if you have lost your senses."

"Oh!" Pocahontas cried. "Prayers! Supper! The news! How could I have forgotten?" She clapped her hands and laughed at herself. "Nuttagwon, here, has taken overlong dressing my hair."

Nuttagwon gasped. "But . . ." she began.

Pocahontas grinned at her and took off one of her own necklaces. "Tomakin will make this official tonight," she told her sister. "Father is adopting this maiden. She will be renamed, as well." When Pocahontas settled the necklace around Nuttagwon's neck, the warmth and weight of the beads felt like a caress. Nuttagwon looked down and gasped. The gods, themselves, used deep purple wampum like this to seal their promises. The necklace was priceless! It circled and dwarfed the gift from her own mother.

"Coming, Nuttagwon?" Pocahontas asked.

4
NEETAH

"THE SUN IS SETTING!" MATACHANNA SAID, PUSHING PAST
the younger girls. "We have no time for beads and paint!"
They ran along the empty pathways of the village out
through the gate of the ruler's stockade and through the
wider town stockade before reaching the riverbank. The
people stood on the shore splashing water on their faces,
washing their hands, and murmuring quietly. Even the lit-
tlest children knew the importance of the ceremony and
were quiet. Nuttagwon followed Pocahontas to the empty
mats spread out on the ground next to a cluster of young
women. The girls washed quickly and settled down as the
sun dropped toward the marshy horizon.

Nuttagwon sat listening to the rush of the water in front
of her knees. Around her, dozens of the Powhatan's daughters, sons, and wives from many tribes sat quietly. They all
wore beads of copper and shell, elaborate headdresses, dangling earrings, and fine smooth leathers. *Was Pocahontas
really her father's favorite among all of these handsome people?*
Neetah wondered. *What did he see in her?*

The worshipers began sprinkling holy tobacco in circles around themselves before the sun slid behind the water. Nuttagwon stopped staring at the huge family and tried to concentrate instead on the gentle god Ahone, giver of all beauty.

Her mind kept wandering. Where were her own mother and father praying? If only she could talk with them about the promises she'd made to Pocahontas! Too much had happened too quickly. Those around her began chanting, and Nuttagwon mouthed the age-old words of praise. The beads around her neck seemed to pull her downward. She shrugged a shoulder to center their unaccustomed weight and noticed Pocahontas's outstretched finger.

Nuttagwon's whole body stiffened. She kept chanting as Pocahontas smiled, her dimples deep shadows in the dusky light. Nuttagwon quickly hooked fingers with her new friend. Just as quickly she let go and struggled to find the calm space within herself.

"Wait here," Pocahontas said as the prayers ended. She darted off toward a group of men. Nuttagwon saw the tall Tomakin lean down to talk with her. His scalp lock bristled with white feathers. *A priest and a warrior*, Nuttagwon thought. She watched the Powhatan's family, trying to observe every detail, the same way Pocahontas had when she'd looked at the strangers near the ships. Nuttagwon noticed that the other men gave Uttamatomakkin space. They did not interrupt his conversation with the High Chief's daughter. *He is a very powerful priest*, Nuttagwon concluded.

Pocahontas strode back. "It is settled. After the feast, you will be given a new name and a new family."

"A new name?" Nuttagwon's skin tingled. "What name

will I have? And changing families, Pocahontas? Am I truly to be adopted?"

"We *did* speak of this," Pocahontas said firmly. "Besides, it will be glorious fun! Now we must hurry to the feast."

Nuttagwon stared for a moment before she ran after Pocahontas, holding the precious necklace to keep it from slapping her chest.

Even through the cloud of tobacco smoke around the royal fire, Nuttagwon could see that nothing here looked like home. The crowd was huge, and people wore the paint and clothing of many tribes. Men and women actually sat side by side on mats as they ate. Instead of sharing from the cook pot, each person held a wooden plate. It seemed that others filled the plates for them, bringing helpings big enough to feed a village family in deep winter. Nuttagwon searched through the smoke for a glimpse of her parents. Had they been invited to this feast?

Beside her, Pocahontas stooped to take a corn cake from Matachanna's plate. "Thank you, sister!" she said gaily, then turned. "Come." She hooked Nuttagwon's finger with her own and pulled her along to the Powhatan's side of the fire. Hisses of disapproval followed them, but Pocahontas did not slow down until she stopped by the High Chief's feet.

Nuttagwon looked up at the Powhatan's face, and a thrill ran through her body. He was smiling openly at Pocahontas from his perch atop dozens of mats. By his side, Uttamatomakkin sat on a single mat. He was not smiling.

"Tomakin," Pocahontas said, "will you introduce my friend?"

The priest handed his plate to Matachanna, seated on the mat beside him. He shook his long-handled rattle and rose to his feet. The oily sheen of his painted body glittered in the light of the fire. So did his white feather and the copper medallions hanging on his broad chest. He spread his arms wide for attention, shaking the turtle shell until the corn kernels inside sounded like the hiss of a snake, although all eyes were already on him. Tomakin waited so long that everyone knew he would announce something of importance.

"Our little visitor from the hills, Nuttagwon, the Appamattuck, has saved Pocahontas's life this day." A chorus of startled whispers circled the fire. The priest waited for silence again. "She showed bravery and cleverness. Most of all, she showed loyalty." Nuttagwon's head swam. She tried to focus on the priest's words. "Often," he went on, "a name is changed to reflect a change or event. Seldom is a new name so well deserved."

"But her name is Nuttagwon." Her mother's voice floated from the back of the crowd. Nuttagwon turned and squinted, trying to see her through the smoke.

Uttamatomakkin waited, then made the announcement. "From this day, she shall be known as Neetah."

Neetah? The very word meant "friend"! Nuttagwon grabbed Pocahontas's arm for support. This meant that everyone who knew her would call her "friend."

"Neetah?" The Powhatan's voice came from above her. It took a moment for Nuttagwon to realize he was speaking to her. She turned so suddenly that her pigtail and beads flew sideways. Many around her laughed, but there was warmth in the sound.

The Powhatan was standing now, and spoke to the crowd over the girls' heads. "Our friend, Neetah, will join my family this night. Her old family will be given much for their poor village." He waved an arm to the side, and deer hides were pulled off three huge baskets of corn. Murmurs of wonder rose in the night sky.

"My daughter Pocahontas and her Neetah have encountered the strangers and have lived to tell of it. They will be of great use to me in the moons to come." Pocahontas grinned at her father. The Powhatan glanced her way and added, "As emissaries, they will be busy doing tribal work. Others will shoulder their chores while they manage a man's job with their young girls' bodies."

Nuttagwon heard sudden whispers from here and there around the fire. "No chores! He can't mean that!"

"What can little girls do?"

"That Pocahontas already thinks she is a Weroansqua."

"She'll be impossible now!"

They are right, Nuttagwon thought.

"Enough of this," the High Chief said. "There are many stories you will want to hear from the girls tonight."

Though Nuttagwon's plate was filled with the most succulent cuts of meat, she was barely able to eat. Beaver tail, juicy and prime; the tenderest part of a deer's loin; the tail of a turkey—it did not matter. Over and over Pocahontas was asked to tell of Neetah's valiant deed, taming the strange giant dog. Every time, Nuttagwon interrupted, trying to make her actions sound less heroic. That only made the listeners revere her more. "More logs on the fire!" someone said, until the blaze made the leaves above rustle from the heat.

Nuttagwon's mother moved to the front of the crowd to sit with her famous daughter. Her father came, too, and, after an awkward moment, sat next to his wife in the very public light of the fire. "Nuttagwon," her father said.

"She is Neetah now," Pocahontas corrected him. Nuttagwon flinched. Although Nuttagwon's mother glared at Pocahontas, her father did not seem angry.

"Neetah, you bring honor to our village, and"—he flashed a look at his wife—"to your clan as well. You will be missed, but your story will live on at our fires."

"Mother?" Neetah said. Words of truth came to her as if from Okeus. "I will remember your lessons. I will hold to the ways of our gods, our clan, our tribe, and always remember the old stories." Neetah dropped her voice to the barest whisper. "I will always be your Wingam, Mother." She lifted the heavy necklace of wampum beads over her head and settled Pocahontas's priceless gift around her mother's neck.

For a moment she held her breath. Her mother finally met her eyes. Then her arms enfolded Neetah in a hug. "Ahone keep you, my daughter," she whispered.

"Neetah?" Uttamatomakkin stood behind her. This time she responded at once. "Come now to the temple. We will conduct this hasty business tonight." Pocahontas grabbed Neetah's hand and motioned her parents to follow them to the holy longhouse at the edge of the village.

By the time they got there, a large party was trailing them. Tomakin entered first, stooping low under the door. Neetah followed, her eyes watering in the dense smoke, full of the incense of sweet grass and sage and tobacco and the singing of an unseen priest. A great statue of Okeus loomed up out of the shadows, his face contorted in rage, his glowing eyes reflecting the ceremonial fire. Fear flooded Neetah's body. She would have to answer to Okeus for her actions this day—and for her decisions. She stopped so suddenly that Pocahontas ran into her back.

"Look away from the statue." Pocahontas pushed her forward.

Neetah took a deep breath and nearly choked on the pungent smoke. For strength, she grabbed at her mother's single wampum bead on the thong around her neck. The ceremony passed in a blur of chants and smoldering herbs, sharp questions, and her stumbled answers. In the dizzying heat of the lodge, faces faded in and out of the shadows around Neetah. Tomakin. Pocahontas. Neetah's soot-streaked mother wearing the promise necklace. The Supreme Chief, Powhatan. The handsome Uttamatomakkin. And Pocahontas, always Pocahontas, straight-faced but dimpling with amusement. Okeus watched it all, too, his eyes unblinking, his face full of anger.

Finally it was over, and Neetah staggered out into the night. The cool spring air hit her face like ice water. She took deep, shuddering breaths as she followed Pocahontas. "Where are we going?" she gasped, as her head began to ache. She pictured the sleeping platform waiting for her, cushioned and covered with furs. Her whole body ached to curl under them, to hide her head from the night and the all-seeing eyes of Okeus.

"Father wishes to speak with us." Pocahontas led her to the dance circle. A large figure waited within the sacred ring of seven posts, carved with the faces of untold ancestors. No one would dare invade this space or pause near it to listen.

"Girls." the Powhatan's voice was low. "I need to hear all of it now. Tell me everything you saw and heard from the strangers, whether or not it seemed important."

"That will take us until dawn, Father," Pocahontas said. Neetah looked at the solemn wooden faces around the fire and swayed on her feet. Pocahontas took her hand and asked, "May we sit?"

"Yes. My first wife will be bringing strong teas and warm robes to ward off the night's chill—and the urge to sleep."

The village slowly quieted around them as women and children retreated to their longhouses to sleep. Some of the men went to the men's sleeping house. Others followed their wives to the women's house. As the Powhatan pumped the girls' memories for every word, gesture, detail, and relationship they might recall, the men drifted back to the men's house, one by one. A sentry walked past, a dark shadow against the night, while the girls described again the long shiny knives and layers of clothing worn by the men. The morning star glowed in the east before they were done.

"I leave it to you to decide what roles you will play with these strangers," the Powhatan said. He rose and stretched. "Whatever it takes, you two must become trusted. You must bring back to me whatever you come to understand of their words, their ways. You will accompany my representatives to the strangers' growing fort. You will pose as innocent children, though you are neither children, nor innocent." He paused and rested one hand on Pocahontas's head. The other weighed heavily on Neetah's. "May Ahone be with you, my daughters, guiding and guarding every step."

Neetah could not block out the image of the glowing eyes in the temple darkness. Okeus would be along, too.

Later in the royal family's longhouse, Neetah cuddled under a feather-soft deer pelt.

Pocahontas untangled the white feather from her hair and set it aside. "Sleep," she said. "We have roles to play out, Neetah. Ahone grant us success." She closed her eyes and turned away. Soon her breathing evened out and deepened into sleep.

Neetah lay watching the dawn sky lighten through the smoke hole. She wondered what would happen if they failed. She was glad she had not the vision to know.

PART II

INSIDE THE FORT

1607~1609

5

THE FORT

June 1607

UTTAMATOMAKKIN AND SIX OTHER PAMUNKEY MEN PADDLED the giant war canoe directly to the strangers' landing place. Neetah leaned from one side to the other, trying to see past Pocahontas and the broad shoulders of the men in front. On the shore, a crowd of the hairy-faced men gathered, staring back at them. Neetah shielded her eyes from the sun reflected by the strange white metal on the men's chests.

More men rushed out of a half-built fortress of sharpened tree trunks. They held tools in their hands that sparkled like their chest plates, as did the long knives hanging from their waistbands. Three youngsters ran down the bank to join them, dogs bounding alongside. "Those boys are our age!" Pocahontas whispered. "We will use them."

Neetah sat back on her heels in the hollowed log canoe, stunned by Pocahontas's fearlessness.

The hairy-faced leader strode to the front, looking tall in his white metal hat. *Kaptinzmit*, Neetah thought, as Pocahontas said it aloud.

"That is Kaptinzmit, Uttamatomakkin. Do your negoti-ating with him, but watch the others."

"And I suppose you expect to be at the center of the dis-cussion?" Uttamatomakkin asked.

"No. Neetah and I have other plans," Pocahontas answered. Neetah blinked in surprise.

Kaptinzmit's voice barked an order, and the men on land formed a line, facing the approaching canoe. After another order, the boys scampered behind the men.

"Muzkets," Uttamatomakkin said. "A band of these strangers used them to kill far to the south. They hunt with them instead of using bows or spears."

"I, too, have heard of these weapons," another man said. "A clan brother died after the stick roared at him. His wound festered and resisted all of our medicine." Neetah watched the muscles ripple across Tomakin's back as he quietly reached for his bow. The canoe stopped surging forward as the men rested their paddles.

"They protect the children," Neetah whispered.

"I see that, too," Pocahontas said. "I will use it." Suddenly she stood tall, mid-boat.

"Get down," Uttamatomakkin commanded, but Pocahontas raised her arm instead, staring at the newcomers.

For a moment, everyone froze. Neetah's skin prickled with excitement. Then, in answer, Kaptinzmit slowly reached his hand out toward Pocahontas. One of the pale-skinned boys pushed between the men in front of him to see. Slowly, the men lowered their knives and their muskets.

Cautiously, the Pamunkeys began sculling the water again

with their paddles, easing the canoe back into motion. As they got closer, Neetah smelled the strangers and nearly gagged.

"Anath." Uttamatomakkin called his greeting, as soon as they were within hearing distance.

"Fayre thiwell," Pocahontas chimed in, her voice high and pure over the priest's low tones. Uttamatomakkin twitched angrily, but a smile flickered across Kaptinzmit's face. He barked something else to his men. Their laughter was rude, but they relaxed.

The canoe slid easily onto the muddy riverbank. Uttamatomakkin stood, his hands spread open at his sides, clearly empty. Neetah drew in her breath. The priest's body filled the sky above her, perfectly tattooed and brightly painted. His short priestly cape fluttered in the breeze. So did the spray of white feathers he wore tucked into the big knot of hair over his left ear. Except for his priest's lock, the right side of his head glistened in the sun like the rest of his body, greased against the early spring chill. Neetah thought Uttamatomakkin looked like one of the gods. She felt a blush creep up her cheeks. *Stop it*, she scolded herself, and glanced away.

The canoe rocked wildly as Uttamatomakkin stepped out. His bodyguards eased themselves over the sides of the boat. One steadied it as Pocahontas followed, her hand still extended toward Kaptinzmit. After an awkward moment of silence, Kaptinzmit greeted them. "Gooday," he said, and, pointing to himself, said his name clearly, plus a string of other words. Neetah tried to hold the sounds in her mind. It was hard when the men smelled so bad. She stared at the fur on their cheeks and upper lips, on their wrists and the backs of their hands. Some even had hairs on their fingers. A few had hair peeking from their noses!

It was easier to look at the boys. They might be just as smothered in clothes, but their cheeks were smooth. One of them, a boy with seawater-green eyes, smiled at her. It was the one who'd played with "Here-boi." Before Neetah could stop herself, she smiled back and offered her open hand to him. "Here-boi," she called, to let him know she knew his dog.

The boy looked startled, but took a few steps toward the canoe. They both glanced at the men. The strangers and the Pamunkeys stood close and tense, trying to communicate. "Powhatan," Neetah heard, and "King Jaimz" and "Chessiopiac." That was the name of the bay beloved by the shoreline tribe. Neetah almost laughed aloud when the strangers tried to say the word. It came out more like *Chessapeek.* "Jaimztown" one man kept saying, as he pointed to the fort. No one was looking at the canoes.

Neetah waded ashore to stand by the nearest boy. "Neetah," she touched her chest by her mother's bead. "Kaptinzmit," she pointed to the leader of the strangers. Then she pointed to the stranger-boy.

"Samuel." He pointed to his own chest. "Samuel Collier, cabinboi." He grinned and stared at her body as if he'd never seen a girl his age before. His face flushed red.

Neetah decided to ignore his stare. "Samallsamallcallcabinboi?"

"Nay." He shook his head. "Just Sam."

"Nayjustsam." Neetah tried again.

46

"Samuel," the boy said firmly, and then pointed to himself, repeating, "Samuel. Neetah."

"Here-boi?" Neetah asked. She looked around for the big black dog. Samuel looked confused, so Neetah made her hands into droopy ears by the sides of her face and quietly mimicked the deep woof.

Sam laughed and looked up toward the fort. "Tucker!" he called. "Here-boi!"

"Here-boi!" Neetah cried. The big black dog barreled out of the fort and thundered down the bank toward them. Samuel knelt to greet the dog, so Neetah knelt as well. She glanced up toward the others. One of the Pamunkeys looked at her sternly. Pocahontas stood next to him. There was approval in Pocahontas's eyes and a dimple playing on her cheek. Suddenly, the dog was upon Neetah and Sam, its hairy body driving them over into the mud.

"Nay!" called Sam, but the dog was licking his face with its big pink tongue. The smells of dog and stranger mingled.

Together, Samuel and Neetah rolled over and over with the dog, laughing and wrestling. Neetah felt suddenly as if she had two spirits. One played like a child. The other noticed Samuel's clothing, some of it smooth and some of it rough. His hard leather moccasins scraped her legs, and there was dirt ground into the skin of his neck. She looked up and saw that Kaptinzmit and some of the other English men had come over and formed a circle around them. Kaptinzmit looked at her and then glanced at Uttamatomakkin and Pocahontas, who had also joined them. The Pamunkey priest met Kaptinzmit's eyes and made a face to dismiss the interruption. Then both turned and walked up the beach, Pocahontas and the others behind them.

Neetah grabbed a piece of driftwood and hurled it into the water. Tucker bounded after it. Neetah and Samuel regained their feet before Tucker galloped back and shook water all over them. Samuel took the stick and threw it farther into the water. When the dog leaped after it, Neetah and Samuel scrambled up the bank. As Neetah tried to wipe water off her face, she brushed some sand into one eye. She rubbed at it and bent over. Suddenly she felt a hand holding her wrist. "Nay," Samuel said. "Don't be a'rubbin' at it." Neetah straightened up, surprised by the kindness in his tone. Her eye closed over the pain, and tears spilled onto her cheek.

"Stand ye still," he said. Even the dog quieted at the gentleness of his voice. Samuel leaned toward Neetah, staring into her eye. Closer and closer he came. Neetah forced herself not to flinch as he reached forward to touch her. She held her breath to keep from smelling him, too. This close, she could see the lice in his hair.

"Nay," he said again.

He backed up a moment and reached his hand into a pouch hidden in his clothing, pulled out a scrap of fabric, and held it toward her eye. Neetah grabbed the scrap and examined it with her good eye. It was woven like grass cloth, not knotted like fish netting, but the fibers were finer than anything she had ever seen. Its edges were folded over and one corner was stitched with a design. She memorized the pattern as she handed the cloth back to Sam.

He folded one corner into a point. Neetah willed herself

to be still and prayed to Ahone for safety in the stranger's hands. Samuel flicked the sand grain out of her eye and stepped back. "Is it gone?" he asked.

Neetah blinked and wiped her eye gently. She grinned at Sam.

Sam did a strange trick to celebrate. He threw his whole body over toward one side, landing on one hand. He spun, heels over head, from one hand to two. Then suddenly he was back up on both feet. Neetah laughed, so he did it again while Tucker barked nearby.

Pocahontas hurried back from where the men were huddled on the beach and tried the trick, too, but tumbled to the ground at Sam's feet. "Pocahontas." Neetah introduced them by pointing. "Samuel." He laughed and showed them the trick again. The other boys gathered and soon all of them were showing off or lying, panting and dizzy, on the ground. None of the boys had begun their man-growth yet and all they could do, it seemed, was stare at the girls' bodies. Neetah wondered if their sisters were always covered in cloth, too, instead of simply wearing a comfortable thong and a patch of moss. She shrugged at their stares and turned to Pocahontas. "Are you hungry?" she asked.

"Samuel?" Pocahontas made the motion of feeding herself. Then she chewed on nothing. He looked at Neetah. She pretended to drink from a gourd. When she was done, she made a mock belch and patted her stomach. Samuel grinned and made a real belch.

"Come," he said, and led them toward the opening in the Jaimztown stockade. Neetah glanced back once. Kaptinzmit was down on the beach, using a feather to scratch at a piece of white leather while Uttamatomakkin spoke. Other Pamunkeys were trying on some hats the strangers had given them or showing off their copper bead earrings.

"Neetah?" Samuel called when they were inside. He held a dipper toward her. It was not made of Ahone's good gourd. Instead it was formed of the strange white metal the men wore on their chests—shiny, but not copper. Neetah tried to see how it had been made. There seemed to be nothing inside but water, so Neetah drank deeply.

The fort walls hid five or six shelters. Instead of the comfortable round homes of the Pamunkeys, Neetah saw logs with fabric stretched over them.

"Neetah?" another boy said. "Pocahontas?" He held out a flat round cake, the size of a corn cake but white. Neetah took it and held it up to Pocahontas, who bit off a piece and kept chewing. The boy laughed. "Hardtack," he said, and broke off another piece of cake. "Snap!" It sounded like a dry stick breaking. Then he pointed to a basket made of dark wood and as tall as a man. Neetah and Pocahontas stepped over and, on tiptoe, looked into the container while the boy held its lid open. It was nearly empty but held layer upon layer of hardtack cakes. "They have not much food left," Neetah said to Pocahontas.

"And no fields planted," Pocahontas said. "No baskets to collect berries, no drying racks full of fish, no deer meat hung to age. This is good. They will not be staying."

"Thanks be to Ahone and Okeus!" Neetah prayed her relief. "These must not be the men who will bring the end of the Powhatan peoples." She felt a weight drop from her shoulders.

"It is too early to be sure." Pocahontas chewed a mouthful of hardtack and grinned at the boys as if it were the finest turtle meat. "Remember everything." She said the Pamunkey words softly against the strange clattering talk of the white boys. Neetah glanced about the inside of the fort walls.

"Stay open and look simple," Pocahontas warned. She tried to tuck herself into a ball to roll over and over as one of the boys was doing. At the end she sprang to her feet. One of the other boys smacked his hands together five times, loudly. The others grinned.

"Pocahontas! Neetah!" Tomakin's voice called from the river. Before the girls could respond, Kaptinzmit walked through the break in the fort wall. He seemed stunned to see them there. Pocahontas ran to the hardtack barrel and nearly fell in as she fished out a dry biscuit. She hurried to Kaptinzmit and gave it to him. "Hardtack, Kaptinzmit," she said. When he took it, she did another of the head-over-heels tricks she had learned from the boys and smacked her hands together quickly, five times. Kaptinzmit laughed. Then Pocahontas pointed to the biggest shelter in Jamestown. The top of this strange fabric house rose to a point with a crosspiece lashed to it. "The four directions," Pocahontas whispered to Neetah.

"The church?" Kaptinzmit asked. "You want to go there?"

"Church," Pocahontas repeated. Kaptinzmit smiled.

"Come with me," he said. The girls followed as he walked to the church and pulled the fabric door aside. Neetah's breath caught as she looked up to the ceiling. The point along the top was three men tall! Huge trees had been felled, stripped, and fastened without cords to make the structure. Then it had been draped in fabric. This church seemed to be a temple of some sort. Spirits hung as strong in the air as the lasting smell of the strangers. The floor was packed solid with the strangers' footprints. Samuel and the other boys stood stiffly by the door, shifting their feet as if afraid.

Chills swept Neetah's body as she faced a raised platform at the far end. It was empty except for wooden tables and stands, smoothed and oiled as carefully as human skin. There were no statues, no offerings, no blessed objects, no bodies of past chief priests—but power hummed in this place.

"Nay, child!" Kaptinzmit cautioned, as Pocahontas strode to the front.

"What is the meaning of this!" A man entered from a side opening. He moved as if he owned the temple. *A priest*, Neetah thought, though he carried no rattle and wore no headdress. "Ah, John Smith," he said. "You bring me heathen souls to convert."

The man's honey-sweet voice made Neetah cringe, but Pocahontas stood tall and offered her hand to the stranger. She gazed back at Kaptinzmit and waited. Her face held no fear and her lips held the hint of a smile. Neetah had seen that look before. When Pocahontas used it on her own father, the Powhatan had smiled back. Now Kaptinzmit's face softened.

"This is no simple heathen," he told the man. "She is Pocahontas, the Powhatan's daughter." Neetah listened intently when she heard her friend's name and that of the

Supreme Chief's. "Master Robert Hunt." Kaptinzmit pointed to the priest. Neetah noted the respect in his voice.

"Pocahontas? A *princess*?" The priest looked at Kaptinzmit, then lowered his eyes and bent his head down toward Pocahontas.

Princess, Neetah repeated to herself. The very word had power for these men. The man turned to her. "And that one?"

Kaptinzmit said, "She is some sort of maid or lady-in-waiting. She is no one."

The dismissal in his voice was cold, and Neetah saw the strange priest's eyes slide past her, as if she had disappeared. *No one*, she thought.

"Neetah!" Samuel's voice at the door was urgent. He pointed outside and, with his hands, pantomimed boats leaving.

Pocahontas rushed toward the door. Samuel took off his hat. "You are a *princess*?" he asked her, his voice strangely quiet. Pocahontas stared at him, and he too, bowed slightly toward her.

"This," Pocahontas whispered to Neetah, "is perfect." She grinned as the two girls hurried out of the church, past the fort walls, and down the hill to the waiting canoes.

6

CHAWNZMIT

Summer 1607

"BUT, POWHATAN, IF THEY THINK OUR *PRINCESS* IS IMPORTANT," Uttamatomakkin argued, "they could kidnap her. It would be too dangerous to take her back to the fort!"

"But it also means you can use me as a messenger," Pocahontas told her father. "I should return to the fort soon, bearing gifts from you. Perhaps food? I have seen their food stores. They are low."

"You did tell us that." They sat amid the elders of the tribe, the priests, and the blessed women, as they had for many nights now, sorting out the information the greeting party had brought back.

"Neetah must come, too," Pocahontas said. "The strangers think nothing of her, so she passes beneath their notice. And think of all the words you have learned from her, the sights you have seen through her eyes!"

Neetah looked down into her lap at this. Even now, things bubbled up in her mind that she had forgotten to tell the council. She picked up a stick and began drawing a pattern in the dusty ground. "This is the shape of their stockade," she said. "Here, here, and here are shelters for the men. And there is something they call a church here, a temple with a sign of the four directions at its very top." She drew the strangers' powerful symbol. "The same sign decorates their ships." Since everyone was looking at her, she shared another memory. "Kaptinzmit," she said, "the stranger in the temple called him Chawnzmit."

"What about the man in that temple," Uttamatomakkin asked. "Did he have a name?"

Neetah thought silently, going over the scene yet again. "Master, um, something-hunt," she said slowly. "He was at home with the spirits in their strange temple. He must be a priest."

"Kaptinzmit spoke to him with respect," Pocahontas added.

The group fell silent as they digested this new observation.

They met the next night and the next before a decision was made. "You will accompany a party to this Jaimztown bearing corn and oysters, Pocahontas, my *princess*." Wahunsenacah used the strange-sounding title for his daughter. "Take strawberries and walnut milk, too."

"You have no choice, Neetah. You must come with us to Jaimztown this day." Pocahontas had stayed on her sleeping platform long after the other women and children had filed out of the longhouse. "I have had dreams . . ." Pocahontas reached out with a finger. Neetah knew her friend had not been sleeping well. She often thrashed on her bunk, sometimes whimpering and crying out loud.

"Sometimes I have nightmares, too," Neetah said gently.

She sat down beside Pocahontas and hooked fingers with her. "Everyone dreams."

"These are night visions," Pocahontas said firmly, "and you always appear. You and me and Chawnzmit and a baby—a child of great importance." Tears spilled onto Pocahontas's cheeks. "It is so sad," she said. Neetah's breath caught in her throat as she tried to imagine whose child Pocahontas had foreseen and what dreadful future she'd glimpsed. She did not dare to ask. Visions were the province of priests and elders. Pocahontas shivered on the bed, her teeth chattering. "Fire," she whispered.

Neetah rose quickly and threw the wolf skin around Pocahontas, though the morning was warm. When that did not stop her friend's shivering, Neetah built up the fire on the floor using the sap-rich light sticks. Then she sat back down, her arm around Pocahontas's shoulders.

"You will be fine," she said, wondering whether to send for a medicine woman or even for Uttamatomakkin himself. Pocahontas did not respond, but sat hunched, facing the fire. Beneath her arm, Neetah felt her friend's shivers stop. Her breathing became slow and shallow, as if she were asleep, though her eyes were open, unblinking, and her tears trickled down her cheeks, unnoticed. "Pocahontas?" she whispered softly, then "Matoaka?" There was no response, even when the fire crackled and shot sparks toward the ceiling. The fire spirits were alarmed, too, Neetah thought. Chill bumps rose on her arms.

Come! Neetah willed someone, anyone, to return to the longhouse, since she did not dare leave Pocahontas in order to fetch help. What if she fell into the fire? *Or,* she thought, *fell away into her vision?* Now Pocahontas was twitching and whimpering as if asleep. Neetah prayed to Ahone for strength to help hold Pocahontas until her spirit returned to earth.

At last Pocahontas took a shuddering breath and shook her head. She threw the wolf skin off and stood blinking in the hot, smoky room. "I must go," she said. "The men are waiting at the riverbank—and Chawn is waiting at the settlement."

"Chawn?" Neetah asked. But Pocahontas had rushed out of the house toward the river. Neetah hurried to catch up. Five men waited on the bank, their canoes ready and loaded with provisions for the hungry strangers at Jaimztown. Spears and bows bristled between the baskets of dried corn and fish. Pocahontas settled into the middle of the largest canoe, with Neetah behind her.

As much as Neetah wanted to ask about this "Chawn" or the waking vision that Pocahontas had seen, it seemed wrong to mention it in front of the warriors.

When they reached Jaimztown and pulled the canoe up on the bank, Pocahontas would not meet Neetah's eyes as she led the men up toward the stockade.

"Neetah!" Samuel yelled joyfully, as he ran out to greet them. When he saw Pocahontas, he stopped short, touched his hat, and said, "My lady."

Neetah heard the whispered word *princess* from the strangers who streamed out to see them. The straighter Pocahontas walked, the more these men nodded to her and the more Neetah heard the strange greeting "My lady."

Kaptinzmit appeared at last, straightening his metal chest plate. Pocahontas hooked fingers with Neetah and pulled her along. The two girls hurried toward the strange leader. As she had with her father during the scene around the fire, Pocahontas smiled and dimpled before this older man. And Kaptinzmit looked at her fondly in response. *Was this part of Pocahontas's vision?* Neetah wondered. She shuddered, watching Kaptinzmit scratch at a flea beneath his smelly clothes.

The strangers laughed and slapped each others' backs when they saw the food. They paraded with it into the fort. A few men stoked a central cook fire with wood and swung a big cook pot into place on a three-legged stand planted right in the middle of the flames. Neetah stepped closer. The raven-black pot was not even smoking! Neetah reached out a finger to touch it, but Samuel pulled her hand away.

"Hot!" he scolded, then beckoned her into a nearby shelter. Neetah noticed that other tools made of this strange black metal lay on a wooden shelf.

"*Hot.*" Neetah tried the stranger's word before she reached out her hand.

Samuel laughed and handed her a piece shaped a little like a drinking gourd. It was cold and heavy.

Neetah struggled to lift a black cook pot as heavy as a boulder from the floor and then ran her hands over pieces of white and black metal. "*Spoon.*" "*Cold.*" "*Iron.*" "*You.*" "*Knife.*" "*Ax.*" "*Pot.*" Neetah tried to hold all the words Samuel taught her safe in her mind, but there were so many! She looked at a metal tool leaning against the shelf. It was as tall as she was. "Muzket?" she asked. Samuel laughed with delight. He looked quickly out the door before handing it to her. Neetah began exploring the weapon, sticking her fingers down a hole at one end, until Samuel suddenly jerked it away and set it back down.

Samuel pushed her out of the shelter toward Pocahontas and the men. The "princess" was still smiling as she spoke with Kaptinzmit. All traces of her dark vision-trance were gone from her face.

Neetah and Samuel spent the afternoon throwing sticks for Tucker. Then they snuck into another one of the shelters, this one with four sides of wood. They climbed onto a sleeping platform with woven bedding as soft as fur pelts.

Neetah sat on the edge of the bed, swinging her bare feet and staring at a fireplace. The flames had gone out, though Samuel didn't seem frightened by the bad luck that would bring. Black pots hung above where the flames would normally be. Strangely, this fireplace was tucked indoors against a wooden wall. Neetah sniffed the air. There was no good smoky smell in this house from a friendly little light fire and no soot stains to make things look homey. She glanced at the ceiling. No smoke hole! Neetah jumped down and ran to investigate. A tunnel led from the fireplace right up through the shelter to the blue sky.

"*Chimney,*" Samuel said. Neetah did not know if he was sharing the word for fire or smoke, ceiling or sky, but she repeated it carefully.

Next, Samuel led her out of the fort to the forest where men were cutting wood. Then they returned to eat some of the corn mush boiled in the black pot.

"*Porridge*," Samuel explained as Neetah tasted it and burned her tongue. "*Hot*." Finally, Neetah understood that word. The men around them ate as if they were starving.

There was little game on this side of the river. Neetah had seen few plucked feathers and no deerskins in the fort.

One of the men made a strange salute to Kaptinzmit. "To Chawnzmit and the little princess!" he said. Many others repeated these words, but two echoed in Neetah's head. "*Princess*," of course. That was Pocahontas's other name. And "*Chawnzmit*." "*Chawn*." Neetah shivered. That word had flown straight from Pocahontas's vision to these strangers' lips.

Neetah's chill lasted all the way back to Werowocomoco.

At the fire that night, Powhatan's elders heard how thankful the strangers acted at the gifts of fresh food. Neetah shared details of their tools. "They use raven-black cook pots and fire tools. That strange metal is many times heavier than copper and cannot be bent. They have tunnels to guide smoke out through the roof of a shelter. *Glass* is their name for a special kind of ice that does not melt. They use it in spy holes and for drinking out of or looking through. They use a feather quill and paint to make fancy little designs on flat sheets, though I did not understand why."

"That is called *writing*," Pocahontas interrupted. "Chawn scratches tiny patterns for every word I say. Then he *reads* my words back to me. They are saved on flat thin sheets of *paper* so he does not have to remember them."

While the others asked about writing and reading, Neetah thought about the change in Pocahontas's voice when she said the word "*Chawn.*" She looked carefully at her friend. After her waking vision of Chawn, Pocahontas had spent the afternoon smiling and laughing aloud with Chawnzmit. *Could she be attracted to the smelly, furry stranger? That is not possible*, Neetah decided, and then rubbed her temples, tired from looking at everything—and everyone—for hidden meanings.

"Hear this," the Powhatan said, after listening to all the reports. "I must have one of those muzkets. If that weapon is as dangerous as we hear from our tribes to the south, I need one. I want a black-copper pot and a long, shiny white copper knife, too. We need to master the crafts of the strangers."

The other elders nodded. "You will want an *ax*," Tomakin said. "This tool slices into oak as our sharpest antler knife carves through fat. An ax is what they used to make points on top of their fortress wall." He shook his head in wonder. "We have much to learn from them."

"While I watched," Neetah reported, "they cut down as many trees as I have fingers."

Around the fire, Pamunkeys gasped. It took days to burn through the trunk of a tree, chipping out the charcoal as it formed. "One of those, too, then. *Ax*," the Powhatan demanded. "We will trade food for these treasures."

"And if they do not trade?" Tomakin asked. "They would not allow me to even touch a muzket."

"The boy Samuel allowed me to hold one," Neetah said. "He is very daring."

The Powhatan sat back. "Let us be generous for now. Each of us will watch and learn as much as we can."

"Neetah and I will learn the language and writing," Pocahontas said. Neetah stared at her. "Neetah has a gift with patterns, and Chawn is already teaching me words. You will need translators."

And, Neetah thought, *Pocahontas wants an excuse to spend more time with Kaptinzmit.*

"Samuel, the boy, learns our words fast," Pocahontas was saying. "Perhaps he could come here? It would not be like letting the stranger men near our homes."

"He is only a young child," Pocahontas said, "several seasons away from huskanaw." Neetah flinched at the thought of the boy's trying time. Not all of them survived the poisons and caging, and all who came out of the ceremonies were changed forever. They were men. The passage to womanhood was easier. At least that was what Neetah's mother had told her.

The Powhatan stroked the copper medallion on his chest. "We will see," he finally spoke. "I do not entirely trust these strangers, even the children."

Later that night, Neetah echoed his words as she combed Pocahontas's hair. "I do not trust Chawnzmit." She felt Pocahontas's body stiffen under her hands, but went on, "You are not yet a woman, though you say Chawn with the same softness as Matachanna speaks of Uttamatomakkin. It worries me."

"No. Chawnzmit is as great a leader as my father,"

Pocahontas said sharply, "and he plays a part in the vision I have been given."

So does a child, Neetah thought, but she pressed her lips together to keep from adding sticks to the fire kindled between them.

"You do not speak?" Pocahontas challenged. "You know the truth of this. And Chawn sees me as a *princess*."

"We do not even know what that word means," Neetah said.

"It means I am special to him, and he is special to me," Pocahontas shot back. Then she stood and stalked out of the sleeping house.

Still holding the comb, Neetah stared at the door. How could Pocahontas be so foolish? Chawnzmit showed off to everyone, a clear sign of weakness in a man. He smelled as the strangers all did. And he was rude. He had dismissed her as—she fished up the word—a *no one*. Now Pocahontas was treating her like that, too. Neetah poked at the fire, then grabbed a turkey-wing brush to sweep the dirt floor clean. Their friendship, she thought, had come on as quickly as a summer shower. It seemed to be passing just as quickly. *Cheawanta warned me*, she thought.

Should I leave? Neetah wondered. *Could I find my way home by myself?* She pictured her mother's face, soot-smudged and tear-streaked in grief. *I have no other home.* The thought chilled Neetah's bones like a winter gale. She held the bead at her neck and took a deep breath. *I am a Pamunkey*, she told herself. *I have my clan. I have my family.* She summoned a picture of the Powhatan and his wives and all of his well-fed children. *Two families*, she corrected, imagining her aunts and uncles, father, and, finally, her mother again, clean-faced and calm.

Neetah sat on a sleeping platform and started pulling tangles out of her own hair with Pocahontas's comb. With each stroke, she thought about how all of them—the tribe, the clan, her family—were in danger. Pocahontas had many flaws, but her visions were powerful, coming with no fasting or ceremony. They had to be honored even though they seemed to hold tragedy. The more Neetah thought about it, the simpler it seemed. Pocahontas faced something terrible. Neetah had to keep her safe—if she could.

Neetah looked up as Pocahontas padded silently back into the longhouse and come over to her. "Give me the comb," she said. "I'll re-braid your hair for you. Father has agreed. We must go back to Jaimztown, and soon."

7
CAPTURE

Summer to Fall 1607

"Why do they not save seed to plant?" Neetah asked Pocahontas. "The English could be raising their own corn by now." They stood with Samuel in Jaimztown watching as, once again, the strangers made porridge with every bit of the corn brought downriver from Werowocomoco. "We have planted four crops of corn while they wait here to be fed."

"They do not fish for themselves, either, or dig clams," Pocahontas complained.

"Or swim," Neetah said. "Are they afraid of the water spirits?"

"*Suck-qua-han?*" Samuel repeated the Pamunkey word Neetah had used, then quickly translated it to English. "Water," he said, pointing to the river. Neetah felt her face redden and looked at Pocahontas. They would have to be careful of what they said around Samuel. After only five visits—three moons—the boy spoke Pamunkey as well as a baby just off the cradle board.

"You and I will practice his English words together on the

long trips here and home," Neetah said. "Who does Samuel work with?"

"Chawn," Pocahontas said. "That man's mind is weasel-quick. Chawn listens, he remembers, and he cares. There is no one like him in the entire Confederacy. . . ." She stopped and blushed when she caught sight of Neetah's face.

"Just do not say these things where Tomakin can hear you," Neetah cautioned. They both looked at the priest, whose body filled the door of the church. He and Master Hunt gestured at the crossed sticks.

Uttamatomakkin wheeled about and stamped over to the girls. "Is this the boy?" He stared at Samuel. "There is room to take him back with us as a guest—or a prisoner."

"A *guest*," Pocahontas said firmly. She turned to Samuel. "Come," she said, then pointed to the canoe in the river.

"Samuel and Pocahontas go?" Samuel Collier stumbled on the Pamunkey words. "And Neetah? Werowocomoco?" The Pamunkey girls smiled at how badly he said the town name.

"Yes," Neetah told him in his language. "To talk. Then you come home." She pointed away and then back again to the spot where they stood.

"I am *princess*," Pocahontas said clearly. "You are safe with me."

Samuel took off his hat and threw it up into the air. "Yes!" he yelped.

"Now?" Chawnzmit asked, when Samuel and the girls met him by the great cook fire and told him of the plan. "No.

What if they kill you?"

Pocahontas said, "Samuel safe" to Chawnzmit. "No kill. Talk talk talk." Chawnzmit's face softened. Pocahontas pointed to her chest. "I am *princess*. No hurt." She put an arm around Samuel.

"We must ask the others," Chawnzmit said.

When he'd gathered five men together, he called for Uttamatomakkin. "You no kill Samuel?" Chawnzmit demanded.

Uttamatomakkin motioned for his pipe. One of the other warriors brought it from the canoe, and Tomakin handed off his rattle. Slowly, grandly, he opened the tobacco pouch he wore draped over his waist string and filled the pipe. Another of the Pamunkeys ran to fetch a flaming stick from the fire. Tomakin lit the pipe, held it out to the four directions for blessing, then announced loudly, "Okeus, hear me. Ahone, mark my words. Before all my ancestors, I say this worthless runt, Samuel, is safe with me—for now." He puffed the pipe and offered it to Chawnzmit with a sly grin.

Chawnzmit made no move to take the pipe. Tomakin's smirk disappeared.

"No kill?" Chawnzmit asked, then demanded it louder. "*No kill?*"

Neetah held her breath. At last, Tomakin repeated the assurance Chawnzmit wanted to hear, and the English man took a puff and passed the pipe. His friends coughed and choked out the holy tobacco smoke, but they were looking at Chawnzmit with admiration.

"Come," Uttamatomakkin barked, and the Pamunkey

party strode out of the stockade behind him. Neetah beckoned to Samuel, and he broke into a run toward the canoes.

Neetah sat beside Samuel that night at his welcome dance. Uttamatomakkin sat in the center of the circle, drumming on a folded rawhide. Other musicians pounded drums or played flutes outside the circle. Samuel clapped in rhythm for each of the townspeople as they danced for him in turn. When at last they all danced together in a circle, Samuel and Neetah joined in. "Good!" Neetah said, as Samuel perfectly copied the steps of the men. He did not know the prayers or signs of the men, though, and he almost followed them to the men's house when it grew late. They pushed him roughly away, and he came back to Neetah looking like a sad puppy.

"Come," she said, and led him to the women's and children's sleeping house. In the night, Neetah listened to Pocahontas having another of her dream-visions and to Samuel sniffling like a baby from his sleeping platform on the other side of the entry room. At last both began breathing smoothly, and Neetah could sleep.

After prayers the next morning, Matachanna pressed a toy bow into Samuel's hands and rolled the target ball in front of him. Samuel looked helplessly at Neetah, then tried to shoot the ball. When other boys—even little ones—hit the moving ball, they were fed breakfast. Again and again, Samuel's arrows flew wildly. No woman would let him eat, and he was staggering when Neetah decided to help him. The sun was high in the sky and a laughing crowd had gathered. Finally, Samuel won a bite of food to end his fast—and the ball wasn't even rolling.

He had no idea how to shape an arrowhead out of a piece of stone, either, or how to track a deer through the woodlands. He didn't know any of the women's tasks. And he did not even know to relieve himself far outside the village.

"Harmless as he is, he is welcome in my family," Powhatan's first wife said at supper. "If this is the skill of a boy child among the strangers, we have nothing to fear from the fathers."

"Remember the prophecy," the Powhatan said.

Within a month, Neetah watched the first warrior being carried home with a wound in his belly. "I was training as a medicine woman in the hills," she told the men who carried him. "Perhaps I can help." They let her take a look, but Neetah knew she was seeing death. This was no simple arrow puncture or war-club gash, no spear slash or knife wound. The man's belly seemed blown apart. Blackened burns ringed the injury.

"Muzket," Samuel told Neetah. "Close range."

The injured Pamunkey made no sound. Neetah knew he would die in silence, his pride unbroken. Any Appamattuck warrior would do the same. Neetah listened to his wife keening her fear as she held his limp hand.

Neetah watched a Pamunkey medicine woman hover by the litter where the fallen warrior lay. The woman sighed deeply, then pressed his guts back into place and tried to staunch the bleeding with spiderwebs. The soothing paste of roots she smeared on the burns around his wound was quickly washed away by his own blood. "Find

Uttamatomakkin," Neetah whispered to Samuel, as the wound wept other fluids.

Neetah and the other medicine woman stood aside while a circle of priests began a chant around the litter. Using their rattles for punctuation, they filled the night with a rhythmic cry for the warrior's spirit to find its balance again. On and on they danced, calling on the spirits to throw their strength into the injured one. Finally, at moon-set, the priests were silent and the women's cries of grief soared over Werowocomoco.

Before winter chill began to color the leaves, Neetah had been called to watch over nine more Pamunkey men with muzket shots. All of them died.

"We *must* have muzkets of our own," the Supreme Chief said, as the tribe's unease grew. Pamunkey men took to shooting arrows at any of the settlers' animals that strayed from the strangers' fort. They shot the hairy men, too, whether they were outside burying their own dead or simply relieving themselves in the woods.

"Do not ask again about taking food to Jaimztown!" the Powhatan raged at Pocahontas in front of everyone at supper one night.

Neetah gasped as Pocahontas rose to her feet. "Father," she pleaded, "Chawnzmit is not our enemy. He is a great leader, like you. Can you not make a friendship with him?"

"We need to kill him and drive all the others away," one of the other priests said. There were many shouts of agreement. "He has sent too many of our warriors through the western sky to the Great Hare." The soot-streaked faces of wives at Werowocomoco, the smell of funeral pyres burning, and the sad ceremonies long into the night made the town tense with anger.

Samuel stood up so he, too, could be seen. The crowd roared for his death, but Uttamatomakkin leaped to his feet and, raising his rattle high overhead, shouted, "This one is under my protection."

"Great Powhatan," Samuel's clear voice rang out. The Pamunkeys quieted at the sound of their language from a stranger's mouth. "If Captain Smith come here," he pointed to the ground by the meeting fire and went on, "he see great Powhatan and many, many, many men. He stop English muzkets." Samuel acted out shooting a muzket at Neetah. She flinched in spite of herself.

"Could he come here for a time, Father?" Pocahontas asked. "Once Chawn has seen our strength and our just ways, he will control his men. He will not hurt us. I know this man."

Wahunsenacah did not answer. Instead he sat silently. When others began making suggestions, he snarled, "Enough!" and waved them off. The men melted away, taking positions at the far edges of the firelight. The Powhatan's wives quietly shooed their children from the clearing. Uttamatomakkin firmly pushed Samuel, Pocahontas, and Neetah toward the sleeping houses. When Neetah looked back, the High Chief sat quietly on his tower of mats, alone and unblinking, staring into the fire.

One frosty morning, Matachanna called Pocahontas and

Neetah out of the cornfield. Pocahontas tossed a handful of withered bean plants toward a waste pile and ran to her sister. Neetah picked one late squash bug from a fat pumpkin and squeezed it between her fingers. She wiped her hands on the dry corn leaves. "I have to go," she apologized to Cheawanta and the other girls, then hurried along to join a council gathered in front of the temple.

Neetah settled on the ground beside Pocahontas and behind a row of broad-backed Pamunkey men. Sunshine gleamed on the thick bear grease they had spread on their skin for warmth. Neetah shifted about, trying to see. The warriors who had visited Jaimztown were all there. So were the elders and priests of the council, sitting behind Uttamatomakkin. They all faced Wahunsenacah, who wore his full headdress as the Powhatan.

He spread his arms for attention and spoke. "Chawnzmit has been taken captive."

"Is Chawn hurt?" Pocahontas asked quickly. Men nearby twisted about to glare at her, and Neetah hooked fingers with her for strength.

The High Chief's eyes narrowed before he said, "No." Pocahontas sighed in obvious relief. "The stranger is being taken from village to village. He has been introduced to our many, many, many people." The High Chief glanced at Samuel and went on. "He has seen our ceremonies, our dances, and our arts. He knows our food. Our priests are watching him and reporting his reactions. Chawnzmit will be brought here by winter's shortest night."

"And then?" Pocahontas asked.

"Then," Uttamatomakkin took over, "I will hold a divining ceremony to judge whether Chawnzmit means us harm." The priest touched the amulet hanging on his neck.

"And then?" Pocahontas asked again. Neetah could not understand why the Powhatan was being so patient with a girl. She glanced toward her friend and then quickly took a second look. Since strawberry time, Pocahontas's body had ripened. Neetah felt a quick stab of envy.

"If he means us ill," Uttamatomakkin said, "I will kill him. If his plans are peaceful, we will smoke pipes together and make treaties."

"Father," Pocahontas said, "what if you were to adopt him? If he were kin, his tribe would be part of the Confederacy. His men would use their muzkets on our enemies instead of on us." Neetah stared at her friend in wonder. "I could stand for him in the ceremony." Pocahontas went on. "I know him well, and I would be his sister."

"You walk the very edge of a cliff," Uttamatomakkin warned. "Choose your path with care, blessed Matoaka." Neetah swallowed hard. Pocahontas was a blessed one? Already? She was clever. And she'd had visions, waking and sleeping. But Pocahontas was far too young to be blessed. That came when a woman was a few years from death.

"Father, think of Neetah." Neetah's whole body jerked as Pocahontas called out her name. "She would be a sister to Chawnzmit as well—and a spy, too."

"As would I," Matachanna said, sitting tall.

"No," said Uttamatomakkin. Matachanna bristled with anger. "You cannot yet speak the stranger's language as

Pocahontas can," he told her. "Neetah has drawn maps of the fort and the inside of their houses. Kaptinzmit and the others already know the two of them and trust them." With every sentence, Matachanna sank lower.

"Our priest wants to keep that one safe for himself," someone said in the back of the crowd. Matachanna blushed and hid her face, but not before Neetah saw her smile.

Tomakin's eyes sought the distance and his body became still. "There will be a place for me and a wife in this, too," he said, as if seeing it, "but far, far from here." Neetah could not help but stare at the tuft of white feathers he wore. How she wished she could see visions, too—even dark ones, like Pocahontas's. Any glimpse of the future would answer so many questions.

"Wait," the High Chief said. "No child can adopt—not even one as spoiled as my own little *princess*."

"I shall make my retreat soon," Pocahontas stated. "I will be a full woman of the tribe by the shortest night." At this impossible statement, men pulled away from Pocahontas. Neetah smiled. They were uncomfortable being close to a vision-seer, and all men were in awe of a woman's life-making power.

8

THE POWER

November 1607

"I WILL BE HUNGRY ONLY FOR THE FIRST DAY," POCAHONTAS reassured Neetah, licking her fingers. "Then the pangs will lessen. I will chant our prayers and finally have the chance to follow my visions wherever they go." Neetah shuddered. The friends squatted together, close to the royal cook fire, picking flakes of hot flesh from a baked fish's bones. Clams and mussels lay on the coals, steamed open in their own juices.

Neetah scooped a gourdful of tea from a pot wedged between burning logs and tried to think of what to say. "Good luck? Be strong? How could you know?" There were so many questions she wanted to ask! Instead she sipped the fragrant tea and looked about the empty royal enclosure. Thick clouds of wood smoke and the murmurs of idle tribespeople rose from the smoke holes of every longhouse. Neetah tilted her head to the sky, letting the weak winter sunshine wash over her face.

"How can you face days in darkness?" she asked.

"Visions bring their own light," Pocahontas explained, loosening a clam from its shell and popping it into her mouth. She handed a clam to Neetah, too, then went on.

"When the blood time has passed, and I hold the force of woman's magic within me, my clanswomen will come and take me to the women's room beyond the stockade. There I will learn lessons and chants, receive clan tattoos, attend ceremonies." She sighed. "Then, finally, Chawn will come." Her voice brightened. "After a sweat bath, I will bind him to me. To *us*," she corrected herself, and ate an oyster.

"How can you know?" Neetah's question burst out. "No one knows the day and time of their womanhood."

"I have seen it in a vision," Pocahontas said, as if it were as natural as breathing. She groaned and rubbed her stomach as she walked to the sleeping house. She scratched on the door politely, then called out, "I am ready."

When the healing woman saw the dark stain on Pocahontas's moss, Pocahontas began singing. Powhatan's wives filed out in a cloud of wood smoke and joined in joyful song. They led Pocahontas around to the far back end of the longhouse to the beat of the ancient chant. The healing woman raised a mat to show a shadowy compartment walled off from the rest of the sleeping rooms. A water pot stood inside along with a reed so Pocahontas could drink without touching water to her lips. Neetah just had time to see pelts and waste pots lying about in the shadows before Pocahontas linked fingers with her for a moment, then ducked inside. The mat was dropped back into place and Powhatan's first wife closed a thick bark door, walling Pocahontas off from all light. She motioned Neetah away, and the women filed off, singing.

As Neetah ground corn or gathered firewood over the next few days, she watched the women and the mothers of the tribe. *What must their power feel like,* she wondered. *The power to make life.*

"Neetah!" Samuel came running to find her a few days later. "I saw Pocahontas! She walks with some women in the woods."

Neetah breathed easier. Pocahontas's door had been opened at last to let in sunshine. Neetah resisted the urge to look for her friend. "She needs many days to learn now. Without us," she explained.

The next day, Neetah kept herself busy at the edge of the stockade wall near the back of the sleeping house. First, she twisted dried bundles of grass into fine, strong cord. It kept her hands busy while she listened to murmurs of conversation coming from inside the women's room. Now and then she heard short bursts of laughter and endless story songs, but she could not make out Pocahontas's voice from the others.

Samuel found Neetah mid-morning. "Is Pocahontas free yet?" he asked.

Neetah pointed through the trees to the end of the sleeping house. "Do not go there!" she cried, as Samuel started down the path. "No man can."

"Why are you not there?" Samuel came back to sit with her. "You and Pocahontas . . . ," he locked his forefingers with hers to show friendship the Pamunkey way.

Neetah felt the familiar pang of envy she had worked all morning to ignore. "My body is not ready."

He paused a moment. "Is she a prisoner," Samuel asked, "like Chawnzmit?" He said it in the Pamunkey way, then picked up a pebble and hurled it at a tree. "Prisoner like me?"

"No, Samuel," Neetah said quickly. "You are no prisoner.

You are here to learn our language and our ways. Chawnzmit is in our towns to learn about the Powhatan's huge Confederacy. When the learning is done, everyone will go home: Pocahontas, Chawnzmit, and you." She hoped he understood half of what she was saying.

"But Pocahontas *is* home."

"After her first stay in the women's room, she can marry and make a home somewhere with another man. But she won't." It was all too complicated. Neetah glanced about, looking for a job that she and Samuel could do together. "Come." Neetah grabbed the new twine she'd made and led Samuel to a large clay pot by the royal sleeping house. "The hide needs scraping. We need words and a job to keep us warm." Together, they pulled a raw deer hide from the pot. When Samuel turned his face away from the smell of the greasy liquid dripping from its hair, Neetah laughed.

She showed him how to string twine through the holes left in its edges from yesterday's cleaning. With the fresh cords, they pulled the hide tight against a square frame.

"*Wood*," Samuel said, tapping the frame.

Neetah repeated the strange word twice, then told him, "*Musheis*." Samuel practiced the new word, while Neetah showed him how to scrape the hide with oyster shells.

"*Deer*," he said, and while Neetah didn't know whether he meant the animal or the leather, she repeated it. "*Shell. Dog. Scrape. Ouch*," she learned. When Samuel pressed too hard and sliced into the precious hide, she didn't scold. No child learned that way. They kept working and Neetah learned the words *hole* and *sorry* from him. Just as fast, Samuel learned a few more Pamunkey words. Wet fur and drippings gathered in the dirt beneath the hide as the afternoon went on. They tested each other on words, and then they tested each other's strength.

Neetah's arms ached, as they always did before a hide was completely scraped. Samuel kept asking if he could sit down. She would only laugh and tell him to keep working. "We stop only when the leather is clean and soft," she said, then checked the hide. It was beginning to look fluffy. She rubbed harder with the edge of the oyster shell and Samuel copied her.

She taught him the word *vebowhass*. He countered with the word *sweat*. Finally, they were finished and it was time for sunset prayers. Neetah realized with surprise that she hadn't thought of Pocahontas for hours. She and Samuel talked easily on the way down to the river. He refused to break through the ice and wash, but sat silent, watching everyone else dust the ground around them with circles of tobacco, then chant to the setting sun.

On the way back uphill, Neetah overheard a group of men talking about a mission to take food to Jaimztown. "Our spies say the English are starving," one man said. "They are burying bodies almost every night."

"If this is true," another said, "they won't kill people who bring them food."

"Imagine how those Chickahominies would feel if they knew the English fought alongside Powhatan's men! Ho! They would give up and join the Confederacy as quickly as rabbits hop."

"The Powhatan is sending us tomorrow to get inside the

gates and see the truth of it ourselves."

Neetah glanced at Samuel. How much had he understood? He should go back to help his friends—if they were still alive. Neetah wanted to go, too, but with Pocahontas still in seclusion, there was no one to convince the Powhatan to send children with his warriors. Neetah tried to think of what Pocahontas would do.

She stopped mid-path and pulled her deerskin cape around her. "Samuel," she said, "we are going to Jaimztown tomorrow. They need us."

The next morning, they were ready by the canoes. "We are going with you," she told Uttamatomakkin. "You need translators." The priest looked at Samuel and scowled. Neetah had an answer ready. "When you show them that you have kept Samuel well-fed and happy, they will know you are a great and good man."

"Huh," Uttamatomakkin grunted. A moment later he pointed to the smaller canoe. "Your place," he said to the children.

It seemed to Neetah that half the men of Jaimztown had vanished. The rest looked haggard. Through an open door she saw a man lying limp, his face covered with red dots. Other spotted men groaned and cradled their bellies. They needed a medicine woman, and Neetah did not know enough to help with this strange English disease. "Master Hunt!" she cried, recognizing the priest wandering from bedside to bedside. His clothes hung on him like the fabric hanging on the men's shelters, still half-finished. Neetah glanced at his church. Unlike the other buildings, it was fully timbered.

"God be with you, Samuel." Two English boys, Henry

and Thomas, drifted up to the landing party. "Have you brought any food?" Their legs looked as thin as cornstalks while the winter wind whipped against their clothes. They stared hungrily as the Pamunkeys unloaded baskets of corn cakes and freshly caught turkeys. The sight of a side of venison and a basket of cornmeal brought one English man to tears. Neetah looked away. These stores had cost her village dearly, too. It was only the beginning of winter and the tributes from other tribes had not filled the huge storage baskets buried underground. The drought had spread hunger, thick as snow, across the land.

Once they had gobbled handfuls of corn cakes, the boys began to relax. "We never should have come here, Samuel," Thomas said haltingly. "I have seen so many die."

Neetah ached as she looked at his face. She, too, had watched friends and relatives die.

"There is not so much hunger in Werowocomoco," she said. She looked from Samuel's strong lean frame to his friends' pinched faces and weak bodies. An idea came to her. "Our tribe sometimes takes in others' children," she said slowly. The boys did not need to know that this was an act of war. The enemy's children and women were kidnapped after their men were killed. They never went home. "They are fed as our own. . . ." Neetah's voice trailed off. "Wait here," she said, trying to think how Pocahontas would get the priest to save these boys.

"Uttamatomakkin . . . " Neetah's voice failed, so she had to repeat herself. "Tomakin?"

The priest turned to look at her. Neetah took a deep

breath. "An Appamattuck warrior would take all the boys home with him, for ransom or for raising." She watched Tomakin's fists clench. "Of course, if the Pamunkey tribe is too poor this winter to feed a few skinny little boys . . . "

"We take them," Uttamatomakkin said sharply.

It took a long time for Neetah's arms to stop trembling. Then she could smile.

"The captive chief!" Cheawanta came running from the outer field to tell the news. "They bring him now!"

Most of the men were out hunting or fishing on the river, but women from all over the town gathered to watch. Neetah glanced toward the back of the women's house for a moment. The elderly blessed women of the village had entered the women's room, but Pocahontas had not come out yet. "Come, Samuel," Neetah said. "They will need our skills."

Followed by Henry and Thomas, Neetah and Samuel scurried through the woods to watch the victory parade. First came warriors acting as bodyguards. They carried bows and arrows, wooden clubs, and tomahawks. Their tattoos identified them as belonging to different clans, but their body paint gave just one message: these were fierce men, tempered by huskanaw and experienced in battle with other tribes. In the middle strutted Opechancanough in a full-feathered cape. "The High Chief's younger brother," Neetah whispered to the boys.

"There's Captain Smith!" Samuel's young voice drifted through the trees. Chawnzmit's head jerked and the bowmen around him glared in their direction. Samuel ducked behind Neetah. The other two crouched behind a bush. "He looks well," Samuel whispered, after he took another peek. Neetah agreed. Not only was Chawn's step firm, but he looked around without fear. A long snakelike row of warriors followed Kaptinzmit, kept in line by another lesser chief. When they all had passed, Samuel asked, "Where have they gone?"

"They will be back," Neetah said. "They will circle the village three times before pausing for a victory dance. Then I think they will take Kaptinzmit to the temple. They want to do ceremonies to foresee his true purpose."

Samuel translated for the other boys, then asked, "Will they hurt him?" Neetah did not answer.

Samuel looked around at the women and children watching from the woods. "Where is Pocahontas?" he asked.

"The women's house," Neetah mumbled. She glanced over her shoulder. How Pocahontas must be suffering, wondering if her Chawn was safe! "I have to tell her," she explained to Samuel. When he got up to follow, she said quietly, "This is not your place."

"I am not Pamunkey," Samuel said and grinned, "and you are not woman. We go together. Stay here," he told the others.

Neetah laughed out loud and led Samuel back through the town and into the woods beyond. They walked around behind the house and stopped. "Chawnzmit has come," Samuel called out, loudly enough to send a flock of winter crows flying.

From inside the hut, an ancient chant broke off midword. A chorus of women's voices began talking. Then Neetah heard Pocahontas, loud and clear. "Is he well?"

"Yes!" Neetah cried, and then she and Samuel sprinted back into the village to watch the victory dance.

9
INITIATION
December 1607

SAMUEL AND NEETAH WATCHED FROM THE WOODS AS THE procession leading Chawnzmit finished circling and entered the village. First came four warriors with bows drawn and arrows ready to fire. Then another six warriors formed a ring around Chawnzmit.

"He looks tired," Samuel said, straining for a clear view.

As Neetah watched, Chawnzmit studied everything as he strutted past. Children peeked at him from bushes and doorways. Women stared and giggled. It was clear that Chawnzmit was searching for someone. Neetah and Samuel left the cover of the woods and stood in plain sight. Samuel jumped up and down, waving.

"God bless you, child!" Chawnzmit called to Samuel. "Neetah . . . ?" he began, but the warriors shoved him along. The relief in his voice was as plain as the question, Neetah thought, watching the stranger's back.

As they followed the parade to the town center, Samuel said, "You and Pocahontas . . ." He hooked his forefingers together in the Pamunkey sign of friendship. Neetah grinned encouragement, wishing she was as quick to learn his gestures. "After her woman time," Samuel went on, "will you call Pocahontas my lady?" The seriousness in Samuel's voice made this sound important.

"Why? She will not get a new name."

"She is a *princess*," Samuel said, "a member of Powhatan royalty." He breathed the word with such respect that Neetah pulled him into a cornfield so they could talk without being interrupted. "In England," Samuel went on. "*Royals* have big names."

Neetah climbed up a watchtower of lashed poles and beckoned Samuel onto the platform. "Does Chawnzmit have a 'royal' name?" she asked.

Samuel shook his head as he climbed to stand beside her. Neetah had learned that this head shaking meant no. "Chawnzmit is a *commoner*." Samuel made the word sound unimportant.

Neetah pointed to herself. "*Commoner?*" she asked.

Samuel laughed aloud. "Nay," he said. "You are just *serving class*." He said it in the same tone that Chawnzmit had used when he had called her *no one*.

"*Serving class*," Neetah repeated. That wasn't quite right, she thought. Her father was a chieftain, though a minor one, and her aunt was a full Weroansqua—but Samuel didn't know that, and Neetah realized she had almost forgotten it herself.

"*Commoner*," Samuel said proudly, pointing at his own chest. "Pocahontas and Wahunsenacah, *royals*. King James in

England. Queen Anne. *Big royal* over all." He swung his arms to include everything. "Over Jamestown. Over the Powhatan." He made a motion of bowing low at the waist, his hands open at his sides, clearly defenseless. "Your Royal Highness, King John." Neetah couldn't wait to tell Wahunsenacah of this. Samuel dipped his head toward the women's room, "My lady, Pocahontas," he said.

"Samuel!" The Chief's first wife dashed up to the platform. "Neetah! Where have you been? They need you to talk for Chawnzmit. In the temple." Neetah blinked. The temple was for the priests, the men, and sacred business. It was not for young girls, yet she had been there three times now. "Hurry!"

Neetah and Samuel rushed to the great longhouse. "Captain Smith!" Samuel said.

The stranger was sitting cross-legged on grass mats before Uttamatomakkin in the big room. The priest was covered, head to foot, with black soot and bear grease. Neetah stared at his headpiece. Snake and weasel skins were woven in and out among white feathers. The animals' tails dangled about Uttamatomakkin's blackened face. He and six other priests stood in a circle around Chawnzmit. The others were painted half-red, half-black. Spirit masks glowered from the walls over their heads. Through the strong odors of sweet-grass incense and tobacco, Neetah could smell the scent of death. Neetah felt clammy as she thought of the bones of all the old chiefs resting in the back rooms.

Tomakin gestured to Samuel and Neetah to sit down.

A drum began a simple throbbing beat. Chawnzmit

stared at Samuel and deliberately closed one eye, then opened it again. Neetah noticed Samuel's body relax beside her. There was a message in that movement.

Tomakin spoke, and then Neetah translated his words. "Tomakin says he will know your mind, Chawnzmit. He will see if your people wish to hurt us. If so," Neetah had to swallow before continuing, "we kill you. If you mean well, you live."

"I mean no harm," Chawnzmit said forcefully, and that was how both Neetah and Samuel translated it for the others. Chawnzmit turned his hands palms up.

"Silence," Uttamatomakkin said, his meaning unmistakable in any language. Now he began a chant in counterpoint to the drum. It was picked up by the circling priests while other drums added layers of intricate rhythms. As the chanting continued, Uttamatomakkin sprinkled a perfect circle of ground corn around Chawnzmit. He painstakingly set a magic number of dried corn kernels on the circle at each of the four directions. Another priest sprinkled tobacco over the light fire, as well as stronger herbs. As the smoke thickened, Uttamatomakkin took a few corn kernels from each pile. Then he added more. The chant ended.

It began again, but the beat was faster this time. Neetah's eyes burned from the smoke and her stomach ached. In the excitement of Chawnzmit's arrival, she'd forgotten to eat. Neetah began swaying with the drumbeat, chanting in her own mind. Besides her hunger, there was no way to tell how fast the day was passing in the flickering, smoky temple. Neetah lost track and soon forgot to think at all.

It was dark when she and Samuel stumbled outside with an elderly priest. The priest walked them to the nearest cook fire and scooped pieces of venison out of the stew. "Eat, children," he said. "You will be needed though the night."

Neetah almost cried from exhaustion, but calmed herself inside. The tribe needed her. Samuel asked for a drink, and the priest gave them both dippers of some sharp-flavored tea. The drink made Neetah feel wide awake again. She continued to feel alert through the night and into the next night, too. She lost track of the number of times the corn kernels were cast or the chanting restarted. Sometimes Uttamatomakkin officiated; sometimes the great Powhatan, Wahunsenacah took over. Although Neetah had to translate for Chawnzmit a few times, he was never asked directly whether he meant harm to the Powhatans. The gods themselves would make it clear through the corn.

At last the chanting stopped. The priests counted the corn kernels and conferred with the Powhatan. When Uttamatomakkin announced, "This is no enemy," whoops of relief and joy and triumph filled the temple.

Samuel lurched to his feet from where he'd finally curled up to sleep. He bolted for the door, but Tomakin grabbed him. The priest held on to his arm long enough for the boy to realize everyone was celebrating, not preparing an attack. The Powhatan raised his pipe to the four directions and passed it to Chawnzmit, who puffed twice and passed the pipe along to Uttamatomakkin. Neetah watched closely. Chawn had done this before, perhaps at the other villages. Pocahontas would be proud of him!

Neetah thought back to Pocahontas's plan. Adoption. Neetah's body sagged with sudden exhaustion. Was that a dream—or was what was happening now real? Samuel had dozed off in the corner during the ceremonies. Neetah knew better than that, but now she *had* to sleep. She took a dipper of stew from a pot and lifted it to her mouth on the way back to her longhouse, but she scarcely tasted it. By the time she entered the house, her legs were numb. By the time her head nestled into the wolf pelt, she was asleep.

"Wingam?" The whisper was insistent. "Wingam, wake up." Neetah sat up, confused. Who was calling her true name? "You have slept enough." Pocahontas grinned at her.

Neetah joyfully hooked fingers with her friend. "My lady," she said, and then suddenly felt shy. Pocahontas had spent her time in the women's room. It was something Neetah could not ask about. She stared at her friend, looking for clues. New tattoos, elegant and intricate, encircled her wrists. A fringed apron shielded the source of her power. The hair on the front of her head was growing in and her skin glowed. Even her fingernails were clean. *Days without work,* Neetah told herself, *and a sweat bath.*

"My lady?" Pocahontas asked. "You call me by English words, Neetah. What do they mean?"

Neetah laughed aloud. How she had missed Pocahontas's endless curiosity! "I learned much while you were gone," Neetah said.

"You will tell me later," Pocahontas said. "Now we must help in the preparations for Chawnzmit's welcome into the tribe." Neetah stared at her friend. "Yes, I am sponsoring him," Pocahontas answered her unspoken question. "We must bind him tightly, you and I, if there is any hope of peace."

"But the priests learned Chawnzmit's intentions," Neetah said. "We have nothing to fear from the English."

Pocahontas did not look relieved at this good news. In the silence that stretched between them, Neetah yearned once again to ask what terrible visions her friend had seen. Instead she pressed her lips together. "The words, *my lady*," she explained to break the silence, "that is how the English refer to a princess. To *royalty*." She mimicked how Samuel had filled the strange word with awe. "To you."

"I like it." Pocahontas smiled and handed her a red paint pot. "We are all to have red faces for this ceremony," she said. "I shall be red to the waist as well."

When Neetah walked into the temple this time, the intense tobacco and sweet-grass scents smelled soothing. She lined up with the High Chief's other young daughters against the far wall. If she stood on tiptoe, Neetah could see the white feather in Pocahontas's hair. Her friend looked small seated on the mats with the other women. They were an island of quiet in a house vibrating with joyful singing and wild drumming. The priests and warriors crowded close, painted to frighten away the old Chawnzmit, English stranger, and welcome Chawnzmit, the new member of the Chief's own Pamunkey tribe. Smith stood on the broad, flat expanse of council rock, both arms held by warriors.

The girls and women quietly watched the pageant, until the question was asked, "Who speaks for this man?" Neetah held her breath as Opechancanough strode to the council rock and spread his arms. Powhatan's younger brother looked so much like the Supreme Chief that it took a moment for Neetah to realize which brother was speaking. Over the drumming, over the singing, Opechancanough roared, "I do not trust this Chawnzmit." The singing died down. "I have watched his tribe," the Powhatan's younger brother went on. "They clear trees and build as if they mean to stay."

Tomakin strode to the council stone at the Powhatan's feet. "We proved his intentions to be peaceful."

Opechancanough snorted. "His ways are stranger than we know. I, for one, will never call him Pamunkey." Neetah saw Pocahontas's head jerk.

"As long as I rule, little brother," the Powhatan said from his pile of mats, "I make decisions. Not you." Now the drums were quiet, too. Everyone watched as Opechancanough pushed Smith down to the rock and stood over him.

"You know the prophecy, Brother. Strangers will come from the sea to bring our world to an end. Those strangers have arrived. If you do not have the strength left—or the wisdom—to end this now, I do." Opechancanough raised his war club, and Neetah held her breath. For the first time she saw fear in Chawnzmit's strange blue eyes.

Suddenly, Neetah saw a flash of movement. Pocahontas darted forward. Pushing herself between the posturing brothers, she wrapped her arms around Chawnzmit's shoulders. "I speak for him," she said, her voice loud and clear in the silent room. "I will adopt this Chawnzmit." She glared about the room. "Who will stand with us?"

The terror in Chawnzmit's face turned to confusion, then

relief. The Powhatan was the first to break the stunned silence. "This was our plan."

Tomakin stepped up. "Let us hope the gods approve," he said.

Neetah found herself stepping through the women seated on the ground. Before she had thought about it, she had announced, "I stand with Pocahontas." Suddenly, Chawnzmit was on his feet again. Warriors from many tribes were welcoming him. The Powhatan stood with a hand on Pocahontas's shoulder. Opechancanough was nowhere to be seen.

Neetah glanced at Pocahontas. Her face was glowing with excitement as she stood next to her new kinsman. Chawnzmit had lost all look of fear, and a toothy smile glinted through the hairs cascading from his upper lip. Neetah touched her own lip with her fingers. She breathed in the good bear-grease scent of her own hand and silently thanked Ahone that she was Pamunkey, clean and open to adoptions that brought such different peoples together. The crowd thinned around them as people headed toward the riverbank.

"My lady Pocahontas," Neetah said, "the sun is near setting." Chawnzmit smiled in response to the English words, and Pocahontas linked fingers with him, pulling him out of the house. Neetah followed, keeping close. Two warriors trailed behind, speaking quietly. Neetah was glad they were there, keeping watch over the stranger. They walked too far back to hear Pocahontas's words to Chawnzmit.

"You and I are family," she said. Chawnzmit looked down at their interlocked fingers. "Yes," Pocahontas said. She stopped walking. So did he. "Chawnzmit," she said formally, "my name is Matoaka." Neetah drew in a breath. The sharing of Pocahontas's first given name handed this stranger power over Pocahontas's spirit, but he seemed only confused.

"But you," he pointed, "are Pocahontas."

Pocahontas looked patiently at him. "Matoaka," she repeated, her voice quiet. He whispered it back to her and Neetah relaxed. He had caught the importance of the secrecy.

Pocahontas asked for his name. "Chawnzmit," he said. A chill breeze seemed to blow down Neetah's back. Pocahontas asked again and again, but still Chawnzmit refused to share his first name. "Kaptin Chawnzmit," he repeated, and "Chawnuithen Smith." Neetah felt the ice of it in her gut, but Pocahontas's voice stayed level and patient.

"My lady," Neetah interrupted, "we must pray." Neetah urged her friend along to the riverbank. Pocahontas truly needed the protection of Ahone now. She had left herself vulnerable to this man. Her name, Matoaka, could be used as a weapon! Sooner or later, Neetah felt sure, Chawnzmit would use Pocahontas's first name against her. The fear burned inside Neetah until they were both seated and Pocahontas had sprinkled a circle of tobacco around herself. Neetah sighed in relief. That was some protection.

Chawnzmit stayed quiet as the Powhatan people prayed together, the sun set, and a pair of warriors arrived and escorted him up to the cook fire. Samuel sprinted to catch up and began translating some Pamunkey phrases for Chawnzmit. The sound of the guards' laughter mingled with Chawnzmit's. Finally, the stiffness in Pocahontas's posture relaxed. "Pocahontas," Neetah whispered sharply, "we must talk."

"Poor man," said Pocahontas, her voice brimming with compassion. "How fragile he is, with no name of his own."

"Pocahontas . . . ," Neetah began, but her voice trailed off. It was not her place to advise a vision-seer, but Pocahontas did not seem to see any of the dangers crouching all around her. "Does your Chawnzmit understand any of this?" Neetah began. "The adoption? What he owes you? What you have done for him—and what you must do?"

Pocahontas smiled. "Did you not see his face, Neetah? When I stepped between him and Opechancanough?" Neetah's muscles tensed at the memory of that scene but Pocahontas went on. "That relief, that thankfulness. If Chawn understands nothing else, it is enough of a bond for our needs."

Our needs. The words echoed in Neetah's mind. Chawnzmit was part of *her* family now, too.

10
JOY

As winter deepened, the dogs' contented sighs were the only sounds Neetah heard in the longhouse at night. At last, Pocahontas seemed free of visions and fears—and Neetah could sleep.

Whenever Chawnzmit spoke with tribal leaders, he asked Pocahontas to translate for him. "They are giving Chawnzmit land for his own tribe," Pocahontas reported to Neetah one day. She also shared Chawnzmit's tall tales about England. "He is so funny!" Pocahontas said. "Listen to these: 'An ocean so wide it takes three moons to cross. A city a thousand times bigger than Werowocomoco. People sitting on the backs of giant servant-animals'?" Pocahontas laughed aloud.

"Why does he not tell you the truth about England?" Neetah asked. "Is he tricking you?"

"Chawn would never do that," Pocahontas said. Neetah stayed silent.

When both girls translated in meetings, Neetah always let Pocahontas interpret Chawn's words first. "Why do you do that?" Pocahontas asked one afternoon, as she sifted the cornmeal that Neetah was grinding. "You have learned as much English as I have."

"You are always sure of the answer," Neetah answered. Standing, she raised the heavy grinding stick and slammed it down on the dry corn kernels deep inside the hollow log, then raised it again. "Besides, you are the Powhatan's daughter," she added. "You are a woman. You have been given visions. You are . . . Pocahontas." With each comment, Neetah raised the stick and landed it again with another satisfying *whmphf.*

Pocahontas pulled her soft deerskin cape tighter around her shoulders and shook the shallow basket of cornmeal in her hands. The finest pieces filtered through the loose weave and landed in a round-bottomed cooking pot propped between her legs on the ground. "I cannot do this alone," she said. Neetah looked at her sharply. Pocahontas's tone was sad, and she was shivering.

"You take over pounding this batch," Neetah offered. "That will make you feel warmer."

"I was not speaking of this simple chore," Pocahontas said.

The girls moved silently to dump the freshly ground corn into the sifter and pour a new measure of dried kernels into the log.

Neetah searched for a way to change Pocahontas's mood as she knelt by the cook pot. Now Pocahontas slammed the stick down. "It has been a moon. Chawn must go back to Jaimztown," Pocahontas said. *Whop!* went the grinding stick.

"That is why your mood has fallen?" Neetah spoke quickly. She began one of the ancient chants to cover her thoughtlessness at asking such a direct question. Pocahontas didn't answer but instead pounded time with her. They sang almost through a full cycle before the grinding stick clattered into its hollow log.

That night Neetah awakened to the sound of Pocahontas's whimpers. Neetah reached down and pulled a puppy up into the bed and cuddled it until Pocahontas's vision-dream passed and they all could sleep again.

The morning dawned gray and cold and windy. After prayers Chawnzmit and Samuel strode toward Neetah and Pocahontas where they stood eating some leftover succotash stew. The two warriors assigned to guard Chawn squatted nearby where they could play chance games and watch the English man, too.

"My lady!" Chawnzmit said, his teeth showing. "The canoes are ready. We go to Jaimztown at mid-day."

Pocahontas dropped her gourd back into the pot. Chawnzmit towered over Neetah, smelling of old sweat and dirt, but he spoke only to Pocahontas. "You will come with us, will you not?"

In answer, Pocahontas offered him a finger. He hooked it with his own. "Wait until the men hear of my adventures!" he said. "The things I have seen! The dangers I've faced!" He was talking so fast now that Samuel gave up trying to translate.

Pocahontas tugged at his finger and said, "We will go, but remember, Chawn, you will give us a huge grindstone to bring home." She turned to Neetah. "No more pounding corn to flour inside of logs! Our Chawn has also agreed to give us powerful muzkets."

Neetah glanced at Chawnzmit's face in time to see his lip

hairs twitch at the word *muzkets*. Samuel had told her that the English man understood much more of their language than he let on. He seemed to be following this discussion. He had certainly understood when the Powhatan had offered him a piece of land. Neetah wondered if Pocahontas knew Chawnzmit was tricking everyone. When Neetah turned to ask, Pocahontas was following Chawn toward the river.

No one was shivering as Opechancanough pushed the canoe into the icy river. The Powhatan had insisted that his sullen younger brother, although still angry, escort Chawnzmit home. Baskets of corn, sides of venison, and dried and fresh fish were heaped high in the center of the canoe. Neetah sat on top of a pile of furs. Every bit of her exposed skin was heavily greased against the winter weather and, as a member of the Powhatan's court, she wore far more clothes than she would have at home. Her soft leather tunic and leggings were tied snugly against her skin. Her moccasins, too, were laced tight and stuffed with sweet grass to hold out the cold.

Pocahontas sat ahead of her, in front of Chawnzmit. She wore a feathered mantle over her winter clothing. He wore only the clothes in which he had been captured two moons earlier.

Neetah noticed that his teeth were chattering when they boarded. It served him right, she thought. He had refused the chance to wash in the river with the tribe before morning and evening prayers. He firmly clung to his own clothing—layer after layer of woven cloth, metal chest plate, and thigh guards, even when offered warmer furs and skins. After the boat landed, his jaw still quivered as he led his Pamunkey escorts toward the Jaimztown gate.

"It's the captain! He's alive!" Happy calls floated from the stockade.

The scene that greeted them inside was even worse than it had been at Neetah's last visit. She could not help but stare at the gaunt English men. They looked ill, all of them—and there were not many left. The settlers fell on the food the Powhatan had sent like crows on a field of ripe corn.

When the men had finished the corn cakes, Opechancanough told Pocahontas to ask for the big muzkets and grindstone so the Pamunkeys could get back to Werowocomoco by nightfall. "It is cold, and I do not trust the weather or the people," he said.

Neetah watched Chawnzmit lead them to the huge circular grindstones. The English men gathered around, gnawing on dried fish as Opechancanough ordered his tribesmen to carry the stones to the canoe.

Neetah looked at the canoe and then caught Pocahontas's eye as four men leaned down to force their fingertips under one of the huge round stones. This was hopeless, and Neetah could see that Pocahontas knew it. The warriors strained and muttered angrily, but they could not move it. Opechancanough ordered the last two of his men to help. A few of the English men began clearing their throats. One or two actually chuckled aloud. Now Opechancanough pushed his warriors aside and pulled until his whole body trembled with the effort. Still the stone did not move. "Too big for the canoe, anyway," Opechancanough snarled. He looked around the circle of English men. "This was a trick from the start."

Neetah tried not to notice the smirks on the faces of the English men. "That was only part of the bargain," Pocahontas said gently. "We will still be taking two of their precious muzkets back to Werowocomoco."

"These are *cannons*." Chawnzmit gestured at two log-sized chunks of the heavy black metal. "Our biggest muzkets. You may take them both to the Powhatan."

Opechancanough's scowl became an open glare. Even Neetah could see the problem. These "gifts," too, were far too large, heavy, and clumsy to be transported in canoes. The English men began muttering under their breaths. Neetah knew Opechancanough did not know enough English to understand the rude insults, but the tone would be clear in any language.

"I will show you the secrets of how they work," Chawnzmit said.

Pocahontas translated, then told Opechancanough, "Once we know the magic of these cannon muzkets, we can make as many as we want for ourselves." She turned to Chawnzmit. "Thank you," she said. "We will watch now." She beckoned Neetah over to the nearest cannon. Neetah stepped close to see and remember everything.

The English men hurried to pour a grainy black powder down the throat of the giant muzket and a tiny bit more into the other end. Then they rammed a scrap of fine-woven fabric with a stick into the cannon and rolled a squash-sized ball into it. Another man brought a lit cord from the nearest house and moved to the back end of the muzket. Too late, Neetah saw the rest of the strangers step away. *Danger!* she thought, but had no time to react before the fire touched the closed end of the cannon.

Suddenly, the cannon roared, as loud as thunder, in her ears. Neetah screamed with the pain of it and ran. It mattered not where she went. The pain burned in her ears. It made a high keening sound that drowned out everything else. She pressed her hands to her ears and looked about. Where was Pocahontas? Where was Chawnzmit? Why couldn't she hear?

Through blue-black clouds of acrid smoke, Neetah saw her friends, scattered about, peeking around trees and from behind bushes. She also saw English men, doubled over with laughter. One pointed at Opechancanough, running toward the canoes. Another put his hands over his ears in imitation of the Pamunkeys. Gradually, Neetah was able to hear the loudest of their taunts.

"Stop your insults!" Chawnzmit was bellowing at his companions. He reached his arms toward the fleeing natives. "Friends, friends! Come back!" his voice filtered through the insect sounds buzzing now in Neetah's ears. "Opechancanough!" he yelled.

"Come back." It was Master Hunt, their holy man, calling, too.

Slowly, the Pamunkeys began returning to the fort. Now the English men brought little gifts for them—beads and trinkets.

"Long knives?" Opechancanough demanded. "Axes?"

Pocahontas translated, but Chawn pretended not to understand and handed her more beads instead of useful tools. The English men began to put the magical black power into the second cannon. Now everyone stood back when fire was added. The roar was no surprise this time, but Neetah still jumped from the power of it.

When it was time to go, Opechancanough had stopped speaking to anyone. Several of the English men were yelling at Chawnzmit. They quarreled over the remaining food, too.

"Chawn," Pocahontas called back from the canoe. "I will bring more food, and soon."

Neetah listened to the high, thin sound of crickets in her ears all the way home. It was winter. There could be no crickets. But the sound of spirit crickets stayed with her all the same.

The crickets went away over the next ten days. They were gone when Neetah traveled again to Jaimztown. Pocahontas had pleaded with her father to let them take more food to the settlers. She became wild when her father wanted to delay the trip a few days. "Now!" she begged. "Chawn needs food *now*. They all do!"

The smell of burned wood hung low over the icy river as the canoes approached the English colony. Smoke floated in the sky. "Hurry!" Pocahontas cried to the Pamunkey warriors as they paddled around the bend. Suddenly, the canoe swerved and stopped as the warriors back-paddled.

A new ship lay next to the Jaimztown stockade. Like the first three, it had great red crosses painted on its sails. Its masts reached upward and dripped with vinelike ropes. And the ship brought many more men. They were wandering here and there on the shore, looking stunned—and very cold. Above them on the bank, smoke swirled from the charred stumps of the stockade. "Where is Chawnzmit?" Pocahontas called out from the canoe.

"Chawn!" someone called up the hill.

"Get Chawn," the word passed on.

"Call Chawn."

"It's Chawn's little princess!"

Finally, Chawnzmit stepped out of the charred stockade, his clothes singed and smeared with soot. Samuel limped out behind him.

"My lady Pocahontas!" Chawnzmit cried. There was desperate relief in his voice.

"Get us to land!" Pocahontas ordered the warriors. They paddled double-time, and the canoe slid halfway up onto the icy shore. Pocahontas scrambled out and ran to Chawnzmit. Neetah hurried along behind but stopped as the English man wrapped his arms around Pocahontas.

"Thank God," he said over and over. "Thank God." Through Chawnzmit's stringy hair, Neetah caught a glimpse of Pocahontas's face glowing with joy as she hugged him tightly.

"Neetah, you came just in time!" Samuel grabbed both her hands and stared into her face. "The settlers were sending John away. He let them starve, see? But then the *Susan Constant* came up the river. That boat. From England and full of food, Neetah. Full. And supplies. We are saved at last! We carried it all to the fort." He looked up at the smoking ruin. Neetah saw tears in his eyes. "It burned, Neetah. All our houses. The church. The beautiful new food. And now . . ."

"Slow down!" Neetah begged.

Beside them, Chawnzmit was telling the whole story, too, in a loud voice. "The fire came from a cook fire? A hearth? A candle? No one knows. It jumped on the wind faster than I could stop it—and all the water I had was frozen."

The horror finally settled into Neetah's bones when she saw the ruins for herself. No building had been left untouched. Fire spirits had eaten up the thatched roofs first, of course, but they had left almost nothing of any walls, either. The storehouse was gone. So was whatever food had been inside. These people had nothing left but ashes.

Neetah thought of the great baskets of corn, acorns, beechnuts, and walnuts that her tribe had buried underground. Fire could never reach them, and they were down too deep for water damage. Last season's corn crop had been small because of the drought, but what had been harvested was stored safely. The tributes brought to the Powhatan had been small, but they were set aside, stored deep underground. Here, they had nothing.

"Can you help us?" Samuel asked as the two of them walked together.

"Yes," Neetah promised, "but you should ask my lady Pocahontas."

"You are steady as a bear, Neetah. Pocahontas is a—a red squirrel flashing through the treetops."

"I am a bear?" Neetah did not laugh aloud. "I do not have that strength, Samuel."

"Did you see John's face today?" Pocahontas asked Neetah. "He was so glad to see me!" Wind whipped the sour smell of burned wood down to the river landing.

"Did you not see the ashes?" Neetah prompted, "or the burns on everyone's hands?"

Pocahontas settled silently into her place in the canoe. She picked absently at the fringe on her winter cloak as the men's paddles slipped in and out of the icy water. Finally, she whispered, "I have seen far more than you have, my friend." Neetah moved close to better hear her secrets. "My visions all show horror and hunger ahead for the English men," Pocahontas went on. "I will *not* let them starve." Neetah flicked her gaze to Opechancanough at the bow of the canoe. "Yes, he would let them all die," Pocahontas said, "but my father will see the sense of providing for them." She paused. "They are kin."

For the rest of the winter, Pocahontas talked the Powhatan into giving the suffering English men turkeys, deer, baskets of corn cakes, and pottery jars of cornmeal. Every four or five days, troops of Powhatan's hunters strode into Jaimztown. One joyful day, they saw that the ship called the *Susan Constant* had sailed away with half of the English men. "You see, they are not going to stay," Pocahontas told everyone who would listen. "We are safe."

Neetah usually followed Pocahontas into Jaimztown, but when Pocahontas was called to the women's room, Neetah took Chawnzmit's supplies to Jaimztown in her place.

• • •

By the last snow of spring, Neetah, too, had become a woman. She fasted in the silence and darkness of the women's room, awaiting a vision of her own. None came. When the medicine woman came to set her free, Neetah pleaded, "One more day." Still no visions appeared, waking or sleeping. When the medicine woman came again, she insisted on putting a healing paste on Neetah's tear-stained cheeks.

"Now," the medicine woman said, a few hours later. "You must come out and let your clanswomen welcome you properly."

Neetah spent more days in the room with kind women who were as gentle with the clan tattoo needle as they were with the secrets of this new life-making power. They shared herbs for teas to relieve cramping and teas to bring on a flow of blood; they taught charms to attract a man and skills to keep him; they shared stories of childbirth and child death. Through it all, Neetah felt the power of womanhood soar within her.

Neetah's skin was still steaming from the woman-making sweat bath when Pocahontas rushed up to her. "Look!" she crowed. Neetah gasped at the ice-blue beads her friend waved before her. "While you were in the women's room, Chawnzmit came to Werowocomoco. He brought a blood-red suit of English clothes, a tall black hat, and a swift white dog for my father."

Neetah staggered to the side of the creek and splashed her steaming skin with handfuls of icy water. Then she rubbed herself with soothing red paste. "You missed a place," Pocahontas said, rubbing the small of her back. "You don't want fleas and lice to find you tasty! When John asked for more food . . ."

"More?" Neetah winced. It had been so peaceful simply

to be a woman before Pocahontas had come with her needs and excitement.

"'*More!*' That was just what father said. Then John brought these beads out." Pocahontas held them up toward the strong spring sun. Lights sparkled on the beads and inside them, too.

Neetah tied a womanly apron around her waist and said quietly, "Matoaka?" Pocahontas's face softened at the sound of her first-given name. "I am a woman now," Neetah went on. She could hear the calmness in her own voice. "I know what that means. So do you."

Pocahontas slowly brought the beads downward. "Not yet, Wingam. There will come a time for us to choose husbands. For now, we . . . "

" . . . are needed by the tribe," Neetah finished her friend's sentence with a sigh. "I have not forgotten your visions and my place in them. But someday soon—"

"A new ship has come to Jaimztown," Pocahontas interrupted, "bigger, and full of new English men and women, too. This time they are farmers. They brought new tools and basketfuls of seeds to plant, and strange animals to raise and even to ride!"

"Pocahontas, listen to yourself," Neetah said. "These English men do intend to stay. They will be the end of us all."

Neetah watched her friend's eyes lose focus and her face relax as she fell into a vision. Then, with a shiver, Pocahontas focused again.

"There is another way," she whispered, but then would say no more.

11
BETRAYAL

Winter 1608 through Winter 1609

"I FEEL AS IF I'VE EATEN AN ENTIRE ELK," NEETAH GROANED, rubbing her belly. Pocahontas laughed, her breath turning to clouds in the wintry air.

"It takes time for your body to come back after a long fast like that," Pocahontas said. "I didn't believe it when the medicine woman told me, either." The new women-friends shuffled through the snow past the temple, fingers locked.

"Pocahontas! Neetah!" The Powhatan stepped through the temple door. "Come and talk with us." Neetah huddled close to the temple wall, out of the wind. "The English gave us twenty long knives for twenty turkeys in mid-winter," the Powhatan said.

"But now," Uttamatomakkin said from inside the doorway, "Chawnzmit will not trade any more tools and weapons. Do you understand this?"

"I do," Pocahontas said. Neetah moved even closer so she could hear. This had all happened when she was in the hut. "It wasn't Chawn," Pocahontas told her father and the priest.

"I understand more now. Chawn is not the only Weroance at Jaimztown. The chief who traded knives with us went back to England on the *Susan Constant*. Now our Chawn is in charge again." Pocahontas sounded pleased at Chawn's success. "Father, remember, Chawn never has traded weapons, knives, or tools with us."

"You speak of Chawn who is Pamunkey?" the Powhatan asked. "Chawn who we adopted into our own family?"

"This worries me," Uttamatomakkin said.

"It enrages our brothers who did not get one of those twenty long knives," the Powhatan said. "They brag of stealing them. They pull axes from the English men's hands as they fell trees. Some even speak of sneaking into the houses to kidnap a muzket. There will be deaths if the English fight back."

"Yes. There will be deaths," Pocahontas said. There was finality in her voice, and weariness. "I am struggling to hold the spirit of peace in our land." Neetah silently hooked fingers with her friend. "*We* are struggling," Pocahontas corrected. "Father, do we no longer share the same vision? Do we not both work for peace?"

Neetah looked from father to daughter in surprise. A *shared* vision? But neither Pamunkey offered an explanation. The Powhatan simply patted the white hound settled at his feet. The dog's whiplike tail beat a happy response. "We will give Chawnzmit and his English men the summer," the Powhatan announced. "You will tell him, Daughter."

Pocahontas pressed her lips together and smiled. Neetah tried to remember how long it had been since she had seen her friend's joyous dimples.

Neetah saw little joy all summer. English men were killed. So were Pamunkeys. There were no major battles, only skirmishes as the tribesmen tried to take what the English men would not give freely. Often Pamunkeys died. Faces appeared around the Werowocomoco cook fires smeared with soot. Women grieved, and anger grew. Neetah and the other healing women were called to tend to muzket wounds while priests burned the warriors whose bodies had been mangled by the English. Some had been disfigured, even after death.

Stories of the English men's savagery passed from friend to friend. Besides destroying the entire Chessiopiac tribe and taking its lands, they were raiding and killing in other villages, too. They took in no women or children, but killed them as well.

Neetah felt Pamunkey anger spread throughout the town. It only grew when the Powhatan called a war council of his elders and declared war on the Piankatanks.

"They control too much territory," he explained later to his wives at dinner. "Yet they do not give tribute to Werowocomoco. I will force them into my Confederacy." Troops of warriors went west to fight. Some did not return. Others did, and Neetah became skilled at tending to warriors' wounds. There were sorrowful new Piankatank slave women working in the village now and frightened children to adopt.

Neetah thought that even the sky spirits were upset. The clouds forgot to rain and the winds blew hot and angry. Through it all, the women's work went on. Neetah helped to plant the corn, though it grew stunted in the drought.

Sunflowers sprouted in their field and grew parched. Few nuts formed on the trees. The beans wilted. The squash were smaller than usual. Finally, Neetah felt the first ripe ears of corn, plump in their husks.

She tucked her hair behind her eyes so she could see Pocahontas across the field. "Dance with me!" she called, and began trying the steps of the Green Corn Dance in the dust. Pocahontas joined in. So did Cheawanta and the other young women. At last, Neetah saw smiles among the Pamunkeys.

Werowocomoco's men traveled far looking for game to fill stew pots for the Green Corn celebrations. Only women, young boys, and old men were in town for the first of the harvest ceremonies. That made no difference to Neetah or the rest of the women. They prepared the Green Corn feast dishes of freshly roasted corn on the cob and boiled new corn, too. They added cornstarch and honey to walnut milk to make a sweet pudding. The smells floating over Werowocomoco made Neetah's mouth water, but she did not sample as much as a sip before the ceremony began.

By mid-afternoon, Neetah had spread paint the color of blue corn over her skin. She began trying to master the sensuous steps the women had danced in other years.

Pocahontas got to wear the silvery yellow color of the tallest kind of corn. Cheawanta and her friends had to choose rust, white, yellow, or red. They all worked together, gathering fresh corn leaves and weaving them together for their skirts.

"I finished first!" Pocahontas announced. She stood up

from the circle where all were squatting, dropped her apron, and wrapped her skirt around her hips. There were great gaps between the leaves. Neetah winced.

"What man would choose you dressed in that?" Cheawanta laughed. "I am making my skirt perfect. It takes longer, but men want wives with skills and patience."

"They also want what Pocahontas is showing," Ofanneis said. Uneasy laughter floated around the circle. "But they don't always marry for it."

"I *will* marry," Pocahontas said, her face flaming. "My husband and I will live on in song and story, long after all the rest of you have been forgotten."

Neetah's face flushed hot in embarrassment for her friend. How could Pocahontas set herself apart from—no, above—the others like that? Neetah busied herself knotting another leaf in the chain. What was Pocahontas thinking? Finally, Ofanneis responded to Pocahontas's prophecy, clearing her throat as if something slimy had caught there, and spitting it out into the cook fire.

"I will finish your skirt, Pocahontas," Neetah offered, "and mine as well—but later. Come away for now." She did not wait for an answer, but rose and started off toward the royal sleeping house. After she'd taken a few steps, the sound of the women's angry hisses died away. Neetah glanced back.

Pocahontas was hurrying to catch up. When they were safely in the house, Neetah turned to her. "You do not make friends that way," she scolded.

"I do not need friends here," Pocahontas said, then paused to lay her hand on Neetah's shoulder, "except for you."

"You do not need more enemies, either," Neetah said, then bit her lip. Who was she to lecture the Supreme Chief's daughter? To change the subject, Neetah looked up at the spears and bows, dried fish, and baskets hanging from the saplings that supported the roof. "Over there!" She pointed to a jumble of antlers tied together with twine. "The headdresses for the dance! I'll climb up and lower them down to you."

"You do believe in my visions, don't you?" Pocahontas asked.

Neetah climbed onto a sleeping platform and shimmied up one of the poles. She sneezed from the smoke near the top of the longhouse. Neetah hooked her toes around a rafter and held on with one hand. With the other, she fought to untie the knots holding the ceremonial gear. When Pocahontas repeated the question, Neetah had to answer.

"Matoaka, you wear the white feather. I do believe you have visions, but you share so little of what you see." She lowered the bundle of antlers to Pocahontas.

"In one vision . . . ," Pocahontas began. Neetah dropped lightly to the dirt floor and held her breath. "I am in a marriage." Pocahontas's voice sounded halting and strained. "It is a marriage unlike any other. I am lonely, but you are there. Many, many lives are saved." Pocahontas opened her mouth to go on, but seemed unable to say more.

Neetah wanted to ask if there were children. If she had a husband, too. And what was the sorrow that made Pocahontas whimper during her night visions. Instead she grabbed a pair of antlers. She put them on her head and began dancing around the fire, singing pieces of the Green Corn chants.

"You cannot sing!" Pocahontas teased. She picked up another pair of antlers, and the two girls danced until they were breathless and sweat streamed down their chests. Finally, they stopped, panting. Neetah gathered the other headdresses where they lay scattered around the floor.

"My poor singing will not matter," Neetah said. "There is no one left in Werowocomoco to dance with tonight but little boys and old men."

"There are visitors on the way, even now," Pocahontas said, her voice deep with importance.

"Oh, Matoaka," Neetah said. She could not keep the irritation out of her voice. "It is not fair to tease me with your vision-knowledge."

Neetah left the longhouse and carried the antlers back to the cook fire. She barely spoke to Pocahontas as the unmarried women prepared their headdresses or left to finish the cooking. Neetah busied herself weaving and re-weaving skirts for the dance, losing herself in the intricacy of the knots and their ancient pattern.

During evening prayers, Neetah heard muzket fire coming from the river. Everyone around her quickly finished their thanks to Ahone and hurried back into the royal stockade.

"Wait," said Pocahontas, her hand on Neetah's arm. Within moments, a sailboat appeared. "Chawn?" Pocahontas called out. "Chawnzmit?"

"Ahoy!" came the answer. "Is that my little princess?"

As the men disembarked and followed the girls back to Werowocomoco, Samuel struggled to translate Neetah's apologies that the Powhatan had not been there to greet them, that the harvest had been poor, that there would be only a small feast at the ceremony, but that, out of common courtesy, all were welcome. Pocahontas simply gazed at Chawnzmit while Neetah watched her friend, stunned. *I am in a marriage, but unlike any other*, Pocahontas had said. Did she expect to *marry* Chawnzmit?

Neetah shuddered, trying to imagine a life spent with his whiskers and sweat and smell and swagger. *Pocahontas did not have visions*, she thought. *The visions had her*. For the first time, Neetah was glad she was not a vision-seer.

"Feasts and dancing for all," Chawnzmit roared. "We stay the night, men!" As the English men piled into the town, Pamunkey boys scoured the forest for more wood to build up the fire. Old men tried to swap stories with the English while the women made extra tea and added more corn to the stew to fill the pots. At the feast, the English men ate as if starved and, indeed, looked even skinnier than Neetah had remembered. Then, while the rest of the tribe entertained these guests, the unmarried girls snuck away to prepare for the dance.

One of the old priests struck up a heavy drumbeat by the dance circle. Another drummer joined him, and then another, and the corn maidens began singing. They entered the circle, their feet moving in small, demure steps. Their leaf skirts swayed along with their hips, celebrating the joy of the first harvest. The corn was finally becoming ripe! There was plenty again—and there would be plenty more to share. Life was coming full cycle and corn spirits of every color whirled and bobbed, swayed and twirled, showing the ripeness of their bodies.

"Do you think Chawn is looking at me?" Pocahontas asked Neetah, when they had completed one set of dances. Neetah had to admit that he was. His eyes followed her with a wild longing.

After the dancing, Neetah thought, *Chawn will follow Pocahontas into the woods, celebrating the harvest in all the ancient ways this hot summer night. That will make Pocahontas happy and honor the gods as well.*

But Pocahontas had spoken of marriage. Neetah could not imagine that. For that, Chawn would have to bring many gifts of deer and turkeys and fish to her family to show that he could support her. After many moons, he might ask to marry her. If the Powhatan and Pocahontas both agreed, Uttamatomakkin could perform a wedding ceremony. But to marry a stranger from a distant land and a different culture? The drumming started up again, urgent as a heartbeat, and Neetah leaped to her feet.

No one but the dancers was supposed to be inside the circle, but the English men did not seem to understand this. Again and again, the women had to push them back to sit on their mats. "Explain to them," Neetah said to Samuel. "That this is not a dance for men and women. Tonight we are the spirits of corn. We dance in thanks to the gods of the harvest."

Samuel's eyes glittered dark and huge in the light of the dance fire. "It looks like you are inviting us to . . . " He looked away and stopped.

Neetah grinned. They had all grown up this past year. "We dance to invite the gods to bring good marriages, too," Neetah said, but Samuel was not listening. He, like most of the men, was up again and dancing with the painted young women in the circle.

As Neetah looked, Pocahontas broke from the circle and danced over to Chawnzmit. Whatever happened later would make a good story to tell by winter fires, Neetah decided, and lost herself in the dance.

There was almost no corn or meat left to send home with Chawnzmit's party the next day. "You are lying," he said. "There is food aplenty hidden here." It seemed the English might search the town by force, until Pocahontas wept and told them to go.

"We will trade with another tribe then," Chawnzmit bellowed, "an enemy tribe!"

Neetah watched as the settlers left. Chawnzmit would find little food elsewhere, she knew. The rains hadn't come this summer and the skies were cloudless again. The harvest was poor everywhere. It would be a hungry winter for all.

Throughout the fall, English men made raids on Powhatan tribes, stealing whatever food they couldn't get through trade. Chawnzmit's men were savage in their demands and brutal in taking what they wanted. Another supply ship full of English men finally arrived in Jaimztown, and the settlers began clearing even more fields. It seemed to Neetah that Opechancanough was right. These English had no interest in leaving—or even in living together peacefully. The Powhatan stopped speaking of his adopted son, Chawn—and he would not listen to Pocahontas, either. Neetah could not find any way to make her friend smile now.

When the Powhatan ordered all of his tribes to stop trading with the English men, Pocahontas wept. "Chawn cannot even get word to me," she sobbed, "and I know he wishes to." Nothing Neetah said made any difference.

"Why not go to Jaimztown alone?" Neetah finally suggested in frustration. "You could take some food and you could see your Chawn." They had all heard the spy's reports. Every day, English men were starving. Every night, more bodies were being buried within the fort walls. It was worse than the dying time of the past winter.

"It is Chawn who must come to *me*," Pocahontas answered, wiping her eyes. "He must ask my father for permission to marry me."

"Is that what you want?" Neetah asked, shivering on the riverbank. Ice was forming again, breaking, and floating up and down the river with the tides.

"It was never what *I* wanted," Pocahontas said. "It was what my visions told me would happen. It was my duty." There was a new uncertainty in her voice. "But now I want this." She took a deep breath and let it out slowly. "Neetah, I have never seen love in my visions, and yet that is what I am feeling." Pocahontas covered her face with her hands. Neetah had never heard her friend sound so stunned, so hurt, so frightened. She wrapped her arms around Pocahontas, rocking her as if she were a baby.

"There, there," Neetah crooned. She tried to imagine what it must be like to be in love. It did make things more complicated. "There was love in Chawn's eyes at the Green Corn ceremony. You will see him again," she promised, "even if I have to paddle you to Jaimztown myself." Pocahontas rewarded her with a shaky smile.

But no one went to Jaimztown that winter. The hunger and the fighting both got worse. The Powhatan announced that famine plans would be put into place. "Our people must split up and move inland to where the game is still plentiful," he said, "or we will starve." Women looked at their warm houses and thought about untying all the cords and packing up the saplings, the furnishings, and the stores and then moving it all through the cold woods. Children whimpered for food. Men watched their families and worried that they would never find enough to feed them. Moving was a hard decision, but everyone agreed it was the right one.

Near the time of the shortest night, Chawnzmit's sailboat appeared again on the river. It was towing a large barge. Neetah grabbed Pocahontas's hands to stop their trembling. "It is coming true," she promised. "Chawn has come to ask for you." Ice clogged the river, coated the bank, and glazed the trees so that the boat could not get near to land. Then the tide turned and the barge hung up on a hidden sandbar.

"Do not unpack. Prepare a feast with whatever you can find," the Powhatan ordered his people. "We are Pamunkeys. We will honor our guests." But extra guards were stationed everywhere in Werowocomoco, arrows ready in their bows.

Neetah waited on the shore next to Pocahontas with some warriors, while the tide swept the ice toward the sea. Finally, the English boat approached without its barge.

"Chawn!" Pocahontas cried. But it was a solemn Chawnzmit and three other strangers, all dressed in extra-fine clothes, who waded ashore. None of them looked at the "princess" in her heavy winter cloak.

"We must see the Powhatan," Chawn demanded. "We bring gifts from King James. And we have muzkets to trade." Pocahontas and Neetah followed behind as the English men and their party slipped up the icy hill into the town. They entered the Chief's longhouse where smoke poured from the smoke hole.

By a blazing fire, Powhatan elders gathered to watch as the Powhatan received a suit of red cloth. He handed it to his third wife, the ugly one. In a corner of the longhouse, Neetah huddled with Pocahontas, their fingers locked together. *Ask about Pocahontas*, Neetah willed Chawnzmit. *At least start the bargaining.*

"Great Powhatan, I leave you Samuel and Henry," Chawnzmit announced, "and Thomas, too. These strong young boys will be a help to you through the winter." Samuel and the taller boys stood. The Powhatan grimaced. So did Neetah. They did not need three more mouths to feed this season. Besides, everyone knew English boys were useless as hunters. Chawn could have brought them only to spy—and to be fed. Neetah's lips tightened in anger.

She and Pocahontas sat rigid, watching as Chawn and his friends tried to get the Powhatan to kneel so a shiny copper crown could be put on his head. Everyone laughed at the struggle, knowing their Supreme Chief would kneel to no one. But the English men would not give up. Finally, the copper circlet landed crookedly on Powhatan's head. It looked worthless above his beautifully beaded winter cloaks.

The Powhatan gave the King Jaimz delegation some old

moccasins and a worn royal cloak in return. Chawnzmit looked furious at the laughter these gifts triggered. After that, the Powhatan would not trade more than a few bushels of corn, even when offered muzkets in return. Chawnzmit clearly wasn't thinking about Pocahontas. In fact, he had not even looked her way. "We will feast tonight," the Powhatan told the English, "and by morning, the tide will free your barge from the sandbar. We will load it with many baskets of corn for you then. Go make your boat secure while we make the feast ready." The English men were ushered out into the cold to tie up the barge, anchor their boat, and gather their crew.

Next, the Powhatan turned to the Pamunkeys and ordered, "Spread the word. We break camp now, now and in silence. We will take the boys with us. Each warrior can set out with his own family. Mine is going to Orapax, up the Chickahominy River. Uttamatomakkin goes with me. Be sure there is a priest and a healer with each group. No one stays behind, save a few of my wives to look busy cooking food here and a few warriors to share a decoy 'feast' with our English *friends*." He said the last with a sneer and several warriors chuckled.

The Powhatan leaned close to the nearest warrior and whispered in his ear. The secret was passed, man to man, around the smoky room. Several raised their bows. Others softly hooted a war chant. One made a crude joke about dawn.

Beside Neetah, Pocahontas hissed, long and low. "What is it?" Neetah asked.

Pocahontas looked at her, eyes full of anger. "My father is going to have the settlers killed," she whispered. "At dawn. After pretending to welcome them with a feast." Neetah felt

Pocahontas's entire body stiffen. "I hate my father."

Neetah felt sick.

Suddenly, the Powhatan strode across the room to Pocahontas and stood towering over her. "You will come to Orapax with the rest of us," he said. "Uttamatomakkin will be watching your moves in case you dare to disobey."

Pocahontas grabbed Neetah's hand and squeezed it so hard that Neetah had to bite her lip not to cry out. When she looked up, Uttamatomakkin raised his rattle in greeting from across the room. "We do this in silence," the Great Chief reminded everyone.

Neetah helped Pocahontas dress in all the clothing they could wear and put the rest on sleds. With the other wives and children, and the English boys, too, they silently untied the lashing that held the royal house together. The sheets of bark, saplings, mats, and furs were bundled carefully and readied for travel. Pots and gourds, herbs and dried fish— everything was divided so the tribe could carry it away.

Once they had all gathered, Uttamatomakkin led them in quiet prayer.

"I will send word at planting time in the spring. We might return here. We might not." The Powhatan's voice barely carried over the hissing of a sudden icy rainstorm. "May Ahone guard all of us." He pointed toward the path for his family to take. Friends stopped to hug silently, children whimpered and were shushed, dogs were gathered, and the group slowly broke up. Neetah walked arm in arm with Pocahontas. When Neetah looked back to see if Chawnzmit was arriving for the fake feast, her eyes met

Uttamatomakkin's as he followed them down the path.

The hard crust on the ground made traveling at night easier, though the ice dripping from tree branches above left everyone cold and wet. Thirty miles was too far to travel at one time, so the Powhatan halted the march at midnight. "Get what rest you can," he commanded. "At daylight we head again to Orapax."

Neetah and Pocahontas lay side by side, cuddled for warmth under a furred deerskin. Just as Neetah began to doze, Pocahontas's body trembled, then shook with stifled sobs. "Hush, now," Neetah said gently under the blankets, wiping tears from her friend's face. "You need to sleep. We face a long, hard carry tomorrow."

But Pocahontas lay rigid and the tears kept flowing. "Matoaka?" Neetah whispered. "I am your friend. Tell me where your thoughts go."

"Did you not hear the plans?" Pocahontas's voice barely carried over the howling wind above. "Chawnzmit will be slain at dawn." Now Neetah's body stiffened. "I must stop this!" Pocahontas said.

"Hush," Neetah cautioned her friend. Then she said more quietly, "It is on your father's orders."

"Yes. I know. I could be killed if I disobey. But Neetah, do I follow my father or my vision?" Under Neetah's hand, Pocahontas's shoulder was shuddering wildly. "I don't know what to do!" The words came between gulps of air. Neetah put her arms around Pocahontas and held her tight, hoping to quiet the storms raging inside her friend.

Neetah whispered, "Tell me your choices. Sometimes

that helps in picking a path."

"I love my father, Wingam," Pocahontas whispered. "How could I betray him? But I have come to love Chawnzmit, too. How could I let him die? I want what the gods want: for me to marry an English man. Chawn!" Pocahontas took a ragged breath before going on. "And, Wingam, how I love my people! My vision says I can save them through Chawn! Oh, what would you do?"

Neetah grabbed the single bead tied around her neck and thought back to the promise she had made to her mother. *I will hold to the ways of our gods, our clan, our tribe, and always remember the old stories.* The gods had given Pocahontas these visions. The old stories prophesied a terrible change coming.

"In your vision, do you help your clan and your tribe?" Neetah asked quietly.

"Yes, oh yes. If all goes right, I save them," Pocahontas said. She wiped her eyes. "Chawnzmit will marry me if I go to him tonight. I am sure. I will live with the English and learn their secrets—then share them with our people. The killings will stop."

"Must it be tonight?" Neetah listened to the sleet hitting the iced twigs above them.

"Do you not want me to save our people? I must warn Chawn and save him, then I must marry him."

"And betray your father? He will never forgive you, you know."

But Pocahontas had thrown off her side of the deerskin and wiggled free of Neetah's clasp. "Are you coming?" she asked.

12
STORM

January 1609

SILENTLY, CAREFULLY, NEETAH AND POCAHONTAS PICKED their way through the sleeping bodies at the camp. They held the deerskin over their heads and leaned down, letting the tanned hide shelter them from the worst of the sleet.

"Who is that?" challenged a guard lying under another skin on the ground. His voice was deep and gruff.

"Two silly girls," Pocahontas replied, her voice light and sweet. "Drank too much at the creek. We need to water the trees, then curl back up and go to sleep." She faked a huge yawn.

"Hurry, then," the guard grumbled, and pulled his buckskin back in place.

The girls did hurry as fast as they could find footing. There was little light and the path was unfamiliar, but it followed the logic of all animal trails. As Neetah jogged along, she pictured the warriors left at Werowocomoco preparing for their raid. Chawnzmit would be sleeping on his boat, unaware of the danger he was in. Neetah followed Pocahontas across small streams and along ridgelines until they came to the heavy rushing sound of the Chickahominy River under its ice shelf. "Shall we risk the ice? It would be faster," Neetah said. Pocahontas agreed, but Neetah insisted that they ask Ahone's blessing first.

Sleet stung their faces as the girls hurried down the river. Their moccasins crunched through the soggy frozen surface of snow, but the ice beneath held. In the end, it was the fierce wind that drove them back into the shelter of the trees on the riverbank. "How much farther?" Neetah gasped, after they'd stopped under an enormous cedar tree.

"We must keep going," Pocahontas said, a catch in her voice. "Chawn could be attacked before dawn. He could be dead now." Pocahontas turned away. "My father, my dear father," she gasped. "He will never forgive me."

Neetah struggled to find an answer. "Your father delights in your tricks," she said. "He will be glad to have a spy living with the English." Pocahontas was silent as they both strode back out into the storm.

Finally, Pocahontas stopped. Wood smoke hung low in the stormy air. She pushed Neetah toward a hollow tree and said, "Wait here. While Chawn is preparing his boat to take us to Jaimztown, I will come back to get you." She took a long shuddering breath. "Pray to Ahone, Wingam. For me. For all of us."

Neetah's mind was too full of anger to pray. She had to go to Jaimztown, too? How dare Pocahontas make such decisions for her?

Neetah summoned up the stink of Chawnzmit, as freezing rain lashed the tree bark. *I'm not the one who wants to marry him. I just want to go home.* She huddled in the hollow tree, listening for any sound of footsteps. As her body shivered, she imagined herself by a warm fire. She was nursing a baby and a tall husband stood nearby. Neetah could not see his face, but his body was smooth and lean and strong.

Tired, she told herself, shivering again. She'd spread enough bear grease on her skin this morning to keep out the chill. *Tired and frightened*. She practiced her good-bye to Pocahontas. "I will think of you by my cook fire, with my husband and babe on a cradle board nearby." Neetah thought of the happiness her mother's eyes would hold as she told her grandchildren the old stories.

Now, as she remembered them, those stories seemed dull. So did the life she was planning out for herself. There were no English men in this future. No supremely powerful chiefs. No excitement. No Pocahontas. Thinking about the adventure that clung to Pocahontas like feathers to a swan made Neetah feel excited and warm even on this cold night. A new idea formed in her mind, and the words to go with it. *Take me with you, Matoaka!*

Neetah smiled and began to doze off. Suddenly, she was awakened by a wild wailing. The little hollow where she'd been sleeping filled with a cold, wet body.

"No! No!" Pocahontas sobbed, keening, cursing the gods and pulling at her hair.

"Stop it!" Neetah grabbed Pocahontas's wrists. "Is Chawn dead?"

"No," Pocahontas said through sobs, "but I am." Neetah struggled to get her friend's story. "Chawn is alive. He is safe. He will escape before Father's men come to kill him." Her voice turned bitter. "And he said, 'Thank you.'"

"'*Thank you*'?" Neetah echoed. "That is all he said? He will not marry you?"

"No. He gave me a handful of beads in thanks for my warning. Then he told me to go away." Her rage filled the hiding place. "Beads, Neetah! Beads? I risked my life for him. I can never return to my father. There is nothing left for me in Jaimztown or Werowocomoco, either. And my vision?" Suddenly, the rage collapsed into sorrow. "Chawn!" Pocahontas cried. She buried her face in her hands. "How will I live without Chawn in my life?"

Neetah held the Supreme Chief's daughter until all her tears were spent. "You are not dead," Neetah said softly. "You have been living a dream, perhaps. But listen to the idea I have." She let her imagination fly free, describing life in a small village with a tall, proud husband. "You and I could make houses beside the same small stream. I would have a child," Neetah said, "or perhaps two. You, too. We could sing them to sleep as my mother did me." Neetah's voice sang a sweet old lullaby. Outside the tree, the storm raged, but the simple melody quieted the last of Pocahontas's hiccuping sighs. "Our husbands will come to us in the day with deer and squirrels to cook," Neetah said. "They will come in the night with comfort and strong loving arms. There will be no worry. No questions. No danger."

"I could do that," Pocahontas said, her voice dull.

"It would be *good*." Neetah fought to convince Pocahontas and herself, too. "A traditional life like that would bring us the comfort that has always been, since the very beginning." The wind shifted then, and a gust of icy sleet splashed into the tree. "Okeus is spitting at us," Neetah said. "He says, 'Hurry home now.'"

"If we can get there before dawn," Pocahontas replied. "Perhaps no one will know of our middle-night travels."

They pushed through the snow and reached the makeshift camp just before dawn. The snow had finally stopped, and the girls crawled under their deerskin, then pretended to awaken with the others. The girls trudged sleepily with the royal family toward Orapax.

In mid-afternoon, a runner overtook their small party. Pocahontas looked at Neetah, her eyes wide. "I have bad news for the Powhatan." The young man panted. "Where is he?"

Pocahontas directed him up toward the middle of the line.

"They know Chawn escaped," Pocahontas whispered.

"But not about us," Neetah said. The cold seeped into her bones.

Within moments, Uttamatomakkin and a warrior strode back to the girls. They blocked the path and Uttamatomakkin turned to his companion. "You were guarding these two last night?"

The warrior coughed and wiped his nose. "Yes." His familiar deep voice brought chills to Neetah's arms. She glanced at Pocahontas. "They slipped out to make water, then came back."

"How long were they gone?" Uttamatomakkin demanded.

The warrior sneezed and looked down miserably. "I dozed. They were in by dawn, but . . ."

"How did you sleep last night?" Tomakin asked Pocahontas.

"Not well," Pocahontas said dully.

"I can see that," the priest said, "and I can see more. Powhatan is too angry to speak just now. It will be worse when I tell him that you two snuck out on a mission last night. He will want to see you both." And he left.

Trapped in the middle of the moving line of Powhatan's warriors and families, the girls kept plodding onward. The afternoon groaned on, step-by-step. Finally, Neetah whispered, "He knows. What will he do to us?"

Pocahontas did not answer, nor did the girls hear anything when they paused at sunset for prayers by the riverside. They had no word at all from the Powhatan until after the longhouses had been erected at Orapax, guards posted, and fires fanned into life.

Wahunsenacah strode past the girls and did not turn to acknowledge them. Neetah saw Pocahontas wilt and felt herself sag, too. The High Chief always bantered with his favorite daughter or paused to discuss some news or practice English with her. This night, she might as well have been a pebble by his path.

He did not speak to her the next day, or the next. Matachanna was little help to her sister. "He seems to have chosen a new favorite," she said to Pocahontas, as the women sat on a sleeping platform. Pocahontas silently threaded an antler needle with deer-gut thread. Neetah kept punching holes through the soft leather piece in her lap. Matachanna made a careful star pattern of dyed porcupine quills in one of the completed moccasins. Pocahontas's stomach grumbled. Outside the house, the winter winds howled.

The women spent most of their days indoors. They stoked the fires and covered the door openings with tightly woven mats. With everyone busy at winter chores inside, the

houses were warm and crowded. Long songs and chants, sto-
ries, and gossip swirled through the humid, smoky air.
Pocahontas's hands stayed as active as any of the other
Pamunkeys', but she did not join in the women's merriment.

Neetah tried to tease Pocahontas, but she would not
smile. Often she simply stayed silent. "Look at how smooth
and strong that hunter's body is," Neetah prodded once. "He
brought in two deer. He would be a good provider." Still no
answer. Another day, Neetah brought a toddler into the longhouse. "Let us teach her to braid hair," she said. Pocahontas
simply walked away.

Winter slowly released its grip on Orapax, but still the
Powhatan did not speak to Pocahontas.

He seemed to delight in warring with the English—and
being sure that Pocahontas heard of it. "Our father has
ordered the killing of all of the English in Jaimztown," her
younger sister came by to tell her one day. Pocahontas did
not respond, but Neetah saw her shoulders stiffen.

"He is punishing me with these messages," she told
Neetah later, when they went down to the river to fetch
water. "This was never supposed to be the way of it. I was not
to *hurt* the English. . . ."

"You did help them," Neetah reminded her. "You saved
Chawn's life, and the lives of the other Werowocomoco visitors." She scooped a huge hollow gourdful of water, then
swung it up to balance it on her hip. "Perhaps you have already
played your role." Pocahontas stared out across the wide river
for a moment before she stooped to fill another gourd.

The girls' steps quickened as they hurried back into the
warmth of the longhouse. "Shall we refill your paint jars

now?" Neetah asked. It seemed a good way to spend the hours until sunset prayers.

Later, a scratching sound drew all eyes to the doorway. "My lady?" Samuel's voice called out. He waited until Pocahontas invited him in, then sat quietly until she had collected her thoughts.

Neetah smiled, as she ground red stone into fine powder. There were many Pamunkey boys whose manners would never be as fine as the English boys. Thomas and Henry felt like part of the tribe now, and Samuel seemed like family. He looked at her sadly until Neetah felt her stomach tighten with alarm. "My lady." He turned to Pocahontas. "Today's travelers came to ask for food, but they brought news you should hear."

Pocahontas kept mashing the red powder into bear grease, but Neetah could see that she was listening. Conversations died all around as others listened, too. "It is Captain Smith," Samuel said. "They say he is dead."

Pocahontas's hands froze, fresh paint blood red on her fingers. "Are you sure?" she whispered.

"That is what they say."

"Was . . ." Pocahontas forced the words through her lips, ". . . was it my father . . . ?"

"No, my lady," Samuel said kindly. "It was an accident."

Neetah watched as Pocahontas pressed her eyes tightly closed. The other women leaned in to watch her reaction. "Look at the fire, Pocahontas!" Neetah said loudly. "It is burning low. Let us fetch more wood before sunset." Pocahontas looked up at her. "Now," Neetah said firmly, holding the door covering open.

Samuel and Neetah stood behind Pocahontas at the cook fire outside. They watched helplessly as she stooped to rub her fingers in the ashes. Then she buried her face in her hands and moaned softly.

"Ah," Samuel said awkwardly, "perhaps I should go back to Henry and Thomas. The guard only let me loose to tell Pocahontas the news." Then he ran off, as Pocahontas, her face soot-streaked with grief, moaned.

For the next moon, Neetah stayed close to Pocahontas as she sat quiet and still in the longhouse. The women's activity swirled around her day after day, but Pocahontas did not respond. She ate far less than her share of the food, too. Everyone's flesh showed the effects of the long winter's hunger, but Pocahontas's seemed to be melting away.

The dawn light of spring began to come earlier and the door mat was often left open for light. The snow melted. Fresh fiddleheads flavored the stew now and birds sang at morning prayers. Neetah left Pocahontas to help the medicine woman prepare the bitter spring drink. After a solemn ceremony to mark the end of winter, they served the tonic to everyone. Soon the woodlands were full of the gagging sounds of people cleansing themselves for the new season. All of the ills and bad spirits, all of the angers and sorrows came up and were left behind to sink away, stinking, into the ground. Wobbly but refreshed, everyone returned for another, more soothing drink and a time of rest. That night Neetah danced with happiness in the warm spring air.

Pocahontas did not come to the dance circle. The next

morning, Neetah pressed shells and a drill into her friend's slender hands. "You must not give up," she said fiercely. "Beads. You love beads. Make some. For me."

For a moment Pocahontas fondled the clamshells, focusing on them. "Here," Neetah said, turning one over. "Add the purple stain here. Three blue beads could be made out of this shell as well as a handful of white." She handed Pocahontas a drill. Pocahontas wedged the shell between her bony knees. She began rolling the drill between her hands, its point slowly gouging a rough bead shape into the clamshell. Neetah smiled and took up another drill. Each bead would give Pocahontas hours of soothing work. Matachanna rose from her seat across the longhouse and walked over to lay a hand approvingly on Neetah's shoulder. The warmth of that touch stayed with Neetah as the beads slowly took shape in her lap.

Near mid-day, someone called from the outside. "The boys! The English boys! They have escaped!"

"Neetah?" Pocahontas said, her voice confused. "Should we . . . ?" Before Neetah could answer, Pocahontas jumped up. Half-drilled beads scattered across the dirt floor. "I have to help them!" She rushed out the open door and stood listening for a moment, then pointed into the distance. Neetah had heard nothing, but she followed at a run. When the sound of shouting drifted back through the trees, the girls ran to the woods and crept along quietly to see what lay ahead. A knot of warriors stood over Samuel's bloody body. Neetah watched one raise a hatchet for the kill. She quickly looked away, biting her lip to keep from crying out. This was no surprise. There was no extra food to feed three growing boys. The villagers had complained until the Powhatan had lost patience. "If they make any trouble, they stop being guests," he said. To Neetah, Sam had felt more like a friend. She blinked hard and turned back to see another man holding Thomas by the arm.

"I told them to go back!" Thomas pleaded. "I want to go home with you now."

"What about Henry?" another warrior asked. "Where did he go?"

"That way," Thomas pointed. "Escaping was his idea. He made Samuel and me go along."

Suddenly, Neetah felt herself being jerked back by her elbow as Pocahontas pulled her behind a tree. "Too late for those boys," Pocahontas whispered. "But we can still save Henry!" Her eyes flashed with an excitement Neetah had not seen in moons. She smiled nervously in response. "Let's go!" Pocahontas said, before Neetah could argue.

It was all Neetah could do to keep up with Pocahontas's wild flight through the spring woodlands. Her friend darted from tree to tree, stopped and crouched behind bushes and boulders, ducked around thornbushes. They outflanked the men who chased Henry and headed down an animal path. Neetah had seen the signs, too. Henry had carelessly broken off new buds and tender twigs in his flight. His path was clear.

Pocahontas slowed to a trot, following the boy's trail. Neetah could hear her own breath, but she could not hear the men behind them anymore.

They tracked Henry until they found him sitting beside

the path, rubbing a sore ankle. "No!" he said, holding his hands up to protect his face.

"We will take you to safety," Pocahontas whispered. For the first time since mid-winter, Neetah saw her friend standing straight and tall.

"To Jaimztown?" Henry asked.

A flicker of pain passed over Pocahontas's face. "No. Not there," she said.

Henry's eyes filled with tears and Neetah looked away, disgusted. This boy would never survive huskanaw, though he was old enough for the test of manhood. A blue jay scolded overhead and Pocahontas grimaced, then pointed silently and headed off the path. Neetah followed her and soon heard Henry behind them, breathing loudly and cracking sticks under his hard-soled boots.

As they fled, Neetah let the animal spirits of the forest fill her mind. A hawk slid through the trees with the swiftness of wind, silent and focused. Neetah borrowed its calm. She caught the skunk scent of fox urine as they passed a huge tree trunk. As Neetah imagined the animal passing in the night, graceful and fleet, her steps grew lighter. She smiled her thanks at the little chipmunk people, standing tall like sentinels on old fallen logs. Not one of them chipped in warning until Henry blundered into sight.

"Wait," Henry gasped. Neetah slowed, then stopped, standing as still and calm as the sapling spirits around her. Pocahontas circled back to see what was wrong. "Have to breathe." Henry bent over, his hands pressed on his knees. Neetah looked from Pocahontas's well-greased skin to the

English boy's heavy clothing. "Is it much farther?" he finally asked.

"Where are we going?" Neetah asked.

"We can hide with the Patowomekes," Pocahontas said. "The Powhatan has no power over their tribe. We will be safe with them on the Patomac River to the north of here." Neetah swallowed. Pocahontas had been ill. Her body was gaunt from winter famine. Could she make the trip? Could Henry? Neetah pressed her lips together. There was no choice but to run. They'd helped a prisoner escape. But to the Patowomekes? Neetah looked at Pocahontas for explanation. "I know the Weroance there," her friend said quietly.

"Will he kill me?" Henry asked.

"No," Pocahontas said quickly. "Japazeus argues every year against sending tribute to my father—food, warriors, or women. He will enjoy hosting those who've slipped from Powhatan's grasp."

"Are we nearly there?" Henry asked, wiping sweat from his forehead.

In answer, Pocahontas just turned and led the way again. "Watch her feet, Henry," Neetah urged. "Step where she steps so you miss fallen branches. You make as much noise as a baby bear cub—and you whimper like a baby, too." A flash of anger showed in Henry's face.

"We are being followed," Neetah explained. She tried not to picture the hatchet falling toward Samuel's head and looked quickly back to Orapax, straining to hear any warning calls from the forest animals. The woods were silent. Neetah smiled. Henry was already matching his steps to

Pocahontas's.

They moved on through the spring afternoon, stopping only to drink from a stream or to pull up dried cattail stalks and nibble at their tender roots. Near sunset, they paused to wash and pray while Henry stood nearby, shivering. Then they moved on. As darkness fell, Henry again asked, "Are we near the Patomac?"

No one answered. Pocahontas looked up through the smooth, wide branches of a persimmon tree. The sky was as purple as wampum and scattered with stars. "We sleep here," she said.

"Where?" Henry looked around. Pocahontas pointed upward. Neetah paused to squat briefly in the shadows to relieve herself, then climbed up after Pocahontas past the first broad branch of the tree. Neetah settled in, leaning against the trunk, listening to Henry's struggles as his clothing snagged on twigs. They heard a sharp ripping sound and a curse when he reached for a branch. Finally, Henry was still, and, one by one, the night spirits let themselves be known: the owls called, a distant wolf howled, a flying squirrel swooped through the tree, and the moth people flew by on soft wings. Neetah smiled in the darkness and let herself sleep.

"My back hurts," Henry said at the base of the tree the next morning. "My legs are too stiff to walk, and I'm hungry." He glared at the girls. "I'm staying here."

Pocahontas looked at Neetah, then turned on her heel and walked away. Neetah patted Henry's shoulder. "Remember, you were not found and killed." Then she joined Pocahontas and a few moments later, she could hear Henry following behind.

After three days, the first Patowomeke guard stopped them. The tall young man spoke the same language as all the Confederacy tribes and seemed to recognize Pocahontas, although he acted wary of Henry limping along behind the girls. He led them all into the hilly little village. A small cluster of longhouses, a newly cleared field ready for planting, a sacred dance circle, and the sound of children playing—it looked like home. Neetah felt the tension leave her shoulders.

Pocahontas, too, seemed relaxed. She teased the guard and asked his name. "Kocoum," he said. "A brave man and a fine hunter." They all laughed at his bold answer. "I will take you to Japazeus," he offered, though his eyes never left Pocahontas's.

Neetah was surprised to see her friend blush. With a grin, Neetah answered for her. "Pocahontas will be happy for your company."

PART III

OUTCASTS
1609 — 1613

13
KOCOUM

"AND SO THE SPIRITS BLEW US HERE," POCAHONTAS FINISHED A long retelling of their story at the main cook fire. Neetah met Kocoum's questioning eyes and smiled to let him know it was all true. The warrior gazed at Pocahontas with respect.

Around them, the Patowomekes sat back on their mats, enjoying the warm evening and their full bellies. Neetah thought the Patowomekes had been very kind. They'd included Henry at their welcoming feast, although they'd never seen an English boy before. Their children were quiet, their women friendly, and their village full of dogs.

Neetah licked her fingertips, savoring the sweet taste of the corn cakes made with honey and walnut pieces, then fried in deer fat.

Japazeus rose to his feet, and Neetah stared in curiosity. This Weroance was younger than her father and far younger than the Powhatan, yet he had managed to keep his tribe independent of the Confederacy. Though he was short, his thick neck, broad shoulders, and muscular legs made him look as strong as any man. Except for the slight dent on the bridge of his nose, Japazeus had perfect features.

"Now tell us your story, Neetah," he prompted.

Neetah felt her face redden. "*My* story?" She was confused. "You just heard it."

Japazeus laughed aloud. "No. *Your* story. I see by your tattoos that you were born to an Appamattuck mother. She lived somewhere inland where the water spirits chuckle and burble as they tumble over rocky falls." At his words Neetah could hear the creeks and brooks of home again. It took her back to her childhood.

"I remember riding on my father's shoulders," she said from her mat. "He carried me over the water spirits to my aunt's town for Green Corn ceremonies. I felt like I was flying. Father's headdress was made of bear claws and mink skins. It was beautiful—but my aunt Totopotomoi's was twice as tall." Neetah stood up and tried to show how tall her aunt had looked to her. "In the firelight, she twinkled all over with copper beads and glossy pigeon feathers." As Neetah continued with her story, a dozen children sat and listened, wide-eyed.

"The Weroansqua Totopotomoi is your aunt?" Japazeus interrupted. "Your mother's sister?"

"Yes," Neetah said, looking at the children. "Do you have sisters?" she asked them. Some said yes, others said no, and one made a rude noise. Everyone laughed. "I have a sister, too," Neetah said. "Pocahontas. We spied on the English together." A flock of questions flew at her. She and Pocahontas talked, Henry added to their story, and they translated, until they were dizzy with exhaustion. Finally, Henry fell asleep where he sat.

"Let him sleep," Japazeus said, as the parents carried their own children off to bed. Kocoum stayed, tall and skinny as a cornstalk. When Pocahontas shivered, he fetched a deerskin and wrapped it around her shoulders. Neetah was glad to see her smile at him.

"Pocahontas, there are questions I must ask," Japazeus said, "before I can allow you to stay." Neetah sat straighter, but Pocahontas yawned. "Does the Powhatan know where you are?"

Pocahontas jerked upright. "No," she said. "That is why I came to you, my friend."

"I have always admired how you defied the great Powhatan, even as a child. And the English. Do they know where their boy is?" Japazeus gestured at Henry, snoring in the warmth beside the fire.

"No. Nor do they know that the boy's two companions died at my father's hand."

"There is risk to me if I shelter you and the boy," Japazeus said. Neetah watched him stroke the bridge of his nose, deep in thought. "But there could be benefits, too."

"Yes," Pocahontas yawned. "We could have beds to sleep in." Japazeus laughed.

"There are extra platforms in the longhouse where my wife, Sitka, and I sleep with our children," Japazeus said. "You may sleep there as long as you need to."

"And Henry?" Neetah prompted.

Japazeus wrinkled his nose, and Neetah laughed. "You will get used to that."

Kocoum helped Pocahontas to her feet and led her to the royal longhouse. The Weroance and Neetah managed to awaken Henry and guide him to a bed in the longhouse as well. He collapsed on top of a heap of mats. Neetah picked a sleeping spot closer to the door and pulled furs over herself. Pocahontas hummed quietly to herself as she slipped into a bed nearby.

Finally, Japazeus entered and ducked through a door to a back room. Neetah heard the sleepy murmurs of his children and the greeting noises of a husband and wife. Neetah smiled in the darkness. This was a safe place. Henry was welcome. And Pocahontas and Kocoum had made a handsome pair in the firelight. Had the "princess" forgotten her English man? "Let it be so, Ahone," Neetah whispered in prayer.

Three days later, Kocoum brought a freshly killed deer to Japazeus's cook fire. "Is there anyone who will help me skin it?" he asked Pocahontas.

Neetah busied herself grinding corn. Japazeus's wife said she had to go gather wood with her children.

"Do you not have things to discuss with the elders?" Sitka asked her husband. When he did not move, she gave him a push. "You *are* the Weroance here." He left, looking back over his shoulder.

It took Kocoum and Pocahontas all day to gut and skin the deer and make the tanning mixture from its brain. Bloody to their elbows, they never ran out of things to talk about. Then they hung the deer to drain so it could be butchered the next day. After morning prayers, they cut up the deer, and Kocoum gave the meat to Japazeus's wife.

"Thank you," Sitka said, "we will enjoy it—but Japazeus is not Pocahontas's father."

Kocoum blushed. "Did you think I was courting her?" His blush deepened. "I simply thought to share the bounty of my hunting with you. You do have extra mouths to feed."

Neetah watched Kocoum and Pocahontas spend the next day scraping the deer hide before Kocoum disappeared into the forest again. In three days he was back with a fat turkey. Before the moon was dark, he had fed Japazeus's family four times over, and his intentions were clear.

When Kocoum had headed out to hunt yet again, Japazeus asked Pocahontas, "Do you wish to marry him?" Neetah wondered why he even bothered to discuss it. The answer was as clear as ice to everyone in the village. Pocahontas looked across the cook fire at Neetah.

"I will be a good wife to him," Pocahontas said. "I will bring joy to the Patowomekes."

Japazeus helped himself to the fresh beaver's tail from Kocoum's most recent offering. "You have surprised me, Pocahontas, with your quiet and womanly ways. After your stories, I thought you'd be wild and foolish." Pocahontas stared at the Weroance until he noticed her gaze. "Yes, yes!" he said. "But you should marry him. After all, we can't keep eating all this meat!"

The Patowomeke priest and Pocahontas's clan members took over as soon as they heard the news. Neetah watched from a distance as the clan shared meals together, visited the sweat lodge, and gave Pocahontas gifts of tools and hides.

They lashed together a new longhouse for the newlyweds. "Near the main path," Pocahontas said. "I want to be in the center of things." They let Neetah help after they saw the clever patterns she wove into a mat for the door.

The wedding feast was held after the second corn planting. That night, after hours of singing and wild dancing in the circle, the priest measured out a full arm's length of beads. The Patowomekes moved closer. Pocahontas called Neetah to stand right beside her as she and Kocoum held hands. Even the young boys listened to the priest's blessing and held their breaths as he wound the beads around the couple's hands. At his word, they pulled their hands apart, and the beads went flying. Laughing with glee, everyone scrambled to gather the wedding beads from the ground. Neetah managed to snatch two of them. Henry joyfully shouted the strange English words, "Huzzah! Huzzah! Huzzah!," though he could not explain what they meant.

Finally, the Patowomekes returned to their own sleeping houses. Neetah's steps dragged as she ducked into the Weroance's house. Sitka was just adding a stick to the light fire on the floor. Neetah held out the two precious beads from her friend's wedding, saying, "These are to thank you for sharing your home."

"No," Sitka insisted, waving them away. "Do not be a silly water bug." Neetah sighed deeply, and Sitka caught her hand and folded it closed over the beads. "Dear Neetah, soon you will use these to catch a bold warrior's eye."

Finally, the night was still. From Japazeus's house, Neetah heard the water spirits chuckling with glee in the nearby stream. Sitka may have called her dear Neetah and made her welcome, but Neetah missed hearing Pocahontas breathing on the nearest sleeping platform. What would Kocoum think, she wondered, of his new wife's night cries? Then Neetah realized that she had not heard any sleeping whimpers from Pocahontas or seen her fire-gazing since they left Orapax. Had the visions stopped?

Three moons later she finally dared to ask. The summer had passed well for the Patowomekes. The harvests were small but better than last year's, and there were no deaths. Pocahontas seemed happy in her marriage to Kocoum. Neetah often sat watching them laugh together. Pocahontas spent evenings and mornings in Kocoum's little longhouse, talking with her husband. She kept stews simmering at his cook fire and mended Kocoum's moccasins with fancy stitching. Pocahontas still stopped work to visit the women's room every moon, so Neetah knew the gods had not sent her a child yet. Kocoum was not visiting other sleeping houses at night, though, and the couple still snuck kisses and touched when they thought no one was looking.

"Pocahontas?" Neetah sat, shaping a pot at her friend's cook fire. "Have you lost your white feather?" Pocahontas's hand rose to touch her hair, then quickly brought it back to roll her own clay. "I ask . . ." Neetah had practiced this part, ". . . I ask only because Japazeus has brought a swan for our cook pot, and we have feathers aplenty."

Pocahontas rolled out a clay snake and wound one end into a small, tight coil. She dipped her fingers into a pot of water and wet the rest of the snake, winding it above the edge of the tight coil and overlapping each layer. Soon Pocahontas had a round-bottomed pot. With her fingers, she pinched the coils together and smoothed out the sides and insides.

When Neetah thought her friend had completely forgotten her question, Pocahontas answered. "I am better off without my visions," she finally said. "Few Patowomekes see dark prophecies like mine. Fewer still are given paths that lead nowhere." She finished her pot, pressing the sides thinner and thinner between her hands until Neetah thought the clay would break. Pocahontas set the bowl aside and got to her feet. "I need to relieve myself in the woods," she explained and left.

While Neetah pressed a pattern into her own bowl, she realized that Pocahontas had not answered her question at all. Was Pocahontas still seeing the future? Neetah left their bowls together in the sunshine. It would be days before the pottery was dry enough for them to work on it again.

"Have you heard anything about the English?" Neetah asked Japazeus. The family was working around the fire in the longhouse while the first of the winter storms lashed the village with cold rain. Henry looked up from the arrow he was supposed to be fletching, a broken feather in one hand and a thread of sinew from a deer in the other.

"Try again," Japazeus said, without looking up from the bow he was shaving down with an antler knife. "But try softening the string first with your teeth. And Neetah, I know nothing beyond the edges of my village."

"That is strange." Neetah took a stitch in the child's moccasin she was embroidering for Japazeus's son. "My father is a Weroance, too, and he knows every rumor in the

Confederacy and from far beyond, too." She picked up the other moccasin.

Sitka hissed and her laughing eyes met Neetah's. "Japazeus," she asked, "was the messenger who arrived last night Chickahominy or was he Mattaponi?" She looked back at the grass she was twisting into cord. "You remember, dear one, it was right before you called a council meeting."

"Huh!" Japazeus filed harder on his new bow.

Neetah snipped the last knot off the moccasins she was making and held them up. "Look what I have for you, Little Cricket!" Henry laughed as the little boy scrambled for the gift, putting the moccasins on his feet and running to show them off to his mother.

"Neetah, you didn't!" Sitka said, as she tied the laces around her child's ankles. "Cricket, go show your father." The little boy swaggered up to Japazeus.

The Weroance stared at his son's feet. "Those aren't the beads from Pocahontas's wedding, are they? The ones Sitka told me about?"

"I think they look good with the porcupine quills," Neetah said. "Don't you?" She put the bone needle she'd been using into her sewing basket.

Japazeus opened his mouth, then closed it.

He looked at the roof over his head and held his hand out. "I think I felt a leak. Neetah, will you come help me find it?"

Instead of laughing at his obvious lie, Neetah followed him into the rain. Japazeus made a tent over their heads with his cape and Neetah stepped close. "Neetah," he said, "there is no leak."

"So you lied?" Before Japazeus could answer, Neetah

laughed. "My father was a Weroance, remember? I know that chiefs and chieftains lie. They must, for the good of their people." She looked up into his eyes. "But there is news, isn't there?"

"Yes," Japazeus said. "And it is bad. Many of the English have died of some spotted sickness. They still have not harvested enough crops to feed themselves. More ships keep coming, and they claim more of our land. That means more blood has been spilled. I wanted to tell you where Henry could not hear."

"You are kind to spare Henry's feelings," said Neetah, smiling. "You have taken Henry into your family, into your heart." Neetah remembered the other flashes of kindness from this man. He had given a huge wedding feast for a woman who was not his own daughter. He had taken smelly Henry into his home and two frightened girls, too—ones wanted by the Supreme Chief of the Powhatan Confederacy. That first night, Neetah remembered, he had insisted in hearing her story, not just Pocahontas's. No one had ever noticed her before when she was with Pocahontas. Somehow Japazeus knew that.

"You are kind," said Neetah. Rising on tiptoe, she kissed him before she knew what she was doing. "Oh!" she said, and covered her mouth in embarrassment. Japazeus simply dropped the cape and enfolded her in his strong, warm arms. They pressed together in the rain, feeling each other's need.

Japazeus, himself, escorted Neetah from prayers the next day. "Like Pocahontas," he said, "you have no father here or chief to ask."

Neetah stopped short to help Little Cricket up from the

ground. "Ask what?" she said, though she knew what was coming. It had been nearly a year since she had become a woman,
and she had not yet chosen a husband. She brushed off Little
Cricket's clothing so she could think before she replied.

This Weroance was handsome and strong, of only middle
age and a fine hunter. He was kind to children and women.
He didn't always speak the truth, but then, he was a
Weroance. Besides, there were no others in this tribe who
appealed to her as much. Her own mother had married a
Weroance and had been happy.

"I can feed and dress a second wife," Japazeus went on. "I
can support more children now, and I find you very pleasing."

"Oh?" Neetah could not believe she was challenging a
powerful man. *I sound like Pocahontas*, she thought.

"You have the strength of silence," Japazeus said. "Deep
and still and sure."

Neetah felt herself blush.

"I like that," he went on. "You listen or sew with the same
intensity as you decorate a new clay pot or pray to the gods.
Sitka sees the same things in you. Will you join us?"

Neetah's entire body felt weak, but she agreed to consider
his offer.

The next day Pocahontas scolded her. "This is your
dream, your vi—" her voice caught but she continued, "—
this is what you have always wanted, but with a Weroance! I
give you permission."

"Why thank you, my lady," Neetah teased, bowing her
head to the "princess" even though no one else in the
Patowomeke tribe did so. "I shall accept his offer."

14
JAPAZEUS
1611–1612

"WILL WE SEND WORD FOR MY FATHER TO COME TO OUR FEAST?"
Neetah asked Japazeus.

He thought for a while before answering. "The more eyes
that come to our town, the greater the danger to
Pocahontas," he said. "To the wrong people, she would be
seen as a valuable hostage. The Supreme Chief might pay a
ransom to get his daughter back, and the English might trade
arms or goods for her. It is better that she stay here, hidden
with me."

Neetah shuddered. "Perhaps the Powhatan has forgiven
her. And the newcomers at Jaimztown may have forgotten
her name by now."

"My dear one, the treason of Pocahontas is spoken of at
campfires everywhere," Japazeus said. "Her tale is likely to
pass from person to person for generations. I prefer to keep
her safe here with me."

"You are generous," Neetah said, running her fingers
along Japazeus's arm, feeling hard muscles beneath the slick

of bear grease. "I feel blessed that I'll have a husband who cares for my friends as well as for me."

"Neetah," Sitka whispered in her ear. "Wake up. You must put this on so Japazeus sees you afresh this dawn.

Neetah stretched and arose in the half light to take a bundle of soft leather from Sitka. She shook it out and held up a deer-skin outfit for winter. It had a ring of beads stitched around the neck and long fringes fluttering from the hem and wrists.

"I made it while you were showing Little Cricket how to set a snare," Sitka explained.

"And wear these." Sitka offered a pair of earrings. When Neetah took them, she gasped at the tinkling sound of tiny bells. She looked closer. Creamy pearls, big enough to drill through, hung on tiny wires alongside copper beads. The hollow beads jingled as they bumped together, making Neetah laugh.

"May the gods always give you laughter," Sitka said, as Neetah put the earrings on, shaking her head to hear the chimes.

When Japazeus saw Neetah in the wedding dress, he stroked the sides of her face as she looked up at him. Neetah longed to caress him in turn, running her hands down his neck, his wide chest, his smooth belly. She swallowed quickly and backed up a step. "Sitka made this dress," she said. "It dances." She twisted and swayed to set the fringe in motion. "And the earrings laugh in happiness."

"You will dance a happy dance for me," Japazeus said, his voice deep. "Later."

During the day, Neetah thanked Sitka for the dress. Other villagers brought Neetah sinews and dyed porcupine quills that she could weave into patterns. They brought vibrantly colored reeds for baskets and tiny shells, too.

"You have a talent unlike any other," they told her and, "you bring joy to our children," and "you honor us by honoring our Chief."

After evening prayers by the stream, the Patowomekes feasted on nut milk and honey, fresh elk, passenger pigeon, and bear until Neetah thought she might burst. She stored the experience away to remember during the hungry times of winter. Her wedding dance and the long chants and songs seemed to be treasures, too, scenes she could recall in times of sorrow and silence. The priest's blessing, the touch of the beads that bound her to Japazeus, and the joyful shouts around them as their string broke did not seem quite real to Neetah.

She hugged Sitka and Little Cricket, glad to be in their family. Pocahontas and Kocoum, her clan members, the priest, the children to whom she had told fireside stories—all welcomed her.

The drummers began again, and flutes played a women's dance. "Watch your husband's eyes," Pocahontas said, dancing beside her in line. Neetah saw, then felt, Japazeus looking only at her and at the fringe swaying and twisting as she dip-step-dipped in the ancient pattern. Her body warmed from the dance or the fire or perhaps her husband's eyes, and she felt the soft leather dress caressing her as it shifted against her skin.

When the men danced, she tried to look only at Japazeus's copper beads jingling and bouncing or the feathers in his headdress swaying. She caught sight of the knot of hair by his temple bobbing heavily to the beat. Neetah stared openly at his painted body gleaming in the firelight. Finally, the ceremony ended, and she and Sitka followed Japazeus to his home. Sitka hooked fingers with Neetah silently, and then she ducked through the back doorway, calling to her son. Henry smirked at them until Japazeus told him to go sleep in Kocoum's longhouse.

When Japazeus joined her between soft bear pelts, it was more wonderful than the clan women had told her, more exciting than Pocahontas had predicted, and more comforting than Neetah had ever imagined. Later, when they threw back the bear pelt, sweating and relaxed, Neetah stroked Japazeus's face, his forehead, his cheekbones, and the precious bridge of his nose.

"Why do I feel as though I watched this day from eagle's wings," she whispered, "instead of from my own two feet?"

"You did not enjoy the power of this Weroance?" Japazeus teased, rising on one arm in mock indignation.

Neetah had to laugh. "Of course, my husband, as you well know." She watched the light fire burn down. "Dear friend, all this day I have been harvesting feelings and sights, smells and memories as if they were acorns to be ground and cooked and enjoyed another day."

"I am an acorn?" Japazeus glanced downward.

Neetah laughed again. "No. You are an oak." She nestled her head into his shoulder so she did not have to look into his eyes as she tried to explain. "You are a joy to me, a husband who was first a friend. And our marriage with Sitka, the village here, Little Cricket, the feast, and the friends—this is all more than one person should have. I feel a strange need to save it for a time of want."

"You are not used to having your own joys, little one," Japazeus said. "How many summers have you seen? Fifteen? And how long have you looked to Pocahontas for all adventure and excitement?"

Neetah drew a sharp breath, but Japazeus went on.

"You are a woman now, wife to a mighty Weroance. And I can prove it." Then he pulled the bearskin back up over them.

It was two moons before Neetah was sure. "Pocahontas," she began one winter morning, "I think that I . . . that Japazeus . . . the gods . . ."

Pocahontas looked up from the corn she was grinding in Kocoum's longhouse. "You are carrying a child," she said flatly. "You have not visited the women's room since your marriage, so, Ahone willing, Japazeus will hold his baby girl by Green Corn time."

"His baby *girl*? You have foreseen this? You are having visions again?"

Pocahontas held her hands up. "No. No. It was a guess."

"It was not! Is she pretty?" Neetah paused. "Oh, Pocahontas, is this the 'important child' of your first visions? Will you have a child here among the Patowomekes, too? Imagine them playing together! What are their names?"

Pocahontas stared down at the crushed corn, silent. She

let Neetah's desperate questions pass by like milkweed fluff floating on a breeze.

"Talk to me!" Neetah finally demanded. "*Matoaka!*"

There was no response.

"I'm leaving," Neetah warned, and then she did.

Back in Japazeus's house, Sitka was thrilled by the news. "Little Cricket!" she called. "You will have a little brother or sister!" Japazeus came out to the front room. "Find the cradle board," Sitka demanded. "Where are the soft little rabbit skins?"

Japazeus hugged his wife and rubbed her flat belly. "Not me, you fool!" she said. "Your second wife." Japazeus looked confused, but only for a moment.

"Neetah!" he cried. She was ready for the hug, but his warm hand rubbing her belly felt strange. Over the next moons, she got used to it. When Neetah sickened, she already knew the teas to calm a mother's nervous stomach. When she slept beyond dawn or knocked over a pot in her awkwardness, Sitka told her these signs would not last. When her belly stretched, the healing woman in the village told her to rub extra grease on the skin. When she snapped or wept at one of his jokes, Japazeus did not seem to mind. She saw little of Pocahontas, but there always seemed to be other friends about. People were nice to her, Neetah knew, because for now she was not just one spirit, but two. The wonder of it followed her like the scent of flowers.

One winter day Neetah gasped, "Oh!" and grabbed at her bulging stomach. Sitka looked up from the stew she was stirring on the cook fire. "Something jerked around deep inside," Neetah explained.

Sitka laughed. "It is your baby." She called to their husband through the snow. "Japezeus! Your baby has much spirit. It is already fighting to get out."

Neetah nearly wept with joy. "More tears?" Japazeus teased, and then the baby moved again.

"She kicked me! She is alive in there!"

Japazeus froze. Sitka stood quickly. "*She*? You cannot know that."

Neetah looked from one to the other in the swirling snow. "Pocahontas knew from a vision that this will be a girl."

Japazeus muttered something under his breath, and Neetah tried to defend herself. "I did not think I believed her, but now it feels right."

"It feels wrong," Sitka said, "for a stranger like Pocahontas to know such a thing."

The baby moved again. "Another kick," Neetah announced. "Does the father wish to rub my belly and feel his little . . . child?"

"After we eat," Japazeus said, stooping for a ladle of stew. "Or tomorrow."

It mattered little that her family's excitement had dimmed, Neetah thought. She sang as she went about her work. If Japazeus made fewer jokes, it made no difference. She smiled with every little message her daughter sent from within.

Henry pretended not to want to feel the child kick, too, until he saw the bulge of a knee or elbow through the thin leather of Neetah's dress. He cautiously pressed his hand on the moving spot and jumped away. "It is hard!" he cried.

"Your belly is as tight as a drumskin!" His face reddened.

"That protects the new spirit as it grows in there," Neetah said.

"I will hunt some food for the little girl, ah, child," Henry said. He grabbed the bow Japazeus had made for him and five carefully feathered arrows.

"Everyone has heard of Pocahontas's rude prophecy," the healing woman told her, as ice melted from the streams. She felt Neetah's belly. "By mid-summer," she predicted, "you shall have this child, girl or boy."

Neetah took a deep breath. "I am afraid," she said.

"You should be," the healer said, "but not of the pain. Wait until you feel the power when this little spirit forces its own birth!" She paused. "It is a woman's gift to work with the gods as they take control of her body to make a new life."

Neetah looked at her squarely. "I, too, am a healer. I have chanted a birth along. With you, I have heard the deep moans of women, and I am afraid."

"Neetah, you know the chants, the soothing teas, and the motions to ease a mother. You have seen how a birth happens. And you have seen the same women, later the same day, well and at ease. In a few more years, they long to hold another spirit within their bodies. You already know your answers. Now go and find some bright green fiddleheads in the woods. They will be good for you—both of you."

Before the fiddleheads uncurled into fern fronds in the woods, Sitka, too, announced she was carrying a child for Japazeus. The Weroance's spirits rose with two bellies to stroke. Laughter returned to the royal household.

Neetah sang often as she worked through the spring, gathering first greens and then berries, later planting corn and beans and squash. By weeding time it was hard for her to squat down to see the undersides of leaves where beetles and caterpillars chewed the crops. As the corncobs swelled full of kernels, it was even harder to get back up.

"Pocahontas!" she cried one day, when it seemed she would never rise to her feet.

"Do you need me?" her old friend called from across the field where she, too, had been weeding. Neetah squatted over a sudden puddle she had made on the ground and closed her eyes. She could not find the breath to answer.

"Lean back," Pocahontas said calmly at her shoulder. "I will catch you. When this passes, we will find the healing woman. She will help us through this birth." Neetah rolled back into Pocahontas's arms and sighed with relief.

"Get the healer," Pocahontas called to Sitka, as she walked down the path arm in arm with Neetah. "The baby is coming!"

"I thought you said it was a girl," Sitka said, walking on Neetah's other side to steady her.

"How could I know that?" Pocahontas answered.

Neetah felt the muscles in her belly cramp again. The clenching was deep, far down below the skin, sharp and strong. Neetah wanted to bend over, to sit down, to curl up like a fiddlehead on the path to protect herself from the spasm. Instead she felt her friend grab her arms, hold her upright, and move her along toward the women's end of the sleeping house.

On one side, Sitka began the birthing song. Pocahontas

joined in. Neetah struggled to get a breath to sing along. "The words," Sitka insisted. "Think about the words." The song was about the struggle of a new spirit. Neetah had known it since childhood. "Make the words," Sitka demanded.

Neetah tried. Her friends were walking in time with the song. They sang loudly now that they could see the door to the woman's room. Neetah's feet picked up the beat; her voice, the words; her lungs, the breaths she needed. She saw the healing woman hurry to enter the doorway before her. "Sing!" Pocahontas demanded when Neetah stopped to focus on the pain. The priest arrived with his rattle, hair knot askew. And, one by one, they entered the room.

In the center of the room, there was a shallow pit, lined with fine white sand. A tall stake had been pounded into the dirt at one edge, painted with red and white and topped with feathers. *When did they do that?* Neetah wondered, and suddenly the pain in her belly was gone. She stood straight again.

"Drink this." The healer held out a dipper full of tea. "You will be glad for this when the spirits fight within you again." Neetah swallowed the entire gourdful, then the cramping began once more. Women's voices rose in a chant, and before she knew it, she was walking in a strange circular dance, fighting to breathe and step and remember the words at the same time.

When the pain eased, the priest pulled a clamshell and a bag from his waist pouch and poured a mix of holy herbs into his shell. He added a cinder from the light fire, and fanned the smoke in each of the four directions. Then he spoke over each woman, so no evil spirits remained. The rest of the incense went into the fire, filling the room with thick scented smoke. A blessing followed, high and wild and ancient. The priest danced around the women, shaking his rattle over each in turn.

"Ack," Neetah said, as a sudden cramp gripped her belly. *Not pain*, she reminded herself, *struggle*. And, thanks to the tea or the blessing, now she could feel it for what it was. Besides, the women were singing again and Neetah knew she had to join in.

The cycle continued on into the evening. Women came in and out, adding their voices to whatever chant was in progress. At last, the gods themselves took over, and Neetah felt their true power. No longer could she sing or chant. Sitka took her hands and put them around the post. "Do not let go," she said.

Pocahontas spun Neetah's body until her backside faced the pit. Neetah knew what to do now. She bent her knees so she was sitting over the clean white sand.

"Push!" the healing woman said from behind her. There was nothing else Neetah could do besides push—or scream with the effort. Neetah took a huge breath and pushed.

The spirit within her gave way, clawing its path out. "It's here," the healer said, somewhere behind her. Neetah stayed half sitting over the sand as the healer cut through the cord and brought the baby around so she could see it. "A girl," she said, handing it to Sitka. Neetah waited for the warm gush of bloody meat that followed a birth to drop.

"I can lie down now," she said, after it slipped out.

"We will take the girl to her father," Sitka announced, wrapping the squalling baby in rabbit furs. "Then you may rest."

Japazeus shouted with joy when he saw his child. "When we are sure she will survive, we will do a naming," he told his wives. "Now I must take her to the stream." Within moments he was back, his daughter shivering, but clean and blessed to the gods. "Hold her to you, dear one." Japazeus handed the baby to Neetah. "Our daughter."

As exhausted as she was, Neetah could not rest. She looked over every bit of her child, a wee one no bigger than a muskrat. The child's tiny fingers clutched at hers and a warmth spread within Neetah's chest. The baby looked into her eyes and Neetah felt weak with love. She held the baby against her and felt it nuzzle, looking for her breast. When the infant found it and began to suckle, a thrill of pleasure traveled from Neetah's nipple to where the child spirit had hidden deep inside her. Afterward, she lay with her baby snuggling close for comfort.

"Are you hungry?" Sitka asked.

Neetah just waved her away, humming to her baby.

Henry came next, holding a flaming light stick so he could see the baby. Neetah felt the sudden rage of a she-bear. "Get that away," she shouted, rolling so that her body protected the wee one's.

"F-forgive me." Henry fumbled his words.

As Henry left with the light stick, Neetah whispered, "Nothing must ever happen to you, my baby. I will protect you with my life."

The next morning Sitka showed Neetah how to strap her baby to the cradle board before dawn so she could hang her child on a tree, leaving her hands free for prayers. Taking the board along, Neetah reported to the healing woman. "May I finish my training with you now?" she asked. "I need to know how to defeat any illness that attacks my family." She looked at the tiny one wrapped in swaddling and tied in place.

"We have limits, Neetah," the healer said. "We can only dose and salve, mend and comfort. Only the priests know ceremonies to balance a person's spirits. That is often what is behind an illness."

"Can we begin now?" Neetah asked, reaching for a pole to steady herself.

"You are still losing blood, woman," the healer said, "as you should. And you are making milk as well." She gestured at the nearest sleeping platform and bustled about, pinching sprigs off the herbs hanging from the rafters. From the bed, Neetah watched her crushing them in a pottery cup. "Drink now, Neetah, and drink water often, too. You must care for yourself if you are to care for a child."

As Neetah's strength returned, she wandered with the healing woman, the cradle board strapped to her back or tied to a nearby tree, and learned the herbs of the forest. "My daughter is Aitowh," Neetah said, glad to hear the sound of her daughter's new name.

Strangers sometimes stopped to talk to the two women in the forest and share news from their travels. "The game is growing scarce in these woods," a hunter told them.

"You will find bloodroot growing in a glade half way up the next hillside," a fellow healer said.

"Beware of the spotted sickness," a messenger from the south warned them. "It comes from the English and has killed many in my tribe."

"I have seen this disease," Neetah said slowly. "In Jaimztown." She pulled Aitowh's cradle board close and gave her a kiss.

"I do not like that news," the healing woman remarked, as she and Neetah started back to the Patowomeke village.

15
KIDNAPPING

Spring 1613

NEETAH BREWED THE TEA FOR SITKA'S BIRTHING. SHE CHANTED and sang and caught Sitka's new baby boy as it dropped toward the sand. Japazeus was wild in his joy, dancing a war dance around the longhouse. Little Cricket followed along, laughing. Even Henry danced with the men, celebrating a new boy in his Patowomeke family.

Before the new child could be named, Little Cricket fell ill. He grew hot, and fluids ran from his nose. Neetah called the healer to the royal longhouse. "It is nothing I have ever seen before," she said.

When Henry brought the priest to look at the child, the old man said, "The moon is full. This will work in our favor. Build up the fire and set Little Cricket on the floor where he will be warm." While Japazeus moved his son, the priest shook his rattle to summon power. Then he smudged everyone present and sprinkled a circle of cornmeal around Little Cricket. As he began the chant of balancing, he pulled off Little Cricket's robe and stepped back, silent.

"Spots," he said, his voice solemn. "I have heard of this."

"Neetah." The healer waved her close. "Is this what you saw in Jaimztown?"

Neetah gazed at the boy lying within a circle of cornmeal. His eyes were red, and he scratched desperately at his belly. Neetah pulled his little hands away and saw a flock of tiny red bumps. The boy's little hands felt hot within hers.

"There were more spots," she said, "but I remember well those red eyes. And I remember many deaths in that town."

The healer drew in her breath. "I have seen another child in the village with this strange wet nose and warm face." She turned to the priest. "Your balancing chant will help Little Cricket's spirit fight. Neetah and I will look for others with this disease."

Within a handful of days, Little Cricket was dead. Sitka wandered about, stunned, her face blackened, and her new baby crying for attention. Neetah spent every moment she could fighting to save three other villagers, but it was different now. Aitowh needed her—and Neetah needed Aitowh. When Neetah's breasts filled with milk, she had to excuse herself, night or day, and feed her baby. Afterward she would return to tending the ill or to napping. Her face showed the strain of sleeplessness and sorrow. Two more children finally died, scratching and coughing and rubbing their eyes. A warrior caught the disease, too.

"His spirit is strong," Japazeus said. "As a hunter, he brings meat for his own family and others as well. He will fight the spots." The heat in the man's body rose until he dropped into a trance, yet still he fought. Neetah, the healer, and the priest worked over him day and night with chants and what medicines they could devise. At last the man awakened, but he was not the same. His mind was weak and he was left blind.

"How can he find game in the forest now?" his wife wailed. "How can he fight our enemies or defend me?" They left her rubbing soot onto her face as if her husband had died.

And then there were no new fevers. The spots had moved on, somehow, taking those it wanted. Neetah finally slept. She played with Aitowh. She welcomed Japazeus in the night and explained more of Powhatan culture to Henry during the day. The longhouse seemed empty without Little Cricket's spirit, but Aitowh and Sitka's new baby boy kept life and joy in the family.

"Neetah?" Villagers came to her with simple needs now. "Have you something for a burn?" or "my husband is not sleeping" or "come quick—my mother has cut herself while scraping a hide!"

One day Pocahontas scratched the door of the Chief's longhouse. "Neetah?" she called. "The healer asks for you!"

Neetah felt a wave of cold fear. "Is it another child?" she called, checking her daughter's cradle board where it hung from a rafter. Little Aitowh lay sleeping, her eyelashes dark against her round cheeks. There were no tiny red bumps on her daughter's skin. Neetah let out her breath.

"Hurry," Pocahontas urged from outside. Neetah paused to stroke Aitowh's petal soft cheek, checking for the fiery heat that had killed Little Cricket. Aitowh's face felt cool. Neetah gazed at her daughter, savoring a flood of happiness. She glanced at Sitka's baby son. He, too, seemed well.

"Did you hear me?" Pocahontas scolded, as Neetah emerged from the Chief's longhouse.

"I heard," Neetah said. "But I had to check Aitowh before I left."

"You have changed," Pocahontas said, as they walked toward the sweat lodge. "A year ago you flew like an arrow to help Henry escape the Pamunkey warriors."

"A year ago I was not a mother," Neetah said. She chose her words carefully. "Every moment now I hurt with fierce love for Aitowh—and a fear for her safety, too."

"Every moment?" Pocahontas asked.

"Yes," Neetah said. "You and Kocoum will have a child soon, I hope. Then you will know this happiness."

Pocahontas abruptly turned away and led Neetah to a little house on the main path. It sat next to where she lived with Kocoum.

"Friends," Pocahontas called, "I have brought Neetah." She waited a moment and held the door back. The sound of coughing filled the small room. Neetah saw the healer sitting on the floor next to a child.

"There has been no new spot sickness since the full moon!" The healer pointed to the rash creeping up the little one's neck and onto his face. "I thought we had sacrificed enough lives to Okeus." She seemed near to tears. "I do not know what to do." Pocahontas wandered in and linked fingers with the child's mother.

"May I bring Henry in here?" Neetah asked. "You did not want the English boy to see your work before, but if he knows anything about this sickness . . ."

The healer lowered her eyes and Neetah ran for Henry.

She quickly explained what had happened.

"I am no doctor," Henry said. "Only a doctor knows when to apply leeches or bleed the sick, when to smear the skin with mercury or cool it with alcohol rubs."

Neetah gazed fiercely at Henry.

"As you wish," he finally said.

When Neetah brought Henry to see the sick little boy, he took one look and said, "He has the measles." Then he backed quickly out of the longhouse. Neetah and the healer followed and Pocahontas tagged along, leaving the sick child with its mother.

"How do you know about *measles*?" Pocahontas asked. She glanced up and down the path as she used the strange English word.

At the same time, the healer demanded, "How do you cure this sickness?" and Neetah asked, "Will everyone get it?"

Henry rubbed the stubborn hairs that had sprouted on his jawline. Then he answered, "There were measles back in England. I had them when I was little. So did my sister and my aunt. They died." He looked at the healer. "I do not know what doctors do for this. Not much works. The measles came in waves when I was little. Many got them, but not all died. Those that lived did not fall to the next wave of the disease. That may be why I did not fall ill when measles hit Jaimztown."

The three women looked sad as they digested the information. "Those that were weak and hungry to start with did not survive," Henry added helpfully. Neetah thought of the widespread hunger the Patowomekes had seen after the last poor harvest, and a chill ran up her spine. Two more women strolled up to see what was happening. A sniffling child followed his mother, who coughed sharply. In the distance, a child cried. Neetah closed her eyes, unwilling to look for new signs of measles.

"Is this an English weapon?" the healer asked sharply. She scratched at her arm. "Have you brought this on us, Henry?" Everyone backed up a step. "Or you, Pocahontas? Or Neetah? It is no secret that you love the English!"

"No!" Henry said loudly. Another Patowomeke stopped on the path to listen. A head peeked out of a nearby long-house.

Neetah hooked fingers with Pocahontas. "My friend and I would never do such a thing," Neetah told everyone, but the group muttered angrily. Neetah raised her voice. "If there is a wave of measles coming," she said, "we should all check our families for the signs. Heat. Red spots. Red eyes. Itch. Cough. Watery nose."

The woman with the cough clapped her hand over her mouth and pulled her child away. After glaring from Henry to Pocahontas, the others left quickly.

"I must confer with the priest," the healer said, and hurried toward the temple.

"I would not bring death to this village," Pocahontas said. "I have betrayed my father and helped his English enemies, then stolen his hostage boy and run away, and married without out his knowledge." She took a deep breath. "I have done so much that hurt our people. I am trying to be different here. You know that, Neetah, do you not?"

But Neetah was heading back to her own house. Japazeus's son was screaming in his cradleboard. Neetah cooed at the boy, then lifted Aitowh from her own cradleboard. Neetah put her cheek on the baby's head and felt extra heat. She quickly unwrapped Aitowh's tight blanket and let it fall to the ground. Carrying the child out into the light, she searched her soft skin for tiny red bumps. There were none.

By that night, Aitowh was as evenly speckled with red as a shorebird's egg is with brown. Neetah refused to put her down. Japazeus's first wife was wild with worry, too. Her little son coughed with every breath. So did she.

For three days, fevers raged in Japazeus's house. Only Neetah, Henry, and the chief were spared. Japazeus and his priest strode from family to family, followed by the healer, giving comfort where they could.

"Neetah," Japazeus said on the third night, "someone in nearly every family has these measles. Many homes have more than one fighting the evil fires from within. Children. Parents. Grandparents. Everyone is suffering."

Neetah clasped Aitowh to her chest and twisted back and forth silently. She could tell that there was more her husband wanted to say.

"There is talk that Pocahontas brought this on us," he said.

"She did *not*," Neetah said firmly. In her arms, Aitowh's breath sounded like an old man's. "Pocahontas would not do this to us. To me."

Sitka darted past to visit the woods again to relieve herself and to change yet again the soiled moss from between her son's legs.

"A runner came today with word that an English ship is heading upriver," Japazeus said. "We are in no state to defend this town if they attack."

Japazeus sent scouts to the river and ordered the ill to stay indoors. Many villagers were losing more water through waste than they could drink. One man began to see visions. There was little hope for him, as his body trembled and shuddered and went limp. Then there were some, like little Aitowh, whose chests gurgled and bubbled with every breath.

Within days, a scout rushed up to Japazeus's doorway. "The ship has dropped anchor," he panted. "The captain and his men have disembarked and are preparing to march this way."

Japazeus had the grieving mothers scrub ashes from their faces and the priests conduct the final blessings of the dead in the dark of night. Although there were many dead, others seemed to be healing, their red spots turning brown and fading into scars where they'd scratched themselves raw. Those people would be allowed to greet the English visitors. "The Patowomekes always welcome travelers," Japazeus reminded his people. "We must throw a feast for the English as if they were welcome guests. Perhaps we can use them against the Powhatan!" Many of the warriors stood taller and stamped their feet in a quick war dance—even the one who had been ill.

Neetah stayed awake the night the English landed, rubbing her little girl's chest. After every wheezing breath, Neetah sat willing her to breathe again and begging Ahone's help. Outside, the sounds of the feast filtered through the open door. Neetah paid no attention.

"It is Captain Argall. He brought supplies to Jaimztown," Pocahontas had stolen into the house to tell her. "He and Japazeus have laughed and smoked pipes on many agreements."

Neetah did not bother to respond. Instead she listened as her baby's breath grew shallower and weaker. Pocahontas watched for a few moments, then sat silently by Neetah's side. Neetah did not move when Sitka came in and lay against the far wall, cradling her little boy. She did not move when Japazeus came in and kissed his first wife and child. She did not move when he kissed Aitowh and then stalked out again. By dawn, Aitowh stopped her desperate fight for breath.

When Neetah pressed her head against her baby's chest, there was no heart beating inside her, no love, no warmth. Pocahontas silently hooked fingers with her as Neetah sat rocking, holding a great aching hollow within herself. Aitowh's spirit had slipped away—the spirit that had once lived inter-twined with her own. Sometime in the long dark pain of the night, Japazeus awoke to take the dead child from her arms. He kissed Aitowh and laid her body beside the light fire.

He turned and glared at Pocahontas, sitting in the shad-ows. "The rumors are true," he hissed. "You have poisoned my people. You have killed two of my children. You must leave my village."

"Where can I go?" Pocahontas asked.

It sounded to Neetah as if they were all speaking at a great distance. *Stop it. You'll wake the baby*, she wanted to scream. But Aitowh was dead. There was no baby now. Neetah longed to rub soot over her face, to pull at her hair, to howl out her pain. But she sat, as lifeless as her daughter, forced to listen.

"Captain Argall will take you back to Jaimztown when he sails, Pocahontas."

Pocahontas stood. "But I have a husband here," she pleaded.

Sitka barked a short laugh at her. "Kocoum has lost a sister," Japazeus told her, "and cousins, too, to the English spirit you brought on us. His father is still wandering amid sick visions as he dies. Kocoum wants nothing to do with you."

Although his words were aimed at Pocahontas, they tore at Neetah like a bear's claws.

"Perhaps it was not Pocahontas's doing," Neetah's voice shook. "Could *I* have brought the measles spirit here?" She looked from one person to another, desperate. "Did *I* kill my baby?"

Pocahontas rushed to her side. Japazeus did not. Sitka hissed at her from her sleeping platform. "You killed *my* babies," she spat. "You nearly killed me. Take your friend and *go*, Neetah. Out of my house, out of my village, out of my life!"

For the next few days, Neetah felt as if she were sleep-walking. No one in the village would speak to her. Japazeus acted as if she was already gone. There was no baby left to love or worry about. Just breasts aching with unneeded milk and a vast hole in her life.

Pocahontas walked by Neetah's side and slept in an empty house with her, but Pocahontas, too, moved as if drugged. Kocoum never came near them.

It was a relief when Captain Argall sent a messenger inviting Pocahontas onboard his ship.

Japazeus and Sitka followed the girls to the river. They did not bother to say good-bye, but stood talking with Captain Argall as Neetah and Pocahontas trudged up the walkway.

The girls stood together watching basket after basket of corn carried below the deck. They watched as the captain gave Japazeus and Sitka a huge copper cook pot. It made no sense, but it did not matter, either.

A sailor led them out of the sunshine, down some steep stairs, and into a little room. He closed the door and rattled it. Neetah glanced around. The smooth wooden walls made the room feel cozy and safe, but it was only three strides from side to side.

Neetah sat on a bench and patted the space beside her. Pocahontas sat down, too, and hooked fingers with her. As the floor beneath them started to sway, Pocahontas began to cry. Without thinking, Neetah whispered an ancient prayer to Okeus, asking for calm water. She also prayed to Ahone for a calm mind.

The timbers creaked, and somewhere sailcloth flapped and strained. The familiar feeling of water under a boat seemed to lift Neetah up. "Feel that?" Neetah asked Pocahontas. "The gods are rocking us just as I used to rock Aitowh." Neetah imagined the gods' arms holding the boat with her inside, rocking, rocking. She sat up straight, flooded with happiness.

"What is wrong with you?" Pocahontas asked. "You have lost your baby and your husband, your tribe and your people."

"I am still held by Ahone and Okeus," Neetah said, swaying with the ship. "They will always hold me, and I, them." With one hand, she grabbed the single promise bead swinging at her neck and put her other arm around Pocahontas's shoulders.

"Wingam," Pocahontas said, wiping her eyes, "I do not feel the gods. But I do feel your friendship. It gives me strength." She laid her head on Neetah's shoulder.

Neetah sat quietly, taking strength from the old ways and giving it to her friend. It felt as if a river ran through her, from the far mountains of her ancestors to the sea, where it bathed Pocahontas. Neetah closed her eyes, seeing it clearly. Under her encircling arm, her friend's breathing settled from raggedy hiccups to a steady, calm pattern. Slowly, the muscles in Pocahontas's shoulders loosened. Neetah sighed in comfort. Then her stomach rumbled, loud and insistent. The river picture vanished.

"Captain Argall will surely have food for us," Neetah said.

They stood and stretched, pressing their hands on the hard wooden roof of the room. Light came through a glass window showing the shoreline of the Patomac. They were sailing downstream. *Toward Jaimztown*, Neetah thought.

Pocahontas moved to the door and scratched it, politely. No one answered.

"Don't the English knock their knuckles against a door to ask for entry?" Neetah asked.

Pocahontas tried that. She pressed against the door. It didn't open.

"Is there a handle?" Neetah asked.

Pocahontas grabbed a hand-shaped knob and pushed. The door didn't move.

"Twist it," Neetah suggested. She watched Pocahontas try twisting, hitting, pulling, and pushing on the door handle. Nothing worked. Neetah pounded on the door with both hands, hoping Captain Argall would hear the noise and come to rescue them.

No one came.

"Are we prisoners?" Pocahontas asked.

Neetah did not answer.

PART IV

AMONG THE ENGLISH

1613—1617

16

HOSTAGE

1613

THE WINDOW SQUARE HAD GONE DARK BEFORE CAPTAIN Argall rattled the door, then opened it. "Welcome to my ship, the *Treasurer*, my lady," he said to Pocahontas. He did not bother to speak to Neetah. She sighed, remembering how she was *no one* in the English world of classes. "Will you do us the honor of dining with us?"

Before Neetah could object, Pocahontas spoke. "I go nowhere without my servant." Neetah blinked. This was the game they had played years earlier. Pretending to be nobody felt like an ill-fitting moccasin now, after being a Weroance's wife and a mother, but Neetah made herself stand back humbly.

"Very well," the captain said. "Follow me." A guard trailed after them up the stairs and through a passageway, his muzket at the ready. They entered a bigger room with many windows and many more English men seated around a wide plank of wood.

"Am I a prisoner?" Pocahontas asked, as she sat down. On

either side of her sat strange English men. Neetah stood behind her friend's chair.

"Much has happened," Captain Argall said. Neetah listened idly, trying to care; trying to ignore her breasts, tight and hot with milk. "When you turned your back on us, Princess, the colony was almost abandoned." A cabinboi reached around Neetah with a ladle of hot stew and poured it into a pottery bowl in front of Pocahontas. Neetah's mouth watered at the smell, as the others were served in turn. "We called it the Starving Time," the captain went on. "You brought us nothing, and none of your father's tribes would trade with us, either."

Neetah watched the men use little ladles to carry soup to their mouths instead of drinking from their bowls. Pocahontas picked up a little ladle, too, and copied their strange manners. The smell of food made Neetah feel weak. "Sickness and hunger killed most of our men." The conversation flowed on around the table. "The few who were left got on a ship and headed back to England."

"But, my friend, you are still here," Pocahontas said.

"Just as we set sail to leave," a man across the table picked up the story, "three new ships turned into the bay, bearing more men and supplies. Still other ships have arrived since then, and we have found different natives to trade with."

"Like Japazeus of the Patowomekes?" Pocahontas asked.

"That is how we discovered where you were hiding, Princess," Captain Argall said. Another servant arrived and took the bowls away. He returned with steaming plates full of meat and gooey sauce and white bread. "Your father will

surely be willing to trade when he hears you are our 'guest.'"
The men around the table laughed.

Neetah could have laughed aloud. They did not know
how wrong they were. The Powhatan cared nothing for
Pocahontas now. She waited for Pocahontas to explain that,
but instead her friend said, "I'm sure my father will agree.
This plan works for all. You will get your fill of corn and I
will learn your wonderful customs."

The men looked at each other, startled. "What do you
call this pretty little ladle?" Pocahontas asked.

"*Spoon*," one of the men answered.

"Spoon? Spoon. Spoon!" Pocahontas repeated in her high
little-girl voice.

"How old are you now, Princess?" The captain sounded
suspicious.

"I have seen the new spring leaves sixteen times,"
Pocahontas answered. Neetah was amazed at how easily her
friend dropped her voice, and how reassuring it sounded.

One of the men leaned over his plate. "And you have no
husband yet?"

Neetah could barely hear Pocahontas's no. She thought
then of Kocoum and Japazeus, both so ready to end their
marriages. Neetah remembered the huge copper kettle
sparkling in the sun and the smile on the first wife's face.
Had she and Pocahontas actually been sold to the English?
Neetah had to talk this over with Pocahontas—yet she could
only stand, mute, behind her friend. She remained hungry
and angry for the rest of the meal.

"My servant will need a plate, too," Pocahontas insisted,

as the English men got up from the table. One was brought in, and Neetah wolfed down the strange food before they were hurried back to their little room by the guard.

Pocahontas flopped down on the bench. It had been covered with thick, soft bedding while they ate. Neetah noticed that a jug of water had been brought to them, too, and a bowl. Another pottery bowl lay under the bed. "I think supper went well," Pocahontas said.

"Matoaka," Neetah said carefully, "at dawn prayers, you were drawn and quiet. Now there is a spark in your eye and joy in your voice."

"English came back to me as I spoke tonight. So did the dance of words with an enemy," Pocahontas said. "Do you not prefer excitement to sorrow?"

Neetah made a show of pouring the bowl full of water and washing her hands and face. "Neetah," Pocahontas finally said, "your strength comes from the gods. Mine from adventure." Yet when Neetah began evening prayers, Pocahontas joined in and they chanted together.

While the ship's bells rang throughout the night, Neetah lay awake, longing for the feel of Aitowh in her arms again.

The next morning, the girls were allowed up on deck. They spoke with the captain and sailors, too. Pocahontas kept calling the English her friends. She asked about everything, from the sails to the buckles on the men's shoes. It was a game they had played before, and soon Neetah made herself pretend to be fascinated by anything the English would tell her. It felt wrong to be sounding like this when she should be wailing and soot-streaked in Aitowh's honor.

When they finally reached Jaimztown, however, it was hard not to be interested in all the changes. Captain Argall had given them no clue aboard ship. "May I present Princess Pocahontas," the captain said to the man who had blustered out to meet them. Captain Argall gave a huge bow and a sweep of his hat toward a tall man in blue whose chest armor sparkled in the sunshine. "This is Governor Gates, my lady," he said to Pocahontas. "He will be your host here in Jamestown." The two men grinned at each other through their beards. Then Governor Gates paused to stare at the girls as if he'd never seen a proper Pamunkey before.

"Ye are welcome to my city, Princess," he said, apparently regaining his wits. "I hope you will be comfortable here. I will assign a guard, of course, at all times, and insist that you sleep upstairs in my house."

Pocahontas said, "Thank you, sir." Neetah deliberately said nothing.

After Governor Gates waved a soldier over and pointed to the girls, he began whispering with Captain Argall. Pocahontas strode confidently about, looking at the changes. The guard, a young soldier with bad teeth, waved at Neetah to stay close to her friend. He rattled his long knife in its sleeve as he followed them while they explored the town.

The fortress walls had been rebuilt since the fire. Three new storage buildings held armor, foods, or tools. The thatch-roofed houses stood square and tidy now, many of them two stories tall. Each was filled with its measure of soldiers. "We even have a glass house here now," the guard said. To their confused looks, he explained, "We blow bottles

186

there and make window glass." Finally, as neither of his charges seemed to understand, he shrugged his shoulders.

"I will take you there, by and by," he said. "And there are more rules you should know. Everyone meets in the church twice daily," he explained, "though the old minister died in the starving time. Miss church once, and you lose a week's food. A second absence gets you a whipping. Men have been shot or burned to death for refusing to attend church. There are to be no more wild games in town, either."

Neetah noticed an English woman stepping out of a doorway and couldn't help staring at her. The fabric she wore fell to the ground and made her look like a mushroom. "Because of *them*," he jerked his thumb at the woman, "we cannot speak as sailors do around here anymore."

"May I talk with her?" Pocahontas begged.

Neetah stood back as the guard introduced Pocahontas to the woman, Mistress George, who smiled at them. Pocahontas touched her skirts. The woman, in turn, felt the fine soft leathers that Pocahontas wore and complimented her on the embroidery that Neetah had done.

"Kindly accept my shawl 'to cover your nakedness,'" Mistress George offered Neetah, even though the afternoon was mild and sunny. Everyone in Jaimztown treated Pocahontas as if she were a Weroansqua, full of power. *My lady*, they called her, or *your highness*. Neetah was simply, "Neetah" or "girl," and she did not complain. Her role was easier—and safer.

Neetah could peek into stew pots while women stirred them, listen to fishermen as they cleaned their catch, or wander down to the docks and watch as ships came in. One day she saw a man stepping from the small boat that had brought him to shore. Feathers fluttered from his hat, and his sky-colored jacket matched his breeches.

Neetah hurried to find her friend. Pocahontas strolled alongside the new minister, her guard following close behind. "Someone important has landed," Neetah said. "He has many servants, and even Governor Gates bowed to him."

"Lord De La Warre must have arrived," the minister said. "He is the colony's patron in King James's court. The minister nodded to Pocahontas. "Forgive me. I must make myself presentable." He scurried off toward the church.

"This man carries himself as your father does," Neetah said. "He has real power."

"A princess should welcome him," Pocahontas said, her dimple showing.

"Perhaps she would present him with a token of her esteem?" Neetah suggested. She took off her wedding earrings and handed them to Pocahontas. "For his favorite wife," she said.

"Does he have a wife?" Pocahontas asked.

"Any man like that has many," Neetah guessed.

Later, at his house, Governor Gates introduced Lord De La Warre to Pocahontas. She and Neetah bowed deeply, mimicking the greeting everyone else gave to this important man. When they rose, the men in the room were laughing at them.

Pocahontas carried on as if she hadn't noticed. "Lord Delaware," she said to more chuckles, "I welcome you to my land." She held out Neetah's earrings, their pearls and copper bells shining softly in the candlelight. "These are for your favorite wife."

Once again men's laughter roared in the room. Lord De La Warre, however, was smiling kindly. "She will be honored," he said, shaking the bells to hear their soft tinkling. Then he tucked them into a pocket on his chest and patted the pocket gently.

"Now go on up to bed." Governor Gates shooed them away. "We have business to discuss here."

As they climbed the steep little stairs, Pocahontas whispered, "We have made a powerful friend this night. Somehow I will get you new earrings."

"A friend is worth more than any jewelry," Neetah said, but she smiled as she pulled her sleeping pallet out from under Pocahontas's bed.

"Pocahontas," she reminded her friend the next morning, "we need to pray." They begged the guard to let them have a bucket of water so they could wash before prayers. He looked both ways and said, "I can sneak you out to the stream beyond the stockade."

After he led them out, Neetah welcomed the familiar ceremony in Ahone's good world. Even with a muzket pointed her way, and without any tobacco to complete the ritual, Neetah felt clean and whole again.

It wasn't hard to get tobacco for the next day's prayers. The English smoked the holy herb almost as if it were a play toy, lighting up pipefuls at any time of day. When Pocahontas asked for some, Governor Gates gave them a twisted wad of the leaves, saying, "This breed comes from islands down south. It's not as hard on the nose or as rough on the throat as what your people smoke."

Pocahontas took a puff from his pipe. "It is indeed different." She handed the pipe to Neetah, who waved it away. The holy herb was just for men!

The governor broke off the tip of the pipe stem where Pocahontas's lips had touched it and let the moistened piece fall to the ground. "The Queen of England and all of the royal court smoke this," he said, taking a puff for himself. "If we could grow this breed here in Jamestown, we could pay our investors back. . . ." His eyes drifted off as the holy weed helped him think.

When Governor Gates had some time off from his duties, he escorted the girls around the compound. "I sent a messenger today to the Powhatan with your ransom demand," he mentioned offhandedly one afternoon. "I told him to release his prisoners, return the guns he has stolen, and send us many bushels of corn. Only then, I told him, would we return his treasured princess." Neetah could not help but glance at Pocahontas's face. She was rewarded by a dimple.

While the governor was distracted for a minute by his secretary, the girls spoke quietly in their own language.

"Can they really think that the Powhatan will trade his goods to get you back?" Neetah asked.

"It seems so," Pocahontas answered. "That is why we are so well treated. I am liking this."

"That is because you are treated like a princess, my lady," Neetah said.

"I would trade places with you as quickly as a frog jumps," Pocahontas said. "Every moment English eyes are studying me. I must take care with each word and movement. Thank Ahone that we have our own language to hide our thoughts in!"

"The sound of it makes them nervous," Neetah said, watching the governor approach them.

"Oh, Governor," Pocahontas said in English. "We were just talking about how big your shoulders are." Neetah blushed at her friend's brazenness, and the governor roared with laughter.

"There is no answer from your father, my lady," Governor Gates commented a few days later. He began letting them know, day by day, that there was no answer from the Supreme Chief. "Do you know why your father is silent?" he asked, when a moon had passed. The girls both swore that they had no idea why the Powhatan hadn't responded.

One night, as they carried a candle up into the loft room where they lived over Governor Gates's quarters, Neetah had to ask, "What will happen to us when the English discover that you are useless to them?"

Pocahontas crawled up onto the strange, soft sleeping platforms the English used, and said, "I will have to become more important to them." She pushed the pillow out of the way, then admitted, "I do not know what that will take. But the Pamunkey attacks are down since Father heard that I am here. Perhaps he still cares for me a bit. I may be doing some good for our people again."

"Do you not think of your husband?" Neetah sighed, settling onto the sleeping pallet on the floor beside Pocahontas's bed. "Do you not long for your people? Have you . . . ," she heard her own voice break, ". . . have you forgotten your sorrow?"

Pocahontas sat up and glared at Neetah. "How can you ask that?"

Neetah spread her hands with palms up to show she was not attacking her friend.

"What you see of me, Wingam, is a pretty shell." Pocahontas still sounded angry. "You may choose to walk clothed in sorrow. I choose to bleed and wail only inside."

Neetah dropped her hands. "I did not know."

"You lost a baby in the last moon," Pocahontas said. "I lost my vision, my destiny. I was meant to bring peace. Instead, I have spawned disease, betrayal, and death. I am worse than nothing." The candle cast deep shadows on her face as she went on, "Even Chawn turned away from me."

Neetah remembered her friend's winter of silence and the slow healing. "But you found happiness since then," she pointed out.

"I painted a mask for myself," Pocahontas said, and blew out the candle.

Neetah was left in the dark silence, imagining all the guilt and emptiness Matoaka kept behind her pretty shell.

"You will be moved upriver to a farming town called Henrico," Governor Gates said at the evening meal one night. To their startled faces, he explained, "Your father must be planning a raid to rescue you, Princess. Guarding you will be easier there." Neetah barely managed to keep from laughing, but there was more. "My lady, the men here are sorely distracted by your indecent clothing." Pocahontas glanced down at her soft cape and apron, leggings and moccasins. "I have told Mistress Edwards," the governor went on, "to dress you as befits your age and importance."

To Neetah's surprise, Pocahontas nodded, in the English way. "I am happy to wear English clothes." Governor Gates looked surprised, too.

When the girls arrived at Mistress Edwards's, the English woman's face looked resentful. She slammed the little doors shut on the windows. With the sunshine entirely blocked out, she lit a candle, turned, and demanded, "Give me your filthy things." Then she muttered, "He wants me to make a lady of you?" She angrily folded and unfolded pieces of clothing piled high on a table.

Neetah held out her hands to take her friend's beautiful clothes. Kocoum had hunted the deer that gave up his skin for these. Neetah and Pocahontas had spent days skinning and curing the leather and cutting it into pieces. Neetah remembered chatting happily over long winter days, stitching in Kocoum's longhouse as wind howled down through the smoke hole. Every piece of Pocahontas's clothing showed Neetah's talent for inventing and repeating tiny patterns in beads or quills.

Filthy things? Neetah struggled against the answers that came to her lips. *Filthy? Your skirts are mud-caked to the knees. The clothing at your armpits stinks as if they have not been washed in many moons. The hair dangling from your soiled bonnet is as greasy as a bear carcass. And you call us filthy?* In the end it was only Pocahontas's warning look as she stripped the sweet-smelling skins from her prayer-cleansed body that kept Neetah quiet. She carefully folded the feather-light leathers. "You may wear all my finery," Pocahontas told Neetah in the Pamunkey language. "It suits you."

"You never intend to go back to our clothes?" Neetah asked, horrified.

"None of that!" Mistress interrupted. "We speak the King's English here. The minister has been telling us of your sneaking, godless ways. Oh my," Mistress Edwards said, as the elegant tattoos on Pocahontas's body and breasts were exposed. "Good gracious me." She seemed unable to say more.

Mistress Edwards took the top layer off a pile of cloth heaped on a table. "*Pantaloons,*" she said, as she showed Pocahontas how to pull the legs up and tie them at her waist. Pocahontas giggled at how exposed it left her in the middle, but Mistress Edwards had turned for more clothes. "Arms up, my lady," she said firmly. She settled a long, wide stiffened skirt over Pocahontas's head and tied the strings at her waist. The skirt seemed afraid to touch Pocahontas's legs, swinging wide around them. "*Farthingale,*" pronounced the English woman. Another skirt was added next, pale and heavy. "*Petticoat,*" Pocahontas was told, and she obediently repeated the word.

Mistress Edwards glanced at Pocahontas's naked breasts and then turned quickly away. "We must cover your pagan wickedness," she scolded and chose another garment from the pile that seemed to have long thin sticks sewn inside it.

When Neetah reached to touch the shiny cords dangling from an edge, the mistress pulled it out of her reach. "*Ribbons*," she said. "*Clean ribbons*."

Neetah watched the English woman help Pocahontas stick her arms through holes and then weave the ribbons up the front of the garment. When she pulled on the ribbons, Pocahontas gasped as the fabric bit in at her waist. "Breathe out!" the English woman said sharply, then demonstrated what she meant. Finally, Mistress Edwards tied the *corset*, as she called it, just above Pocahontas's breasts, flattening their normal curve and leaving her flesh to bulge out above the intricately knotted border. "*Lace*." The woman sniffed. "Few among us are so lucky."

Pocahontas's eyes widened as she looked at Neetah. "Breathe, you fool!" Mistress Edwards said, and Neetah heard her friend begin to pant in little gasps. "You'll get used to it, my lady," the English woman said. "We all did."

She glared at Neetah for a moment, then settled a great shirt over Pocahontas's head, followed by a heavy top skirt, a jerkin, a stiff ruffled collar, and a thick apron. "Sit now," the mistress said. Pocahontas did, and her skirt swung up wildly. The English woman demonstrated how to raise the back of the hoops and drape the skirt as she sat.

"*Stockings*," she said next, pulling thick woven white foot covers over Pocahontas's tattooed calves. "*Shoes*."

Pocahontas tried to see which foot fit which of the thick black moccasins. "They are both the same," the mistress said. "They will take the shape of your feet, once the blisters and bruises heal."

Neetah winced. So did Pocahontas as the English woman tightened the shoe buckles. Now the woman moved behind the chair. She wound Pocahontas's long hair into a knot such as only men wore, then covered it with a cloth pouch, saying, "*Bonnet*. It will keep your hair clean and your head covered in God's eyes." The bonnet edges framed Pocahontas's creamy tan face with ruffles and made the tattoos on her cheeks stand out. "You will have to wear powders to cover these." Mistress Edwards's fingertips touched the ancient clan markings as if she were patting a poisonous snake.

"I can do that," Pocahontas said helpfully. "I often paint my face red."

"This is hopeless," the mistress said, spinning about to open the windows. "The Reverend Whittaker requires you to present yourself at the church as soon as I am finished." She gazed at Pocahontas, sitting on the chair. "Tell him I have done my best." She stalked out of the house, leaving Neetah and Pocahontas alone.

"Do I look English?" Pocahontas asked.

Neetah gazed at her a moment. "You look like a deer stuffed into a turtle shell. Can you walk in those moccasins?"

"Walk?" Pocahontas tried to laugh. It came out a strangled chuckle. "I can't even breathe!" She reached her hands out to Neetah and struggled to her feet. "Oh!" she gasped, her knees sagging.

"What is it, my lady?" Neetah asked, as her friend's hands clamped down on hers.

"Nothing," Pocahontas said, releasing her hold. Neetah watched as Pocahontas smoothed the pain creases from her face. She straightened her body and staggered forward before tottering a few steps. She seemed to be walking on thorns. Neetah reached out to help again, but Pocahontas waved her away. "Okeus is giving me nothing more than I deserve for what I have done to our people."

Neetah's eyes filled with tears as she watched her friend hobble out the door.

17

INSTRUCTION

1614

"THOU SHALT HAVE NO OTHER GODS BEFORE ME," Reverend Whittaker intoned. "Now repeat that."

Pocahontas, sitting primly across the table from the minister, repeated the words. Neetah sat in the corner, horrified by the day's lesson. Instead of listening, she tried looking through the opening of the guardhouse towering over the corner of Henrico's stockade wall and the green hills rising beyond. She played idly with the fringes of Pocahontas's apron, tied around her own waist.

"Be still!" Sir Thomas Dale scolded her, before taking his turn with Pocahontas. At first, Neetah had been glad for a second teacher, but this one was even stricter. He leaned across the table and said, "Thou shalt not make unto thee any graven images." While Pocahontas recited, Neetah pictured the glorious statue of Okeus, his eyes glowing in the firelight of the temple. She imagined it leading the way into battle, giving courage to every warrior. "Now repeat both commandments, Lady Pocahontas," Sir Thomas insisted.

Neetah fought to hold her hands still while the men badgered Pocahontas to memorize rule after rule and repeat them in order. Neetah's fingers ached to weave mats or work clay, twist cord or sew bead patterns onto leather. She could be searching the hills for fresh spring herbs or climbing trees to harvest honey.

Her body yearned to run, to swim, to dance in the warm spring air. Instead she sat useless and invisible, learning along with Pocahontas.

"God bless you, child," the minister said when Pocahontas managed to repeat the entire list of commandments. "Now we will drill on the Nicene Creed that we learned yesterday." Pocahontas's stomach growled. "This is good," the minister said. "Your very body hungers for the word of Christ. Now repeat the creed."

"I believe . . . ," Pocahontas began. She stopped and pushed a lock of hair back up under the edge of her bonnet.

"We believe in one God, the Father, the Almighty," Sir Thomas prompted sharply, "maker of heaven and earth. . . . "

Neetah could have recited the entire creed, she had heard it so often. Pocahontas was able to recall only a few more words before she stopped again.

"You will have nothing to eat until you repeat all of your lessons." The minister rose to his feet. "You are not applying yourself."

Pocahontas looked from one man to the other. "I need to visit the outhouse," she said, her voice small, "or use the chamber pot."

"Not until you repeat your lessons," Sir Thomas said.

Neetah's muscles tensed, but she forced herself not to react. The men had to see how exhausted Pocahontas was and how desperately hard she was trying. They must want her that way—and Pocahontas had turned as meek as a rabbit since dressing in English clothes.

"English clothes make me feel closer to Chawn," she told Neetah once, then corrected herself. "Not Chawn. *John. John Smith*, not Chawnzmit. How could I have been so, so . . . ?" Pocahontas sighed like an old woman.

Another time she said, "If I can learn their magic, I can take it back to our people. They can use it against the English." Once she said, "It keeps me from thinking about the pain I have caused." Only Neetah knew the flock of reasons circling in her friend's mind.

". . . and forever and ever, amen." Pocahontas finally finished the Creed.

"God is surely moving you," the minister said. "Do you feel His touch?"

When Pocahontas nodded dutifully, Sir Thomas clapped his hands in glee. "A true convert! In my own town! Do you know what this will mean when they hear of it in England?"

"And she being a savage princess," Reverend Whittaker gloated. "The daughter of the heathen king himself. Praise God!"

A knock sounded at the door. "Enter and be glad!" Sir Thomas called out.

"Why the merriment, friends?" a local landowner stepped in. Neetah recognized his bright blue eyes and extra-deep voice from the church services. He had often spoken to

Pocahontas. He had even spoken to Neetah, inquiring about her health as if he cared.

"I am converting the first soul to God, John!" the minister crowed. *John Rolfe*, Neetah remembered. His farm was across the river, up on the bank.

"Congratulations!" John's deep voice boomed in the little room. "But," he looked down at Pocahontas, "your convert seems to be in some distress."

"Oh-ho!" Sir Thomas Dale laughed. "You may go now, Princess," he said. Pocahontas rose unsteadily, curtsied, and darted out the door. Neetah followed, nodding to John Rolfe in thanks. His sky-colored eyes sparkled in response.

Pocahontas was already in the privy house, holding her skirts up and sitting over one of the holes carved through the long bench. Neetah lowered herself to another hole and sighed in relief. "That John is a kind man," she said. "Different from the others."

"And handsome," Pocahontas said.

Neetah imagined Japazeus's body, short and thick and tight, and Uttamatomakkin's, bulky with muscle, but graceful. Neetah drew in a quick breath. She hadn't had those sorts of thoughts in many moons now. "How can you tell how John looks under all those clothes and whiskers?" she teased her friend.

"I see it in his eyes," Pocahontas answered. She stood and re-draped her skirts. "I do hope he will stay for supper." She hurried back indoors.

Neetah took her time walking back to the parsonage. It was good to hear her friend bantering about men again.

Neetah breathed in deep chestfuls of fresh air and gazed at the tiny green leaves tinting the tree line. Spring birdcalls sounded from beyond the stockade and frog calls rang from the riverbank. Neetah rubbed her hands over her upper arms, brushing off the scent of the outhouse and chamber pot, of cooking smoke and stale bodies.

A bird called to her, more insistent than the others. Neetah spread her arms in its direction. *If only I could fly*, she thought, and then suddenly dropped her arms. That was no bird calling—it was a signal whistle. She listened more carefully, and then smiled in recognition. There were friends out there. She looked around the compound quickly and whistled a cheerful answer. The "bird" stopped singing, and Neetah walked back into the parsonage with quick happy steps.

"That is a good idea," Sir Thomas Dale was saying. The men were seated around the table with Pocahontas, wolfing down salt-cured beef and cabbage. No one noticed Neetah, so she took her place behind her friend's chair. She rested her fingertips on Pocahontas's shoulder, wishing she could pass the news to her by touch. She saw John Rolfe's eyes follow her gesture and dropped her hand to her side. "But," Sir Thomas went on, "can a savage actually be taught that?"

The minister wiped his mouth on his cuff. "She is picking up the Christian catechism quickly." He stared at Pocahontas speculatively. "It would help if she could read it for herself."

"She has long wanted to read!" Neetah blurted, then put her hand over her mouth.

The minister and Sir Thomas glared at her, but John Rolfe laughed aloud. "She speaks," he announced. "Tell me," he addressed Neetah, "do you, too, wish to read?"

"Don't be foolish!" Sir Thomas snapped. "She is but a girl and a servant."

Neetah thought quickly. "Only if it would help my lady Pocahontas," she answered, then relaxed as the men's attention shifted to her friend.

"I would be happy to read," Pocahontas said. "There seems to be magic in reading and in writing, too."

"There is no magic," Reverend Whittaker scolded. "Magic is the Devil's doing. But God's Word is written in the Bible. And our good King James has just offered a new translation! Imagine." He turned to the other men. "Just imagine if I could teach an ignorant savage to read his majesty's Bible!"

Dale pounded his thighs with his hands, but John Rolfe's low voice rolled across the table. "I'm not sure how ignorant they are, gentlemen." There was a stunned silence as everyone froze. "I only meant," John Rolfe explained, "that I feel these people are brighter than we credit them."

"These *people?*" Sir Thomas spat the word out. "They are animal savages. Further, they are *females*. Thus far, Pocahontas has only proven she can parrot our words. *People?* Ha!"

"Yet you seem to believe she has a soul to save," John Rolfe countered. Neetah noticed Pocahontas's head rising as she straightened her back.

The minister stroked his bushy moustache. "I see your

logic," he said. "I will have to study the scriptures more closely before I have a complete answer." He stared at Pocahontas. "Meantime, I will try to teach her to read."

"May I help?" John Rolfe asked.

"I would be honored," Pocahontas answered.

"This is the letter *A*." John Rolfe leaned over Pocahontas's shoulder a few days later, pointing to the first mark on a paddle he had given to her. "It stands for two sounds," he said. "*Ay* and *ah*." Pocahontas repeated the sounds. So did Neetah, but more quietly.

"Do you want to look at the hornbook, too?" John Rolfe asked. Though the Reverend Whittaker scowled, Neetah darted over, stared at the letters for a moment, and then returned to her seat by the fire. She went back to stirring the porridge but pictured the *A* and the next three patterns as well, memorizing them for later.

"Reading is harder than I had hoped," Pocahontas said in the town square after the first lesson. "The letters all run together in my head and the sounds get twisted."

Neetah bit back the impulse to say how easy she found it. "The first letter is *ah* or *ay*." She drew the pattern in the dirt with a stick. "It starts softly like our gentle God Ahone or hard like Aitowh's death."

Pocahontas nodded. "That is easy. But *A* is an English letter for English words, Neetah, not for Pamunkey names."

Neetah tried again. "You draw the letter this time." When a presentable *A* lay in the dirt, Neetah said, "*Ah* for *apple* and *ay* for *able-bodied*."

"Able-bodied, like John," Pocahontas answered quickly.

"You must keep helping me," she said. "I don't want to let John down." She paused. "Not after how kindly he spoke of us."

Neetah tutored her friend after every class. Together they memorized everything asked of Pocahontas but in the privacy of the bedroom or the privy. "I am so tired of this!" Pocahontas confided. Neetah was exhausted, too, but she hoped it did not show as much on her face as it did on her friend's. The men kept close watch over their princess, so Neetah was able to sneak out to walk, to think, and to pray.

Pocahontas faced a new assignment every morning, then an hour of church after that. Before Reverend Whittaker allowed her a mid-day meal, she had to recite perfectly for him from the morning's lesson. He or Sir Thomas drilled her in the afternoon until evening services began.

There were long, hungry stretches for Pocahontas, when her mind simply would not work as the English men expected it to. She lost the roundness of her cheekbones and her corset closed with fewer struggles. The girls reviewed lessons after supper, too, long into the night. Shadows gathered under Pocahontas's eyes, but her smile was back. Whenever John Rolfe could leave his farm work, he joined the minister and Pocahontas at lessons. He always sat with her in the church pew, his big baritone voice covering the mistakes she made in recitations and hymn singing, too.

Neetah did not go to church. Somehow, she was allowed to spend the hours watching stew pots or minding little babies without facing any penalties. "Come," Pocahontas begged her. "I am finding comfort there."

Neetah laughed. "You find your new John there." It troubled her that Pocahontas had ceased sprinkling a tobacco circle for herself and had stopped washing at dawn and dusk. When they spoke of the growing difference, their voices always rose toward anger. "Their God is no different from Ahone," Neetah said. "And that spooky Devil is just another name for Okeus."

"No, there is a difference," Pocahontas would answer. "Their God had a son who lived on after He died."

"Don't all of our spirits live on in the green meadows of the Great Hare after we die?" Neetah would challenge. "And the English have dozens of saints to speak to, like the spirits who fill our lives."

"The difference," Pocahontas always insisted, "is that the Son, Jesus Christ, will forgive my sins." Neetah knew how desperate her friend was for forgiveness, so she would change the subject.

One day, though, Pocahontas pressed on. "John would be happy if I joined his church, Wingam." Neetah waited silently to hear what that meant. "There would be a ceremony, a *baptism*," Pocahontas plunged on. "I would be splashed with holy water and given a new name, a Christian one. I would at last be able to eat the sacred foods with the other church members."

"A washing. A renaming. A feasting." Neetah nodded in the English way, and then caught herself. "But these sound just like what we do, Matoaka."

"I would lose the name Matoaka," Pocahontas said. "And I would have to renounce my faith in Ahone and Okeus and all the old beliefs before the baptism."

Neetah pulled back. "You would do that?" she asked, horrified.

"It would mean so much to John," Pocahontas gushed. "And I would be able to get right inside the English men's source of power. As a Christian, I could be accepted here, at last." Neetah thought of their flight from the Powhatan Confederacy and the cruel silence of the Patowomekes. Pocahontas went on, "What the Christians say makes much sense to me. I would like to be safe with Jesus."

Neetah looked at her friend. Pocahontas's posture, once proud, looked stooped. Her cheeks were still hollow and her eyes were now dull from stress and sleeplessness. Neetah rubbed her own tired eyes. What these men had done to Pocahontas was not fair, unless . . . She decided to ask. "Matoaka, do you think that you and John might marry if you become Christian?"

Pocahontas nodded ever so slightly.

"But . . . ," Neetah paused, ". . . hasn't he a wife?"

"She died, Neetah, along with a child on their way here from England."

"Then I will support your baptism," Neetah said. "In all your wild thoughts, you have missed the most important truth. You are finally living your vision again—the one that will bring peace to our people. A strange husband, a precious child, and an end to the killing." Pocahontas opened her mouth to argue, but Neetah put her fingers on her friend's lips. "Christian prophets saw visions as you do. I heard this when I sat outside your church. Your visions will be welcome there and your marriage will be, too." The friends locked fingers in the old way.

"Oh, wait," Neetah said. "Do you remember the story of Rebecca in the Bible?"

"She married a stranger to her land, didn't she?" Pocahontas said. "You read it to me from the same book as the Commandments."

"And Rebecca's blessing," Neetah said, "was to be 'the mother of thousands of millions who would possess the gate of those who hate them.'" Neetah thought she had the words right. The two girls were silent for a few moments in wonder.

"*Rebecca*," Pocahontas said aloud, clearly savoring the sound.

When Pocahontas told Reverend Whittaker that she wanted to be baptized, he sent for John Rolfe and Sir Thomas Dale immediately. The three men filled the dining room, waving tankards of ale and praising God and each other. They made plans and chose dates. Then they lit their pipes, and smoke filled the room.

The men composed letters to the king and Lord De La Warre and the other investors in the Virginia Company. They toasted each other's success. Sometimes they smiled at Pocahontas, too. Neetah slipped out to get away from the noise.

A familiar birdcall was coming from beyond the stockade again. Neetah wandered idly toward the sound and leaned against the fence in the shadows. "Tell Pocahontas," a voice whispered through the cracks between logs, "her father sends greetings." Neetah's eyes watered at the beauty of her own language.

"Has he sent a ransom for her freedom?" Neetah asked through the crack. "There is not much time left to get Pocahontas back from the English."

"No. He delivered an insult instead." Neetah tried to place the voice in the darkness. Uttamatomakkin, she guessed. "The High Chief returned a few sick prisoners, not the full number demanded. He sent back only some rusty muzkets and a basket of wormy corn."

Neetah sighed. This was not good. "Tell him," she paused, "yes, tell him that Pocahontas will soon be inducted into the inner circle of their magic. She will share the power once she has it mastered."

"Ho!" Tomakin could not keep his surprise silent. "I will tell the Powhatan." There was no more sound beyond the fence. Neetah leaned her forehead against the good strong wood, feeling for the spirit within. She saw the tree standing tall in the forest, shading longhouses full of children.

There was no time for Neetah to pine for her people. Through the next six Sundays, she had to help scrub the church clean; the parsonage, too. As she swept the church-yard, Neetah listened always for Tomakin's birdcall, but none came. Indoors, fields of new cloth were stitched into gowns for Pocahontas. A new, smaller corset was created for her and bigger, stiffer neck ruffs.

A tall black hat was crafted of beaver-fur felt and ringed with a wide ribbon. Neetah made sure to tuck a white feather into the brim. "Oh, how pretty!" Mistress Edwards clapped her hands. "Perhaps we should all wear white feathers for the baptism."

The catechism classes with John, the Reverend, and Sir Thomas increased in length as Pocahontas memorized all she had to declare as truth.

Finally, the day arrived. The church was packed with settlers, farmers, soldiers, and scouts. Candles burned everywhere, adding to the heat. Neetah could smell the crowd through the open window. When she stood on tiptoe, she could see Governor Gates sitting in the front pew, along with Sir Thomas Dale. Next to them, John Rolfe leaned toward the altar, watching Pocahontas. Neetah strained to hear but could only catch snatches of what they were saying. She mouthed the words along with Pocahontas and said a prayer of apology to Okeus before the churchgoers streamed out into the fresh air.

"Congratulations, Lady Rebecca," people said to Pocahontas.

"God bless you, Rebecca" and "welcome."

Neetah made her way between the frock coats and fancy skirts and tried to hook fingers with her friend. English men and women kept stepping in her way, blocking even a view of Pocahontas. Neetah finally gave up and retreated to the parsonage where a feast had been spread. The noise and the stink of ale sickened her, so she snuck away to hide in the shadows by the gatehouse. She said her prayers and then listened to the evening bird chorus. Still she did not want to enter the house. Pocahontas was gone and Matoaka, too, replaced by a Christian named Rebecca. Neetah wondered how much the ceremony had really changed her friend.

"There you are!" the new Rebecca cried. She held a torch aloft instead of relying on starlight. "I have such news! You and I will be visiting John Rolfe's farm tomorrow. John wants to show me his new tobacco plants. He thinks I might teach him how we grow whole fields of tobacco." The baptized Rebecca was flush with excitement, Neetah thought, and perhaps with ale, too. "He speaks to me differently now," she gushed.

Neetah could hear the change in John Rolfe's tone, too, as he escorted the girls to the front door of his farmhouse the next day. He gazed at Pocahontas with longing—a look she returned whenever their eyes met. "Go out and lie together in the summer air with him," Neetah teased, when the girls visited the privy together. "You know you both will feel better." She shut one eye in the English way of winking. Rebecca looked away without smiling so Neetah made her voice formal and tried again. "My lady Pocahontas, you two could create a bond between our peoples with your bodies!"

"John is a Christian," the lady Rebecca scolded. "They have many rules about such things." Neetah laughed in disbelief until Rebecca reminded her, "I am bound by those rules now."

Neetah watched the couple trade hungry looks for many more moons. Now it was John who grew wan, even though his tobacco fields prospered with Rebecca's help. "John was able to smuggle out some of those Bermuda Island tobacco seeds," Rebecca told everyone proudly. "He will have our first full crop to send to England by next fall." Still John pined for her, his eyes following her figure. At night, Rebecca sighed in her bed in the parsonage.

"Have you spoken to him of your love?" Neetah finally asked her friend. "Have you told him you wish to marry? It is your right, as a Pamunkey woman."

"I am no longer Pamunkey."

Neetah looked at her with disgust. "You are Matoaka, daughter of the Powhatan. You strap on English clothes but underneath are the tattoos of your clan. Beneath the tattoos hides my friend—a woman in love." Neetah took a deep breath and tried to control her anger. "Tell him," she said, her voice quivering.

"I cannot," Rebecca said. "He would turn from me."

"An English woman is allowed no wants of her own?" Neetah argued. "Has she no power at all?" When Rebecca folded her hands tidily in her lap and turned to gaze out the window, Neetah tried again. "You have simply found a new shell to hide in." Rebecca's face hardened, and she did not turn to look at her old friend.

Neetah passed the news of the love-struck couple to the messengers who whistled birdcalls beyond the fence. She did not tell them that Rebecca had stopped talking to her, even in the dark of the night. From Tomakin, she learned that the Powhatan was allowing his younger brother, Opechancanough, to kill any English man caught hunting beyond the stockade of Jaimztown or Henrico. And she learned that her mother had died of the spotted sickness. "Measles," Neetah corrected, trying not to feel the pain.

"Your aunt died, too, Neetah. She had no children, so the position of Weroansqua flows to her nearest female relative."

"That is my mother," Neetah whispered. "*Was* my mother. And now . . ."

"With her gone, too," Uttamatomakkin confirmed her thoughts, "you are, by rights, the Weroansqua of a thriving village, if you wish to return and claim it."

Neetah stepped back, her mind churning like a river about to turn tide. *Go or stay?* There was too much to think about and this was too important to decide all at once. Tomakin slipped away on silent moccasins.

Now Neetah's sighs floated along with Rebecca's in the dark of the upstairs bedroom. How lonely it was to worry alone! Should she return to her aunt's village in the hills? Neetah wondered, turning over restlessly. She remembered visiting on her father's shoulders. The town had seemed grand then, but it would look small now, and dull, after Werowocomoco and Jaimztown. But she would be Weroansqua in her aunt's place. *Only a minor Weroansqua,* Neetah reminded herself, *but a true leader*. She could make treaties and demand tribute, at least from her own villagers.

She tugged at the covers and thought of the Appamattuck people she would rule. They had never seen an English man. Not one of them could read or write or even speak English. They had only heard rumors of the exciting things Neetah saw every day.

She sighed again and looked toward Rebecca in the dark. *No one*, Neetah thought. That's all she was here. A shadow slipping around after the lady Rebecca. And "my lady," the Christian, was still not speaking to her. Neetah felt a hot flush of anger climb over her cheeks. If she went home and became Weroansqua, she would eat first at every meal. She would have friends and husbands, perhaps. People would come to her with their problems. And she could solve them, Neetah realized. She lay silently, imagining herself shedding *no one* like a snake sheds its skin. Underneath her dusty old scales a glossy new Weroansqua glowed—her true self. Wingam.

Go now or later? Another decision. Neetah turned over and pulled the cloth cover up to her chin. *A Weroansqua*, she thought, and smiled. Neetah nestled her head into the soft pillow. Before she left to go home, she had one last problem to solve right here in Henrico.

18
PEACE
1615

NEETAH TAPPED JOHN ROLFE'S COAT SLEEVE AS HE WALKED from church one morning. "I must speak with you," she whispered. John looked alarmed. He glanced about the group of settlers talking in the spring sunshine. When he saw Rebecca intently discussing the sermon with Reverend Whittaker, his face relaxed.

"Very well," he said, and followed Neetah back into the empty church. "Is something wrong with Rebecca?"

"No," Neetah said, and then silently reminded herself, *I am Weroansqua.* Her nerves steadied and she launched into the speech she'd been practicing for days. "This is your church, John, the home of your customs. Our customs are different." She paused, silently begging Okeus's forgiveness for the lie she was about to tell. "In our tribe, a woman's spirit-friend must tell her deepest secrets to the man she loves."

John froze and his face reddened as he thought over what she had said. "And you are Rebecca's spirit-friend?"

"Rebecca dreams of marrying you," Neetah said, not bothering to answer him.

"Does she think I have not considered this?" John's voice sounded tortured. "She knows what is written in the Bible. We are forbidden to take strange wives."

"Rebecca longs for your children," Neetah said. John coughed awkwardly, but Neetah went on. "She believes you to be the kindest, grandest of all the English men—but this is not the secret I must share."

"I cannot speak of this," John said, when he was able to talk.

"Nor can Rebecca," Neetah said. "But I must. My lady, Pocahontas, daughter of the Supreme Chief of the Confederacy, believes your marriage could act as a treaty between her people and yours."

"Well," John Rolfe said, "I could pray on this." He glanced nervously around the church, and then, without excusing himself, rushed to kneel in front of the altar. Neetah watched for a moment, then slipped silently out into the courtyard.

One moon passed, and another. Neetah and Rebecca began speaking again as they helped John with his crops. The tobacco fields were a man's work, but John seemed delighted to try everything the girls suggested, making hills around his plants and sowing beans and squash among them, shading and watering as necessary. The tobacco plants grew tall, their leaves a pale golden green instead of the hearty color Neetah was used to. In another moon, the plants were taller than Neetah's head. Next, they flowered—but with wide blossoms the color of summer sunshine. Then they grew still taller, towering even over John Rolfe's head. The Pamunkey tobacco, flowering pink in a little plot in the next field, looked stunted by comparison.

"We pile straw on tobacco leaves after harvest," Rebecca told John. "It cures the herb for smoking later."

When John asked for directions, Neetah helped to spread the straw. The dirt felt cool and solid under her feet, and the sun washed her back with warmth. She glanced at Rebecca, corseted and bound, dressed, shod, and bonneted, sitting beside the field. She was gazing at John, as the English man tried to spread straw evenly. *Her eyes*, Neetah thought, *looked like a puppy's. Why doesn't he just marry her?* Neetah thought. She grabbed an armful of straw and hurled it across the holy herb, then stood watching the golden grasses spread and sparkle in the sun as they fell.

Every time she visited John's farm, Rebecca tripped out in her English shoes to check on the curing progress. "John!" she called two Sundays after spreading straw. "The tobacco is rotting!" John and Neetah pulled straw away frantically, exposing the precious harvest to the sun and drying breeze.

"We have to think of some way to air cure this kind of tobacco," John said. Together the three talked about using racks like the Pamunkeys used for drying fish and flesh into jerky. Rebecca told John how healing women hung herbs inside their houses from rafters. Neetah pulled another armful and wondered about re-wetting the leaves as they dried, the way basket-weavers did with their splints. John told them about smokehouses hung with hams, salt pork, fish, and pickled eggs. By the time the tobacco crop was saved, Neetah had stored away information from many hours of work to whisper through the fence to the next Pamunkey messenger.

On the way home from moving the tobacco to the new drying racks, Rebecca announced, "John has decided, Neetah. He feels God wants us to marry. He has gotten permission from the governor and from the bishop in England, too."

"At last!" Neetah said and—proper though she might try to be—Rebecca collapsed in giggles with her old friend. "At eighteen turns of the leaf, you are an old woman." Neetah teased, "You and John will need a child soon!" She was glad to see a flush rise on Rebecca's cheeks and dimples play at the corners of her smile again.

"Will you go with John to speak with your father?" Neetah prompted. Rebecca's smile disappeared. At the doorway of Reverend Whittaker's house, Neetah demanded, "You must go and settle this properly with the Powhatan."

Rebecca stared at her.

"There are several ships readying to leave Jaimztown within the week. Any one of them could take you to him," Neetah said.

Rebecca still refused to answer, yes or no.

"I will help you pack," Neetah said. She headed up to their bedroom, Rebecca's shoes clattering on the stairs behind her.

It felt strange to be sailing up a river again, sharing a little room with Rebecca. There were a hundred and fifty soldiers along this time—divided between two ships—the governor, and, of course, John Rolfe. Rebecca spent most of her waking time on deck with John. Neetah imagined seeing Tomakin again, but in the daylight.

They dropped anchor and looked for Pamunkeys. There were no greeters at the riverbank. Neither on the first day nor the second. Rebecca refused to go on deck to show herself. "You see why I did not wish to come, Neetah?" Rebecca's voice trembled. "Father has not forgiven me. He never will."

The governor sent runners with invitations to the Powhatan, telling him that his daughter was aboard. He offered to trade her for hostages.

"I don't care, Neetah," Rebecca explained. "Perhaps my mission is simply to save a few souls from my father."

Three days later, Rebecca agreed to go ashore.

Neetah and John stood with her as Opechancanough and a dozen men approached. Neetah wished to run to camp and find the women, to tell everyone of the coming marriage, to smell bear-greased hair and hear little children laughing. Rebecca stood as stiff as an oak tree beside John, so Neetah held back.

The greetings were formal as the messengers stared openly at Rebecca's English clothing. They delivered Powhatan's refusal to meet with the English.

"What did they think?" Rebecca asked. "People are to come to my father, not the other way around." The English handed out blue beads. "I am well treated," Rebecca told Opechancanough. "I am happy. Tell my father that I am to be married."

"And tell him he is welcome at the ceremony," John said. Rebecca did not bother to translate as they watched the messengers leave.

The next day the Pamunkeys were back. Neetah was down in the ship's hold when she heard the first shot. She and Rebecca watched from the deck as a party of English soldiers rushed inland, guns at the ready. "Why must they do this?" Neetah watched, sick at the thought of medicine women struggling to heal muzket wounds, priests chanting through sleepless nights, warriors grimly dying in silence, and widows smearing their faces with ash. "Why?"

"Perhaps it is the only way to get my father to listen," Rebecca said. She stared out over the water, silent, eyes unblinking. Neetah stood beside her, staring until her eyes watered over, searching for a vision like the one Rebecca was seeing. There was only marsh and field, forest, and endless blue sky.

"You cannot hurry a vision," Rebecca whispered by her ear. "It will come when you most need it."

For the next few days, the smell of smoke and the pop-pop of distant muzket-fire floated over the river. Finally, the English returned to the boat. They carried one body and two wounded soldiers.

"We have a truce," the Governor announced. "We will be trading with the Powhatan tribes again. And the Powhatan sent a wedding gift to you, Lady Rebecca."

Neetah watched her friend rise to her feet, skirts rustling. "Oh, I did not keep it, my lady. It seemed closer to an insult."

"What was it?" Rebecca demanded.

"Only a wide flat basket full of dirt," a soldier said.

John clenched his fists. "What does he have against me?" he asked.

Neetah put her hand on Rebecca's arm, then explained to cover her friend's quick tears. "In our tribes, the gift of soil stands for a gift of land," she said. "What message, exactly, came with the basket?"

"Something about 'between the rivers and to the tides,'" the soldier said. "Made no sense to me."

Rebecca looked up at John. "My father has given us rights forever to use all the lands around your farm. We can grow far more crops than we can use and tobacco enough for you to supply all of England."

John swallowed visibly and Governor Dale slapped him on the back. "What did I tell you?" he asked. "Your sacrifice will pay off for all of us and your descendants, too!" He called for wine and raised his glass to toast the Virginia Company. "Our prayers are answered," he said.

Neetah snuck out of the boisterous group. She climbed to the top of a barrel stowed in the stern of the ship and sat down. John's *sacrifice*? The word burned like a wasp sting as she watched the familiar riverbank fall away behind the ship.

In the middle of a sea of wedding guests, Neetah stood staring at the record book propped open amid platters of feast foods on the parsonage table. No Pamunkey wedding had ever been recorded, she thought. Ignoring the joy all around, she let herself feel a pinch of sorrow. There was nothing left to prove she was ever married to Japazeus. That joy and the terrible sorrow might never have happened. Perhaps, she thought, she could write it in this book. "April 1, 1614," Neetah read aloud, "Johnathan and Rebecca Rolfe, married."

"You can read?!" The Reverend Whittaker pulled the book out from under her eyes and checked it. "*She can read*! The little servant-girl can read!" he announced to the room full of Virginia gentlemen and women. He swung back at her. "What kind of trick is this? Who taught you?"

"Easy, dear friend," John Rolfe said. "You taught her, yourself, while your attention was on our lady Rebecca. There is more to this Neetah than meets the eye."

"She means everything to me," Rebecca said generously, the ring sparkling on her hand against John's sleeve.

"This little one has been in constant touch with the Werowocomoco tribe," John said, "though she is very clever at it." Neetah stared at John. "It is she who has conveyed messages about Pocahontas's well-being to her people. That is why we have had so few attacks of late."

"But she is not Christian," Governor Dale said. "She is a naked heathen savage. She cannot possibly read."

All of Jaimztown's leaders crowded around Neetah. She wished she could melt away like deer lard in succotash stew. "She must be baptized," the minister said.

"She must be clothed!"

"She is a spy!"

"Hang her for treason to King James!" someone said. The words fell on her from every direction.

"How *dare* she!"

"Even *I* cannot read."

"Send the savage back to her people."

"Wait," John said. "Think. Gentlemen, her connections within the tribe have kept us safe. Neetah has taught me much about the growing of tobacco. That will profit one and all. And my new wife, Mrs. Jonathan Rolfe, wishes her dear friend to stay with her." Rebecca nodded and smiled. "Surely," John went on, "we cannot deny my new bride this wedding gift?"

"Well, if she is a friend, not just a servant . . ."

"Perhaps it was a trick of memory. She did not truly read just now."

"I wondered why the attacks had stopped."

"Perhaps, if the lady Rebecca desires it . . ."

"But a heathen?"

The men moved off, mumbling among themselves, and Neetah's breathing returned to normal. "You have been a spy, Wingam?" Rebecca whispered. The old dimple danced in her cheek and her eyes looked merrier than could be explained by the wine. "That was to be my life."

Neetah reached out a finger, and Rebecca hooked hers to it. "My lady," Neetah said, "I carried the vision while you could not. It is your turn again."

"The burden will sit more lightly if there are two to carry it," Rebecca said.

"I will share in your peacemaking until you have a child," Neetah promised and watched Rebecca blush.

"Mrs. Wolfe?" the Reverend Whittaker interrupted, glaring at their interlocked fingers. "When will your friend be seeking baptism?" He could not bring himself to look directly at Neetah.

"It will be some time after I visit the Great Hare," Neetah

said. Rebecca's dimple deepened as the minister nodded wisely.

"Whenever you are ready to begin instruction, I am ready," he said, and smiled when Neetah agreed.

The Reverend Whittaker seldom saw Neetah after that. She moved to the Rolfe farm with Rebecca. Pamunkey visitors often stopped there, openly discussing news with the girls in their own language. Tomakin came. Healing women visited to learn healing cures from Neetah. Tribal elders used the house as a base while they held negotiations. Curious tribesmen came to stare at the foreigners. At Rebecca's request, John built a small women's hut for visitors who might need it. At sunrise and sunset, the natives made their way to the water together and gave thanks. Trade flourished between the settlement and the neighboring tribes. The drought was over, so everyone had the strength and the goods for bargaining.

John wrote to the stockholders of the Virginia Company about his new wife and the fabulous tobacco crop growing in his field. "The Peace of Pocahontas," John told the girls one night. "That's what they are calling it. Rebecca, dear, you are the talk of London." He looked at Neetah and explained, "That is where our king lives."

He never asked how long Neetah would be staying or wondered about her family. He took his wife to church, but did not press for her friend to accompany them or to convert to Christianity. He seemed unaware of much of what was happening in his own house.

Neetah gave the huge spinning wheel a turn and backed away, feeling the sheep's wool between her fingers twist smoothly. Then she walked back, as the wheel spun the yarn onto a pole. "Rebecca," she began carefully, "you have not come to the women's hut in nearly two moons."

Rebecca pulled the shuttle on the loom and glanced through the window at the small thatch-roofed shed John had built for them beyond the field. "That hut has been a comfort to the guests who have needed it and a blessing to me."

"It seems you will have another blessing to thank Ahone for," Neetah said.

"I do feel it," Rebecca said. "I carry John's child. Imagine . . ." Her voice trailed off in wonder. Neetah kept spinning, remembering the secret joy and the feelings of blessedness, clumsiness, and sickness, too.

"May I send for a healing woman from your own clan?" she asked. "New life seems to sit uneasy in the mornings, and there are herbs for that." Rebecca nodded so vigorously that both girls laughed. "Oh, my friend!" Neetah said, suddenly. "I am so happy for you!" She left the wheel and hugged Rebecca. "Have you spoken with John about this?" Neetah asked. When there was no reply, she grinned and said, "It is time."

"Wingam, you will be here, won't you?" Rebecca asked suddenly. "After the child comes? You have given birth and nursed a child. I will need your help."

Neetah thought about her plan to return to the hill village of her father. Then she considered the English men's medicine: knives and leeches and dangerous powders. No doctor should be allowed near Rebecca and a new baby. "I will be here for you," Neetah said. She told herself that being Weroansqua could wait another few moons.

Rebecca gave birth in the woman's hut one morning while John was writing letters at his desk. Neetah was by her side and a circle of Pamunkey women were all around, encouraging and patting Rebecca, bringing teas and lighting sweet-grass smudge to drive away any evil spirits.

"A boy!" Neetah cried, when the infant dropped toward the sand. Before Rebecca could object, Neetah grabbed the baby boy and darted to the creek. The infant howled as he felt cold water close about him, but quieted as soon as Neetah began to sway, chanting the old blessings over him. "I will protect you," Neetah vowed to the child. "Under Ahone and Okeus, I swear it."

By the time she was done, Rebecca's afterbirth was buried and she was ready to present herself to John. Neetah held her arm to steady her as she walked to the house. The other women followed in a joyful procession. "John!" Rebecca called at the door. "A new guest has come to stay!"

When the baby cried, John dropped his feather pen and jumped up so fast that his chair toppled over backward. "The baby!" he shouted. "You had the baby?" His words tumbled over each other. "When? Where? Is it . . ."

"A boy," Rebecca said. "Your boy."

"You should be abed," John said. "I thought . . . A boy!"

The laughter of women drowned out his startled babbling as Rebecca handed the naked child to his father. "A blanket," John said. "He needs clothing. He needs . . . he needs . . ."

"A name," Neetah prompted. "The first name is important, given when it is clear a child will survive." John looked at the baby in fear.

"Oh, this one is strong enough." Neetah looked directly into Rebecca's eyes. "And it has been blessed."

"It will also be baptized," Rebecca said, her voice equally firm. "John and I have already chosen the name Thomas for him."

"Oh-ho!" John said. "The other men must know of this! And you, dear, must go to bed." He stared at Rebecca standing proudly before him, her eyes sparkling.

"Thomas will be hungry soon," she said. John looked confused and awkwardly handed the baby back to her.

"I will go, then," he said. "There will be rejoicing in Jamestown tonight! The town, the colony, the tribal villages, and all of London will rejoice when they hear of the birth."

"A child born of English and Powhatan blood. It is an omen," Uttamatomakkin said. The natives and the English both felt they had left their mark upon the other and all had a stake, now, in the peace that surrounded little Thomas.

"I will raise him adored, as is his right as a Pamunkey child," Neetah said, whenever she found Thomas crying from a scolding. She unwrapped the layers of clothing that made the child look more like a grown man—an English man—than a toddler. She took Thomas out into the dirt yard in the morning, "to let you sleep," she told Rebecca and John. First, she always stripped off his clothing and washed with him, then prayed as the sun rose. At sundown, she took him out again, telling his parents, "This way you can eat supper without interruption." The sun set after Pamunkey language lessons, ancient finger games, and the old prayers.

When Neetah thought of reclaiming her life as

Weroansqua, all she had to do was look at little Thomas. This child of two worlds needed a Pamunkey mother to balance his English upbringing. Perhaps when the child was older, she told herself, she would leave.

In the evenings, John read the women letters he had gotten from England, praising the new tobacco. He shared the news of the Virginia Company's success. He told of new plays by a playwright named William Shakespeare and of music by John Bull. Rebecca and Neetah talked about London as Thomas played by the loom. They asked John to draw maps and prodded him to describe the king and the queen's clothing. "London is big," he said. "Bigger and fancier than you can imagine."

Neetah pictured the Powhatan's beaded cloaks and copper jewelry, his headdress and intricate tattoos, and knew that John was wrong.

"I have been to Werowocomoco," she told him.

"Perhaps you will see London someday," he said.

A year later, John told Rebecca, "You must decide which Pamunkeys to take to London with us." His family looked at him across the table in surprise. "The Virginia Company is paying for the trip," he announced. "They feel we can help raise funds for the colony."

"But Thomas is too young for me to leave him alone yet," Rebecca said. "He is happy here, and safe."

"It is of great importance that we take our child, Rebecca. People will see him—and you—and know that our experiment here in Virginia is a success." John's voice rose, trying to convince her. At last he announced, "Wife, you *will* go with me to London, and we *will* take Thomas." He turned to Neetah. "You will come, too, of course."

Neetah did not respond. She remembered a phrase Pocahontas had used years earlier as she described her visions. "*There will be a child of great importance.*"

"Neetah!" John demanded.

"I will go," Neetah said quietly, "of course."

19
ENGLAND
1616

"ARE WE ALMOST THERE?" TOMAKIN HUNG OVER THE RAILING of the *Treasurer*, gagging and coughing up nothing but mucus. He spat it into the heaving water below. Neetah winced in sympathy as the ship pitched over another wave and Uttamatomakkin's stomach convulsed again.

"The captain says we might spend two full moons crossing this ocean." Neetah spoke in Pamunkey so Matachanna and the others would understand. "I do not know whether to believe him."

"At least we will be putting ashore every night," Matachanna said. "We will escape the stink of this ship and the endless rolling. Your stomach will settle." She patted her husband's shoulder and grabbed the railing to steady herself.

"Matachanna," Rebecca said gently, "Captain Argall said we will see no land until we near England."

"No lake is that wide. The English exaggerate everything." Tomakin wiped his mouth with the back of his hand and stood shakily. "They may have intimidated you, Rebecca, but it will not work with me. I have heard their tales of huge cities and thousands of people. They speak of ships beyond count and temples that soar into the sky. It is a child's fiction."

"What they have told me seems always to be true," Rebecca said.

"They have told you lies about the gods."

"I believe in the Church of England," Rebecca said, "and their risen Christ."

Tomakin rolled his eyes and turned to heave over the side again. The ship swayed and lurched against cross waves all night long. Neetah awoke at every signal bell. She would look about the little cabin where she and Pocahontas had once been held prisoner. Now, Rebecca and John Rolfe had the bed and blankets. Little Thomas slept in a cradle nearby. A hammock had been rigged for Neetah, "so you can be near your mistress," Captain Argall had explained. "It is a good thing the lady Rebecca has to have so many servants. It will make her look important to our friends in London. A shame you all don't wear proper clothes, though."

Neetah had hidden a smile, imagining Uttamatomakkin's priestly fury at hearing he was considered a "servant" to Pocahontas.

Every morning and every afternoon, the sailors and natives were called to worship on the deck. Captain Argall or Governor Dale preached and prayed. There were no pews, but that would not have mattered to Tomakin. He stood stiff, arms crossed over his chest, facing west, toward home and the Great Hare. He scowled but he listened, too. Neetah knew that because he often sought her out.

"Our young ones should know English, too," he said on the third morning, "so that they can listen and remember things to tell the elders."

"Children make the best spies," Neetah agreed.

"But they are not all as strong as you," the priest said. "You grew up walking the true path. Others wander."

Neetah stood tall and felt the priest's sweet words blow against her like a spring wind. "I will give lessons," she said. "There are things our delegation needs to know about these English."

"And I will make offerings to the spirits," Uttamatomakkin said, his face pale, "and focus my prayers on quieting the waters."

Over the next weeks, Neetah worked with the dozen unmarried maidens and boys who had come on the boat. They learned English, but they also learned to flatter and wheedle and ask about everything. "This is not how we act among our people," she reminded them. "But the English will think you simple and rude and harmless."

The children learned. They also grew quieter. "I miss home," Neetah heard.

"I am tired."

"My lips are cracked."

But mostly Neetah heard, "I am hungry." The venison they had brought along was gone in a week. Their dried fish lasted almost a moon. The English shared hardtack biscuits and corn porridge, beans and water, but it did not satisfy. As the weeks stretched on, the water took on the stagnant taste of the inside of old barrels. Maggots, grubs, and roaches shared the food-storage hold with rats. And still there was no land.

There were endless waves and fierce storms, prayers and chants. The natives grew tired and ill. So did the settlers, increasingly frantic to get home. The sailors were losing patience. Only little Thomas's cheery voice brought smiles to everyone's faces. Rebecca's body still fed him milk, so his health bloomed. She seldom walked about on deck now and even her hair looked drab and lifeless.

"Land-ho!" When the call came at last, many of the travelers could only stagger to the rail. "*That* is London?" Rebecca asked. She sighed. "Tomakin was right." There were only a few houses along a shoreline and two boats at the dock.

"No," John Rolfe explained. "These are the Canary Islands. We'll stop and get food here."

"And fresh water?" Neetah could not help herself. There had been no clean water to drink in weeks and none at all for washing or worship.

"Yes, yes," John said, his voice gaining strength as the islands came into focus. "And fruit and meat and . . ."

"If that is not London," Rebecca asked, "how much longer until I meet the queen?"

"A month," John said. "A moon," he translated for Neetah.

"I know that!" Neetah snapped. She stepped away from the rail. "Forgive me," she said, scolding herself. The strain of the trip was showing on everyone. "I will go below to tell Tomakin that we are near land."

The space under the deck was dark and dank and stank of unwashed bodies and rotting grain. Neetah had to duck her head to keep from brushing it on the floorboards above. Hammocks swung everywhere in front of her. "Where is the priest?" Neetah called. "Matachanna!"

"Here, Neetah!"

Neetah picked her way around crates and ropes in the dim light. "We are approaching land," she said.

"And are there ships without number in the harbor?" Uttamatomakkin snarled. As he pulled himself out of the hammock, Neetah could not help but stare. The fine muscles were gone and Uttamatomakkin looked only tall. Neetah felt her own arm. There was no meat to it. She sighed.

"We are stopping for food and water here," she reported, "and perhaps a rest from this endless swaying. Then we will sail on to London." She stared at Uttamatomakkin. "They have called a church service to celebrate, but I think Ahone deserves a prayer of thanks. We must plead with Okeus, too, for safe passage on the rest of the trip."

"You are right," Uttamatomakkin said. "I will lead the ceremonies." He pushed himself up, grabbing his formal headdress from the ledge.

Neetah felt Matachanna's finger touch hers. "Thank you," the woman said, and Neetah locked fingers with her.

"I will gather the others," Neetah said, and left.

Finally, once they had landed, the Pamunkeys could bathe in the water at sunset. The Canary Island English watched in horror. "Don't you know that the dirt on your skin is for protection?" one of them yelled from the bank. The natives ignored the dockhand and kept splashing and playing, diving into the water and rubbing at their skin to rid themselves of the smell of bilge and sweat and rotten food.

"All aboard!" Captain Argall yelled. Neetah looked up toward the dock. Rebecca stood silhouetted against the spring evening sky next to John Rolfe and the captain.

"We must leave," Rebecca called.

"We must pray," Neetah yelled back. "You, too. Then we will get back into the boat." She watched Lady Rebecca sag against John's shoulder. Neetah turned back to Uttamatomakkin. He slogged through the water back to the bank and picked up his bag. The others gathered around as he shared pinches of holy tobacco. They knelt and sprinkled the herb in circles around themselves on the sand. Then Tomakin began the chant. The strange island seemed to disappear in Neetah's mind. All that was left were the gods and the age-old tradition of her tribe. At last she stood, clean and refreshed, and ready to sail on to England.

"That's Plymouth," Captain Argall announced a week later, pointing to the cliffs they were passing. He laughed as Uttamatomakkin leaned against the railing and groaned. "This choppy water means we are in the English Channel," the captain said. "Another three days, and we'll be met at Gravesend."

"Who will be greeting us?" Rebecca asked. "The queen?"

John Rolfe laughed aloud. "Not likely. I've never met her." Neetah thought of the Powhatan and his wives. Everyone in Werowocomoco knew them. Everyone in the Confederacy had met them, and many from beyond, too.

"To meet the monarchs, first someone very important must agree to present you at court," John said.

"You are important, my husband!" Rebecca exclaimed.

Once again John laughed aloud. "Rebecca, I do not think you understand yet how many people live in England. There are a quarter of a million people in the city alone."

"A million?" Uttamatomakkin turned to Neetah. "Is he still saying that their king's village is bigger than Werowocomoco?"

"It has a hundred thousand times more people than our biggest city," Neetah translated for him. Uttamatomakkin stared out over the water, mumbling about white men's lies.

"They didn't lie about the size of this ocean," Rebecca said to Neetah. "The corn we planted before we left must be shoulder high by now." She paused. "Do they have corn in England?" Neetah's mouth watered at the thought.

Once they reached London, Neetah leaned against Matachanna and kept her eyes straight ahead, begging Okeus for safety. Beneath her thighs, a rough wagon seat bounced and jolted on strange wheels that rolled along over a stone-paved path. So many new words—each with an idea never imagined by a Pamunkey. How would she explain it all to her people back home? *Wheels!* Neetah stared at them until her head felt dizzy. Stranger still, the wagon was pulled by giant deerlike animals called *horses*.

Other English people passed, actually sitting astride these animals. But most people walked. Around the wagon, a sea of people moved along, bobbing, stinking, and wearing so many colors and patterns that Neetah's eyes ached.

Houses rose on both sides of the stony path, houses pressed close together and built one on top of another to a dizzying height. More English people leaned out of the windows above her head, pointing and screeching.

"Indians!" a woman yelled.

Another called out, "Come look at the heathens!"

"They can't be heathens," a man walking by the wagon called back. "Look at them. They're not even human."

"There's the child!" There was awe in the old woman's voice as she waved at Thomas. "Hold him up for us, you!"

"Half English, half savage. A miracle."

Thomas stood braced between Neetah and Matachanna and waved back at the old woman while the crowd around the wagon cheered.

"A monkey," the man sneered.

In one hand, Neetah gripped the wampum bead strung around her neck and leaned across little Thomas to link fingers with Matachanna. The two women stared at Tomakin's broad back and his beautiful headdress. He'd chosen to wear the one with snakes and weasel skins intertwined. Red paint colored his chest from his breechcloth to the copper plate hanging at his neck. Uttamatomakkin sat so stiffly beside Rebecca that only his dangling earrings swayed with the wagon's movements.

"He is magnificent," Neetah whispered to Matachanna, her body humming with pride in her people.

Suddenly, the driver pulled back on the ropes tied to the horses. The animals stopped, and everyone in the wagon lurched forward. As Neetah picked Thomas up and resettled him on the bench, a richly dressed man stepped over to the side of the wagon where John Rolfe sat and bowed. "Welcome to the *Belle Sauvage.*"

"Lord De La Warre!" John stood and bowed quickly. "This is my wife," he began, but Lord De La Warre had already swept off his hat and was bowing to Rebecca.

"Dear lady," he said, "welcome to London. The Virginia Company has secured the best of rooms for you above the tavern."

"We are staying in a tavern?" John Rolfe sputtered.

"And you, dear," the gentleman went on, addressing Rebecca as if John had not spoken. "It is good to see you again. You were so kind to me in Jamestown a few years back. May I also welcome your son to London?" And he bowed again, this time nearly touching his forehead to his velvet-bowed knee.

Neetah turned to see what Rebecca would do.

"Thank you, kind sir," said Rebecca, making a proper curtsy. "This time, instead of mere earrings, I carry greetings from my father, Wahunsenacah, Supreme Chief of all of the Powhatan tribes." Neetah blinked in surprise. The Powhatan had sent no such greeting. It must have been the right thing to say, though, for Lord De La Warre smiled and reached a gloved hand across John Rolfe's knees toward Rebecca. She stood, smoothed her long skirt, and used his hand to steady herself as she eased past John and stepped down from the wagon.

John, Neetah, and the rest of the party from Virginia hur-

riedly followed Rebecca through tall gates and into a courtyard full of more white-faced people. Neetah did not know
where to look first. Big animals slobbered over water ponds,
women howled with laughter at men's comments, a juggler
tossed knives up on a stage, and a child with one arm begged
for food.

"Will I have the pleasure of meeting Lady De La Warre?"
Neetah heard Rebecca ask.

Lord De La Warre turned to her suddenly. "I had not
thought to speak of this in front of your husband," he told
Rebecca, "but it seems you are to be presented at court.
Queen Anne loves to have interesting women around for
amusement. My own lady will help dress you appropriately
to meet the king and queen."

"Rebecca!" John said, his voice full of excitement. "We
will have an audience with the queen!"

"Ah, John," Lord De La Warre said, as if he'd just noticed
John Rolfe standing beside his wife. "You should know that
the king is greatly displeased with you. I doubt you will be
invited to the palace."

"Because I produce a better tobacco?" John asked. "I
heard that the King finds smoking a disgusting habit. Rumor
has it, though, that Queen Anne and her ladies are smoking
along with all of London society."

Neetah stepped back in surprise, holding Thomas tightly.
The queen smoked? But the holy weed was not for women!

Lord De LaWarre went on, "But King James is deeply
offended that you, a mere commoner, would marry a royal
princess. Apparently, you did not bother to get his permission."

"Oh." John's deep voice suddenly sounded very small. He turned to follow his wife and the lord into the *Belle Sauvage*. Neetah walked behind, carrying Thomas. She felt dizzy as she looked up at walls that stood as tall as any tree. Even Uttamatomakkin was able to step through the door without stooping although he held himself rigid. They all did.

Once Lord De La Warre and Rebecca passed, the English people pressed close around the Pamunkeys, making rude remarks and reaching out to touch their naked skin.

"I suppose this is the best the Virginia Company could afford," John said to Rebecca, when they had settled into a small room.

Neetah set Thomas down and began unwrapping his layers of dirty clothing.

"You, my dear," John took both of Rebecca's hands into his, "were marvelous! I would have thought you a real princess!" Rebecca snatched both hands back and whipped around, unpinning her hat and laying it on the only table.

Neetah felt stung, too. John was proving to be a different person here in England. Rebecca was a true daughter of a Supreme Chief. Neetah knew the spirit of leadership, too. She was a Weroansqua and her people had a mission here in London. She sniffed the foul tavern odors of stale ale and sweat and knew it would be easy to leave the English behind when she got home. It would be time to claim her birthright.

"Your trunks," a voice outside the door called. John opened the door and a pair of young men slid their heavy wooden boxes into the room. Neetah laughed aloud at the absurdity of fitting three adults, a baby, and all their trunks into such a small room.

There were many times over the next months that Neetah had to pretend not to see the tension that was growing between Thomas's parents. It was not hard, since the two were seldom together. John had many meetings with the Virginia Company's sponsors, trying to raise enough money to keep the Jamestown Colony supplied. Rebecca was invited to parties and teas, receptions and dances all over London. Everyone wanted to claim that they had met the charming Indian princess. "How do you always know what to say?" Neetah asked one night, as she helped Rebecca out of her clothing.

"I listened to my father," Rebecca said. "He taught me how to see what others want in a negotiation and to seem to give it to them."

"There must be more. Everyone loves you!"

"They love you, too, Neetah, although your nakedness makes them shy around you. And I love you!" Rebecca reached out her finger in the old gesture. "Who else would have practiced the English dance steps with me until I could spin without tottering? Who else could I trust with Thomas while I went off wooing England?" Rebecca clapped her hands together in the English gesture. "And, finally, I am to meet the queen!"

"Oh, Matoaka!" Neetah slipped, and used her friend's secret name. "This is your deepest desire, is it not?"

Rebecca was dancing with Thomas in circles. "She is twice my age," Rebecca said, "and twice as playful, if the rumors are true."

"You should have a good friendship, then," Neetah said. "Will King James be as easy to please as his wife?"

Rebecca closed one eye at Neetah in the English wink. "Now that they have two sons to be king someday, James has no more interest in Queen Anne or her friends." She kept spinning with Thomas and explained, "King James is like the Pamunkey men who do not marry women, but spend their lives in magic and name giving."

"Rebecca . . ." Neetah began to scold, but bit her lip. When was the last time she had seen her friend so happy? When she'd first gone to Jaimztown? When she'd fallen in love with John Smith? Neetah thought about that. "You are in love with London!" she said, amazed.

Rebecca set Thomas down on the floor and paused to straighten her corset. "Yes, I suppose I am," she said. Thomas took three dizzy steps and fell over, laughing. Neetah and Rebecca had to join in. "There are so many new things here, Neetah; I am as dizzy with joy as Thomas is right now." Rebecca tickled her little boy's belly until he screamed with laughter.

Neetah was right. Once the lady Rebecca had been formally received at court, she and the queen became fast friends. Nearly every week through the summer and fall, Rebecca joined the queen and her ladies at frolics in the castle or at the royal park. Often she brought Thomas, and then Neetah would go along, too.

"You must be quite comfortable," Queen Anne said to Neetah, looking up and down her body.

"Yes, your highness," Neetah answered with a clumsy curtsy. The ladies in waiting and even Rebecca laughed until Neetah, too, laughed. A curtsy in a short leather apron would have to look very different from one in a wide skirt of lace and bows and ribbons. Neetah tried a bow instead and they laughed even louder. Thomas ran around the lawn, bowing and curtsying to everyone until he was out of breath.

"You were wonderful," Rebecca said in the wagon on the way home. Neetah sat silent, thinking over the laughter. Her face burned.

"I cannot do that again," she said. "It is not laughable to be a Pamunkey."

"Then you must stand as Uttamatomakkin does, stiff and silent, pretending that there is no joy alive inside of him."

"I will show joy," Neetah said. "And dignity. Something you have lost." She tightened her lips to keep from apologizing. It didn't matter if the words had stung. Neetah knew she was right. There was only silence between the old friends for the long ride back to the *Belle Sauvage*. In the courtyard, they stopped with Thomas to watch a juggler up on the stage. The clown kept dropping balls instead of catching them, making Thomas choke with laughter. The crowd around them roared and applauded.

Later, in the room upstairs, Rebecca held Thomas in her lap. She stared as Neetah washed in the little basin, then knelt to pray. Neetah ignored her friend and spoke to Ahone in the sunset glowing through the grimy windowpanes.

Finally, Rebecca spoke. "The queen has a juggler, too. She also keeps a fool whose only purpose is to make her laugh." Rebecca stepped past Neetah to the basin and said, "She does not need two fools."

Neetah watched as Rebecca splashed her face clean in the old way and stood gazing out the window.

20
GOING HOME
1616–1617

"OH, THOMAS," NEETAH SAID. "LOOK UP!" THE CEILING AT Lord De La Warre's was painted to look like a pale blue sky, studded with puffy white clouds. "That is how the sky looks in Virginia," Neetah told the little boy.

"Give him to me for a moment!" Rebecca said, and hurried off to stand with Thomas under a great ball of pine branches. "Merry Christmas, Thomas!" Rebecca rubbed noses with her son. "That is a kissing ball, so we can . . ." She kissed the little boy up and down his neck. Thomas squealed with delight, and the brightly dressed guests nearby turned to laugh.

"My lady," said John Rolfe, swooping from behind to plant a kiss on Rebecca's nose. "I do love Christmas here in England. May I have this dance?" The orchestra in the corner was tuning their instruments again.

"Here." Rebecca handed Thomas back to Neetah and turned to take her husband's arm.

Neetah shifted the cloak over her shoulders, and

coughed. Like most English buildings, this ballroom was drafty. "We will get you a nice mince tart then watch Mama and Daddy dancing from the corner by the fireplace," she told Thomas, and shivered. The morning services at Westminster Cathedral had been long and the vast stone church unheated.

"It is Neetah, isn't it?" Lady De La Warre stood close, holding a cup of punch. The smell of perfume wafted from the woman's gloves and flowery scents flowed from the bouquet stuffed into her cleavage, but they did little to cover her body's odors. Neetah wondered how long it had been since the woman had washed. "Merry Christmas, my dear," Lady De La Warre said. "Only, since you're not Christian, perhaps I should say, perhaps . . . Oh, do give me little Thomas!"

Once again Neetah handed the child over. "Merry Christmas, m'lady," she said with a curtsey. "This is a grand party. Thank you for inviting us all."

"Tommy, Tommy," the great lady bounced the baby in her arms. "Everybody loves you and your mama, too." She glanced at Neetah. "The throne is behind your Virginia Company, dear, and the investors have pitched in again. But I am worried."

Neetah coughed again. "That," said the Lady De La Warre, "is what worries me. Many of your party are sick, are they not?"

"Yes, ma'am," Neetah said. "Three Pamunkeys have died in this cold, wet land."

"I do not like the cast of Lady Rebecca's skin," the lady said. "And she seems less lively. Is she well?"

"We all are worn-out from the trip and new foods, but my lady Rebecca most of all." Neetah chose her words carefully. "This winter season of partying has been exhausting for her."

"Well, tomorrow is Boxing Day, when we exchange Christmas gifts, and then comes a last flurry of holiday events. We are taking the Rolfes to Shakespeare's new play, *The Tempest*. It is about John's dreadful voyage to the New World." The lady stopped for a moment to untangle Thomas's sticky hand from her wide lace collar. "Neetah, I suppose I should call it your world. Er, our world now. In any event, this season is a happy whirl until Twelfth Night. I know that our dear Rebecca and her husband have been invited to the royal masked ball that night." She gave Thomas another hug and handed him back. "You will let me know if this is too much for Lady Rebecca, won't you, Neetah?"

"Could you send her home then?" Neetah asked. The word, even in English, brought a stab of longing.

"Oh dear, no," the lady said. "That is not up to me. But we could have you moved to the country. It is quiet there and the air is clearer."

Quiet. Neetah tried to imagine an end to the endless bells of London, the shrill calls of grocers, the clatter of wheels and hooves on stone pavement, and the voices of uncountable numbers of people. Even the bands of Christmas carolers, so lovely when they had first begun to walk the streets, had become just another layer of noise.

There was no sleeping after the Twelfth Night party. Revelers in the pub downstairs were rowdy and loud until dawn. On top of the street noises, Rebecca's coughing kept Neetah awake. Air! Neetah staggered toward the window at dawn, still coughing. Fine gray grit lay thick along the *Belle Sauvage*'s windowsill and shadowed the glass. She opened the window and leaned out for a breath of fresh air. Instead the room was flooded with the stink of sewage in the gutters mixed with the smells of a thousand cook pots, streets full of horse droppings, and decaying food from the marketplace. Buildings stretched as far as she could see, each topped with a chimney, and every chimney was belching gritty black coal smoke. Neetah watched a cold gray breeze blow across London. She closed the window and turned to John Rolfe, sitting on the edge of his bed, bleary-eyed.

"Your lady Rebecca is very sick. Did you not hear her coughing through the night?"

"Aye," John Rolfe said. "But your lungs seem worse and your cough is deeper."

"It only sounds that way. As tightly as Rebecca's under-things are strapped, she cannot take a deep breath to clear her chest. She has a gurgling sound within."

"I will ask the innkeeper to summon a doctor," John said. He was gone before Neetah could ask for a healer instead.

She ran to the next door down the hall. "There is an

English doctor on the way to treat Rebecca," Neetah told Uttamatomakkin. "You must come and care for her first."

Uttamatomakkin scowled. "Matoaka's spirit is so far out of balance that I do not think my chants and prayers can reach her now. But your spirit is in need, too."

Neetah coughed and agreed to a healing ceremony with him later in the day. "I will get word to the De La Warres this morning that we all must move out of this city." Neetah wrote a note and sent it with the innkeeper's son.

The doctor arrived. He listened to Rebecca's chest through a tube held to his ear. "Pleurisy," he said. "Pneumonia, too. Perhaps worse."

Neetah stood back and watched the strange medicine of the white men. The doctor took a big leech from a jar and waited as it attached itself to the side of Rebecca's ribs while she coughed. Then he cut into her wrist with a sharp lancet to draw out still more blood. As the blood pooled in a dish, the man nodded. "This will allow the bad humors to escape and give her more room to breathe." He rubbed a foul-smelling ointment on her neck and fed her two spoons of some medicine that made her gag. "This will make her sleep deeply," he said. "She needs rest." He left the bottle with John.

"It is her spirit that makes her ill," Neetah said, as soon as he left. "It is confused and homesick. She needs a healing ceremony and herbs from a wise woman."

"Heathen talk," John said. He and Neetah watched

Rebecca drift into sleep, her face pale, and with blood seeping from her fresh wounds.

Neetah prayed silently to Okeus to forgive him, then said, "The De La Warres have offered to move us out to the country. At least there we can breathe clean air and wash away our evils in streams." She shuddered, thinking of the raw sewage floating in the Thames River.

"She is *my* lady Rebecca," John spat back. "She has important meetings this week, and so do I. Our work in London is not finished."

Neetah stood tall and faced him. "I must protect my lady Rebecca as I swore to do, for life. She needs fresh air to get well."

On the bed, Rebecca coughed in her sleep. She hacked and gagged until John and Neetah raised her to a sitting position. Finally, she drew a gurgling breath. A trickle of blood escaped from the corner of her lips. Neetah looked across her at John.

"Fine," he grumbled. "But we will stay with *my* relatives in the county. I will arrange it immediately. Will you wait here with Rebecca?"

Neetah did not bother to answer.

Nor did she bother to say anything to John about the good effects of fresh air and sunshine on his wife, once the Virginia party was moved to the Rolfe's Brentwood estate. Rebecca's color came back and her cough improved. During a healing ceremony Tomakin finally held for Neetah, her spirit floated away and returned, whole. Now the Pamunkeys could bathe every sunset in a nearby stream, even when they had to break a skin of ice. Neetah felt clean at last.

One morning she looked up from her prayers to see a ghost walking across the lawn.

"No!" she screamed. "Do not return to haunt Pocahontas!" She ran across the estate's wide yard to stop the spirit of Captain John Smith before it could infect the house. "Stop!" she screeched to its face. This ghost looked older and very real, but Neetah did not let that stop her. "Uttamatomakkin!" she yelled. "Help!"

By now, the Pamunkeys had gathered about the spirit, wailing and cursing it. Uttamatomakkin had begun an exorcising chant. Aunts and uncles of the Rolfe family stood on the porch, staring. "Good day, John!" one of them called. "What have you done to so upset our savages?"

"Good day, friends!" John Smith called back, ignoring the Pamunkey crowd around him. "I have no idea. I simply stopped by to see my old friends from Virginia."

"But you are dead!" Neetah said in English.

"Is that what they told you?" John Smith laughed. "That figures, as much as they hated me. But I am very much alive. Touch me." He held out a hand. Neetah would not touch him, but she smelled his familiar scent and her heart flew to Rebecca. John Smith! How Rebecca had loved this man! This English man who had befriended her, encouraged her, and then rejected her when she'd given up everything to save his life. How Rebecca had grieved! Hatred burned through Neetah's body.

"May I go up to the house now?" John asked the group. "I have waited long for this." All Neetah could remember were the months Rebecca had spent in sorrow.

She matched his long strides as he walked toward the house. "Where did you go? And why did you choose now to hurt her again?" she challenged. "You had to know the lady Rebecca was in England. Everyone has known for months."

"Not 'moons'?" John Smith stopped to grin at her. "You may still dress in skins, dear, but you have become as English as I am."

"Never!" Neetah screeched at him. John Smith roared with laughter and strode past her up the stairs of the porch.

Neetah froze and so did the scene before her. Rebecca stepped out of the door. Neetah watched the color leave her friend's face and her shoulders begin to tremble.

"It's my little Matoaka!" John Smith roared.

Neetah stopped breathing. In front of all these people, John Smith had exposed Rebecca's private name. Now they knew. They all knew. Neetah felt an icy breeze blow right through her, and things began to move very fast. Rebecca's knees buckled. Neetah leaped up onto the porch and grabbed her friend's shoulders. She spun Rebecca around and pushed her back in through the open door.

"Neetah!" John Rolfe shouted. "Rebecca?"

"She will see him later," Neetah called, as she guided

Rebecca to a chair. "Not now!" Rebecca took a ragged breath and began coughing. Neetah sat beside her friend and threw an arm around her shoulders to shelter her. The coughs wracked Rebecca's chest, mingled with sobs. Neetah brushed away the tears as they fell and glared up at John Rolfe. "Later," she demanded. "Tell everyone to leave us alone for a time."

Her voice must have been truly fierce, for Neetah was aware of bodies moving silently past on the far side of the wide hallway. The hall around them was quiet for a time. Slowly Rebecca's sobs turned to sighs, and those sighs triggered fewer coughs. Neetah looked up. John Rolfe was simply sitting on a chair against the opposite wall. His face was filled with a shameful display of pain. *English men*, Neetah thought with disgust. *They all needed a good huskanaw to toughen them up. Everything John felt was written large in his eyes. He really loves her*, Neetah realized.

"Come take my place," she told him softly. "I will get Thomas ready to meet Captain Smith." Neetah took her single wampum bead off and settled it around Rebecca's neck. With a last squeeze of her friend's shoulders, Neetah went into the house.

By the time she had returned with Thomas, dressed in his best velvet suit, the door to the front parlor was closed. "We will wait here," Neetah said, "quietly." She sat with Thomas in the chair.

The boy wiggled. "Where is Mama?" he asked. Neetah pulled him back to sit still. Voices rose and fell from behind the parlor door. Someone coughed. "Mama!" Thomas cried, and pointed to the door. "Mama in there." He wiggled his way off the chair and tried to peek through the keyhole. Neetah wished he had been raised as a proper Pamunkey, knowing silence, enjoying stillness. "Mama!" he called through the keyhole.

Suddenly, the door opened.

Rebecca knelt and opened her arms to hug the child. Over her head, Neetah could see Captain Smith. Behind him, John Rolfe paced. *Did he know?* Neetah wondered. Had John Rolfe known that Captain Smith was alive all along? Was *everything* a lie?

Neetah felt sick. She left them all and went outside. The cold air made her breath catch, and she started to cough, but the sky arched above her, wide and pure and blue. Neetah could almost pretend she was on the shore of the Patomac with Japazeus, holding little Aitowh in her arms. Those were happy days, she reminded herself. She had known happiness.

"Neetah?" Matachanna strode across the lawn from the gatehouse where the Pamunkeys lived at Brentwood. "Wingam?" Matachanna's voice rang with love. "Uttamatomakkin wishes to know if you need another chant."

"At sunset," Neetah said. "There is much I will pray. But may I simply come and sit with you now?"

In the next days, Neetah watched Rebecca grow quiet again, as she had once long ago when she was Pocahontas. She stopped playing with Thomas. Her cough worsened. Rebecca sat still, watching the water flow past the Rolfes' estate. The first early greening of spring made no difference to her spirits. Neither did her husband's loving care.

"We will go home," he announced one day. He looked at his wife, sitting listlessly. "We must." He explained how the tobacco had to be planted and his farm overseen, but Neetah knew differently. A new sickness was sweeping England. Many people had fallen ill. Yet another of the Pamunkeys had died and now Matachanna was sick. Little Thomas was coughing and hot with fevers. The lady Rebecca seemed too weak to survive anything else.

"We will sail as soon as the weather allows," John said. "The end of February at the latest."

But February 1617 was cold and rainy. March began worse. Not until the second week could the Virginians head home. Neetah was glad to see the end of London and England. She lay on her bunk in the Rolfes' cabin as the ship hurried down the Thames River toward the sea. Even before she felt the roll of ocean waves, Neetah was up on deck. "Captain Argall?" she began.

"It is Admiral Argall now, dear," the old captain said, kindly. "Is there a problem?"

"It is Pocahontas. No, it's Rebecca," Neetah corrected herself. "You should, perhaps . . ." she lost the rest in a spasm of coughing.

Captain Argall hurried toward the Rolfes' cabin. Neetah made her way after him, leaning heavily on the railings. The scene was worse than the one she had left. Rebecca's night-clothes were spattered with blood. Her coughing only brought more to the surface.

"We will put in at Gravesend," the admiral said. "Both of you women need medical care before we attempt the crossing."

"Thank you, sir," John Rolfe said, his voice heavy with sorrow.

Neetah had to be helped down the walkway to shore. Uttamatomakkin carried Rebecca in his arms. They were led to the nearest inn. When Neetah heard them call for a doctor, she was too weak to argue.

"She needs to be bled," the doctor said. "And she needs to see a priest for last rites."

Uttamatomakkin's shape darkened the doorway. "You, there," the doctor said. "Go and get us a priest." Instead, Tomakin stepped in, crossing his arms over his broad chest.

Neetah fell asleep, then staggered across the room to Rebecca's bedside. Someone had washed the blood from her face and hands. John Rolfe sat beside the bed, rocking a sleeping Thomas.

"Matoaka?" Neetah said softly.

Rebecca's eyes fluttered. "Wingam," she whispered, and smiled.

"You have done it." Neetah stroked her friend's cheek. "Your vision. A bridge between cultures. Lives saved. A precious child." Neetah forced down a pang of sorrow. "I always wanted to see visions with you."

Rebecca turned and smiled at her husband and son. "It is enough that the child lives," she said.

Her eyes opened wide and she looked at Neetah. Then she looked through her as if Neetah were made of water. Finally, the spirit of Matoaka seemed to focus on a vision far beyond her. Did she see the Great Hare—or Jesus Christ? It didn't matter. Her spirit was gone.

John Rolfe held his wife's limp hands and wept openly. Uttamatomakkin raised his rattle and began the death prayer to the old Gods. Thomas crawled into Neetah's lap, and she tried to chant along with Uttamatomakkin. A fit of coughing stopped her, tore through her aching chest, and silenced the chant. Neetah fought for gasps of air between rasping coughs that brought blood to her mouth.

"Give me the boy." John's voice came from a great distance. "Take my chair." The weight and warmth on Neetah's lap floated away and a warm hand took hers.

Rebecca seemed to be floating before her eyes as the bed faded out of focus. Neetah could feel herself falling, but she hit no floor.

She lay on her side, looking through soft marsh grasses. A river before her reflected a sunset sky. Neetah looked up at a short, slender girl sneaking through the reeds to the river's edge to stand behind her. The girl's eyes held mischief and her cheeks were dimpled, but her tattoos made Nuttagwon's mind race. *Pamunkey.* She read the tribal pattern. *The vision people. Beaver Clan, like me.*

Matoaka.

"What," Neetah tried to say, "wha . . . ," but she could not make words.

A vision, she realized, as the world tilted her up onto her feet. *I am having my vision at last.* Calm flooded the marsh as the sun set, brilliant and blindingly white.

"Come," Matoaka said, extending her finger. Neetah hooked fingers with her in the old way, and they set off toward the light together.

AFTERWORD

BOTH POCAHONTAS AND AN UNNAMED SERVANT WERE BURIED at Gravesend, England, on March 21, 1617. Rebecca's was a proper Christian burial, while her companion was laid to rest in a paupers' field.

John Rolfe sailed home to Virginia. The priest, Uttamatomakkin, and his wife, Matachanna, sailed home, too, to find that the Powhatan had given his power over to his younger brothers.

The peace of Pocahontas lasted for five more years.

Thomas was sent to live with the Rolfe relatives in England until he recovered from his illness. He returned to Virginia in his mid-twenties to claim the lands left to him by his parents and to meet his great-uncle, Opechancanough. Later he enlisted in Virginia's colonial militia as Lieutenant Thomas Rolfe to fight against the native people.

Sixteen generations after Pocahontas met John Rolfe, there are more than two million people who can claim Rebecca as their ancestor.

There are only about three dozen Pamunkey Indian families left living on a small reservation on the Pamunkey River in coastal Virginia.

The strain of tobacco that John Rolfe had planted on his farm made him a rich man and financed the entire colony. Within four years of Pocahontas's death, the settlers began bringing in African slaves to work the tobacco fields. Today the "holy herb" kills five million smokers every year worldwide.

AUTHOR'S NOTE

I AM FASCINATED BY POCAHONTAS. THIS REAL GIRL, CAUGHT in the collision of two great civilizations, has become part of the folklore of our country. Her story has been told and retold for four hundred years in scholarly books, movies, musicals, comic books, picture books, and novels, and yet it moves us with every retelling.

How could one real-live girl so thoroughly capture our imaginations? A dozen years ago, I decided to explore what is known about her and to write a book in which I would share what I found out.

Reading original source material and biographies made me feel so sorry for "Matoaka" that I began to hope she had had a friend with whom to share her sorrows. My own friends buoy me up, urge me on; strengthen, challenge, and tease me. I looked for evidence of girlfriends in Pocahontas's life. I found accounts in which settlers mentioned that she was attended by loyal "servants," though the class-obsessed English did not bother to record their names. That left me room to invent a friend for Pocahontas, who so needed company. I chose the name Neetah from John Smith's handwritten dictionary of native words. It meant "friend" in a language now dead.

I read everything I could find about Pocahontas, the Powhatan Confederacy, and early seventeenth-century England. I also took my reporter's notebook, my camera, and a sketchbook with me on visits to the Mashantucket Pequot Museum's life-sized native village, to Jamestown, the Jamestown Reconstruction, Williamsburg, to the Pamunkey Reservation in Virginia, and to England. Being there and actually seeing the marshes and slow rivers of Virginia, the palaces and tiny back streets of London, and the look of a corn-husk doll against a black wolf's pelt helped me to fill in some of the blanks in Pocahontas's poorly documented story.

At every stop at a historic place, the staff and guides helped me to "feel" the period. I hefted muskets to my shoulder, felt the fine balance of rapiers and the incredible weight of armor. I crawled down into reconstructed ships like those that carried Pocahontas, and I learned how to paddle a canoe. I twisted cord from grasses, lit fire with friction, ground corn in a log, and lay on a low sleeping platform in a reconstructed longhouse. I fingered an actual lancet used for bloodletting in the 1600s. Back home I found a road-killed deer, gutted it, and skinned it with a small dull knife—then slept under its tanned hide. I tasted venison and beaver, corn cakes, and walnut milk.

All the while, I read. What gave Pocahontas the courage, I wondered, to make so many hard choices? I read that her birth name, Matoaka, means "white feather." This is the symbol carried by a "beloved woman," a kind of priestess or medicine woman of the Algonkian   tribes. These women were trained to seek visions, using *powa*, the intelligent energy of the earth. A white feather appears in every written account and portrait of Pocahontas, so it was not too much of a stretch to imagine her making choices based on a vision of peace for her culture and that of the English settlers.

I cannot know how Indians felt in the early 1600s; what, precisely, they believed or how they worshiped. After four centuries, no one knows for sure. But as I walked in Pocahontas's steps, I discovered that she was no innocent child. She was far from helpless. Her actions were heroic. And, as my story grew, they inspired heroism in my Neetah character, too. Perhaps that is why the Pocahontas legend survives. She inspires all of us.

September 14, 2005

ALGONKIAN CHARACTERS

Members of the Algonkian tribes had several names, each of which had a special meaning. The list below is a guide to the Algonkian characters who appear in *My Lady Pocahontas*, although some of them are referred to by only one name.

Ahone—loving creator god worshiped by the Pamunkeys

Aitowh—Neetah's daughter

Cheawanta—Pamunkey girl

Japazeus—leader of Patowomekes

Kocoum—Pocahontas's first husband and a Patowomeke

Matachanna—Pocahontas's older sister

Nuttagwon or Neetah or Wingam—Pocahontas's closest friend and servant

Ofanneis—Pamunkey girl

Okeus—harsh, judgmental god worshiped by the Pamunkeys

Opechancanough—Powhatan's younger brother

Pocahontas or Matoaka or Rebecca—Powhatan's daughter

Powhatan, the, or Wahunsenacah—leader of the Confederacy of many Virginian Algonkian tribes

Sitka—Japazeus's first wife

Totopotomoi—Neetah's aunt

Uttamatomakkin or Tomakin—priest

SELECTED SOURCES

Books

Allen, Paula Gunn. *Pocahontas, Medicine Woman, Spy, Entrepreneur, Diplomat.* San Francisco: HarperCollins, 2003.

Feest, Christian, ed. *The Cultures of Native North Americans.* New York: Konemann, 2000.

Feest, Christian, and Frank W. Porter III. *The Powhatan Tribes.* Indians of North America series. New York: Chelsea House, 1989.

Fritz, Jean. *The Double Life of Pocahontas.* New York: G. P. Putnam's Sons, 1983.

Haile, Edward Wright, ed. *Jamestown Narratives, Eyewitness Accounts of the Virginia Colony, The First Decade 1607-1617.* Champlain, VA: RoundHouse, 1998.

Hassrick, Royal. *The Colorful Story of North American Indians.* London: Octopus Books, 1974.

Hirschfelder, Arlene, and Paulette Molin. *Encyclopedia of Native American Religions,* updated edition. New York: Benchmark Books, 2000.

Kritcher, John. *A Field Guide to Eastern Forests.* Boston: Houghton Mifflin, 1988.

Mossiker, Frances. *Pocahontas, The Life and the Legend.* New York: Da Capo.

Roberts, Elizabeth, and Elias Amidon, eds. *Earth Prayers from Around the World.* San Francisco: HarperSanFrancisco, 1991.

Rountree, Helen C. *Pocahontas's People, The Powhatan Indians of Virginia Through Four Centuries.* Norman, OK: University of Oklahoma Press, 1990.

_____. *The Powhatan Indians of Virginia, Their Traditional Culture.* Norman, OK: University of Oklahoma Press, 1989.

_____. *Young Pocahontas in the Indian World.* Yorktown, VA: J & R Graphic Services, 1995.

Sakurai, Gail. *The Jamestown Colony.* New York: Children's Press, 1997.

Smith, Patricia Clark. *Weetamoo, Child of the Pocassets,* New York: Scholastic, 2003.

Swann, Brian, ed. *Native American Songs and Poems, An Anthology.* Mineola, NY: Dover, 1996.

Tayac, Gabrielle. *Meet Naich, A Native Boy from the Chesapeake Bay Area.* Hillsboro, OR: Beyond Words Publishing, 2002.

Waldman, Carl. *Encyclopedia of North American Tribes.* New York: Checkmark Books, 1999.

Research Sites Visited:
Colonial Jamestown, Virginia, National Historical Park, National Park Service, U.S. Department of the Interior

Colonial Williamsburg, Williamsburg, Virginia

Jamestown Rediscovery, an archaeological site administered by the Association for the Preservation of Virginia Antiquities

Jamestown Settlement, 1607-1630, Jamestown, Virginia; reconstructions of James Fort, Powhatan Indian village, and ships administered by the Jamestown-Yorktown Foundation, an agency of the Commonwealth of Virginia

London, England

Mashantucket Pequot Museum and Research Center, Mashantucket, Connecticut

National Museum of the American Indian on the National Mall, Fourth Street and Independence Avenue, SW, Washington, D.C., and at the George Gustaf Heye Center, 1 Bowling Green near Battery Park in lower Manhattan, NewYork, New York

Pamunkey Indian Reservation, King William, Virginia

Web Sites
Colonial National Historical Park, United States Park
Service
http://www.nps.gov/colo/

Jamestown 1607-1630, photos of Jamestown reconstructions by Ginny LoDuca
http://ab.mec.edu/jamestown/jamestown.html

Jamestown Rediscovery, the Association for the Preservation of
Virginia Antiquities' *Jamestown Rediscovery* archaeological
project
http://www.apva.org/jr.html

Mashantucket Pequot Museum
http://www.pequotmuseum.org/

National Museum of the American Indian
http://www.nmai.si.edu/